A LONG WAY HOME

ISBN: 978-1-64456-561-2 [Hardcover]
ISBN: 978-1-64456-562-9 [Paperback]
ISBNi: 978-1-64456-563-6 [Mob]
ISBN: 978-1-64456-564-3 [ePub]

Library of Congress Control Number: 2022948617

INDIES UNITED PUBLISHING HOUSE, LLC
P.O. BOX 3071
QUINCY, IL 62305-3071
indiesunited.net

Dedication

TO STROUD

Acknowledgements

The horror of 9/11 prompted me to begin this tale as a short story. It felt so raw that I put it away, but I did not forget the woman I named Meredith Haggerty and the forces that drove her. A few years ago, I heard a radio program on which postcards were read from people who shared their darkest secrets. One of those messages said, "Everyone thinks I died on 9/11." Those chilling words shook me, and A LONG WAY HOME began to come alive.

I am proud of my granddaughter, artist and art teacher Lori Lockhart, who created the book cover, a collage portraying images from the story.

I owe special thanks to Barbara Wagner, my best buddy, who continues to read my book manuscripts with a careful eye to my many errors. She is a dear friend who sticks with me and claims to never tire of slogging through all the rewrites.

Novelcrafters is my critique group. Over the years, we have become friends— scrutinizing our manuscripts—pointing out what works and what misses the mark. We celebrate our successes and our failures. Of course, lots of laughter and a little wine makes it all better.

And finally, I offer enduring gratitude for my husband Stroud who never complains when I move into that other world of my imagination and tune out everyone and everything.

Also By Myra Hargrave McIlvain:

Stein House

The Doctor's Wife

Waters Plantation

Texas Tales

Legacy

Shadows On The Land:
An Anthology of Texas Historical Marker Stories

Texas Auto Trails: The South and Rio Grande Valley

Texas Auto Trails: The Northeast

Texas Auto Trails: The Southeast

6 Central Texas Auto Tours

A LONG WAY HOME

Myra Hargrave McIlvain

INDIES UNITED PUBLISHING HOUSE, LLC

Chapter One

Meredith jerked awake, sharply aware that the bus lumbered along a city street.

"Excuse me," a man said. Lights reflected off his priest's collar onto his face. "You were having a terrible dream. I probably made it worse by sitting here."

Had she screamed? She had been dreaming of the man with the red tie hurtling toward the pavement. The thud, the hideous bursting of his body, had jolted her awake, rigid with terror. She forced a courteous smile, slipped fingers beneath the tortoise rim of her glasses, wiping tears, and scooted over to offer space for the priest. The chill of the metal strip under the window made her shudder. Her arm ached, felt as if it were stiffening; maybe the burns were weeping through the bandage. "Where are we?"

"Baltimore. This was the only empty seat. The buses headed south are all packed after the horror of the plane attacks."

"Those poor people. I can't imagine how they suffered." She clenched her teeth, willing herself to the present, willing the tears to stop.

"I'm Jacques Richelieu." Thin lips, spread into parenthesis smile lines, made his black eyes squeeze almost shut as he extended a packet of tissues. "I mostly go by Rich."

Rich? Not Father Richelieu? She'd never talked to a priest, and as she accepted his kind offer of tissue, she began with a lie. "I'm Shannon Staples." She liked the name—a good invention. It had popped into her head at the women's shelter which she stumbled across before leaving the city. The clerk had asked for her name. When Meredith hesitated, the girl explained that the auxiliary ladies wanted to pray individually for all who came through the door. *Shannon* popped into her head. Then she noticed the box on the counter with *Staples* printed across its top.

"I'm headed back to Brownsville," the priest said. "After all that's happened, running a community center on the Texas border feels like a safe haven."

"I'll feel safer in Mexico." *Why did I blurt that?*

"Mexico?" The priest asked. "Won't you have trouble crossing? That's why I'm on this god-awful bus. Planes are grounded. I doubt anyone can drive over the border for some time."

God-awful? She'd heard that priests drank, but imagined them too pious to swear. "I may have to wait for a time in Brownsville." Lies were coming easier. But controlling herself was not. "Sorry, I can't stop the tears." She dug for another tissue.

"Don't apologize. Everybody on this bus is having trouble settling down. We all need a good cry." His smile, flash-lit by a freeway power light, looked as much like an angel's as Meredith could imagine.

"I can't stop thinking about it." That was the truth.

"We're fortunate to be on this bus. Thousands are trapped in the city. Is someone expecting you in Mexico?"

"Yes, a teaching job." *That lie came easy enough.* She tossed her glasses in her satchel, bunched her coat up against the window, and closed her eyes. Maybe he would get the message that she intended to sleep.

It had been less than twenty-four hours since she had arrived at her new office on the twenty-seventh floor. She wanted to get a head start on paperwork before her first oral progress report as the new director of international claims. After spending the weekend practicing her presentation, she felt ready, even excited. She had made herself indispensable to this multi-national corporation with her proficiency in German, French, and Spanish—languages absorbed as she and her mom followed her dad's army career around the world. Work had become her life, and it was looking up. She removed the folder of reports, adjusted her new glasses, and began to read.

The blast hit outside her window like a sonic boom. Her corner of the building shook; the floor shuddered and began to tilt. She gripped her desk, disoriented. Her office door slammed against the wall as screams, like shrieks on a carnival ride, changed to guttural urgency. Ceiling tiles rained down in pieces, whiting her computer screen. Shelves buckled, slamming heavy files across her desk. She seemed to glide in slow motion as she grabbed for the tumbled mass of gold and orange mums—a gift from the staff in her old office. A shard of glass stabbed the photo of Harvey triumphantly waving his golf trophy over his head, as he sat in his wheelchair at his Westchester club. Water from the vase streaked his cocky grin.

"Could this be it? My chance?" The sound of her voice made her throat convulse. Her hands trembled. She drove her feet into her lunchtime jogging shoes, shoved her glasses into her mahogany leather satchel—her ticket to freedom. Pulling its strap over her head, she clutched its supple smoothness against her chest. Since the '93 bombing, she had kept it with her—contoured to her body like a backpack even when she jogged—certain the time would come. Certain that she would see an opening into which she could vanish.

In the outer office, employees grabbed coats and bags as they fled their cubicles. A woman yelled from the windows at the far end of the room, "A body fell...it's black all over." People rushed to look.

"Get out! Everybody, get out!" The exploding voice of authority turned the crowd as smoothly as the deep bark of a sheepdog, herding them back toward the doors at the center of the building. "Take the stairs. The elevators aren't working."

"It had to be a bomb," someone shouted. "Must have blown out a whole wall."

Meredith had moved up to this floor in the tower just last week. She gazed into a sea of unfamiliar faces. They looked like a subway crowd—slightly jostled, close enough to smell the after-shave, the hair spray—locked together in a common link. Only this time, she wanted to touch someone, to know that they were in it together.

Even after the '93 bombing, she had felt safe here. The towers were so big, so solid. And the numbers added to her security—strangers that nodded at the same time each morning at the coffee shop, on the elevator, in the halls. It was a big impersonal sharing like her train ride into town—the same faces reading the *Times*, clutching the same worn briefcase, swinging the plastic bag with one apple and one banana—part of the unchanging landscape of her life.

The hand on her shoulder felt like a blessing. She turned to the familiar face of Pierre, the new transfer from their Paris office. His black beard looked peppered with ceiling dust. "Tie this piece of my t-shirt around your face. I wet it with my water bottle."

She nodded, weak with relief at seeing someone she knew. She knotted the white mask. "Another bomb?"

He bowed his head as he punched in the numbers on his Nokia and held it close to his lips. "*Bien-aimée,* I can't talk. Turn on the news. A bomb's gone off upstairs. We're getting out." His voice softened, "*Je t'adore.*" He disconnected and stared at the phone like he could see her in the palm of his hand. Then he looked up. "Did you reach your husband?"

"My cell's dead," she lied. She had left it on her desk.

"Use mine."

She hesitated, the trembling started again. "He's playing golf." She punched in the number, holding her breath, praying that he was on the course by now. When the machine clicked on, his charming public voice crooned his message of delight at hearing from her and wished she'd please leave a message. Callers never dreamed how much he hated to be bothered. "A cripple is reduced to limited pleasures," he always said. "Talking on the phone is not one of them."

She spoke to the recorder, only a few sentences about the evacuation. She could not utter, "I love you," as Pierre had done. She had an obligation to Harvey. The love they shared, the delight in each other's company disappeared after the crash. It was her fault he had lost the use of his legs, and she had faithfully paid her debt.

Inching closer to the door, she could see thick white smoke billowing down the stairwell, a roiling, stinking fog spreading over them. The coughing started and grew more intense.

A giant woman who was head of accounting stopped suddenly. "I'm not walking into all that smoke. It'll set off my asthma."

"It's the only way out."

"Well, I'm not going." She turned, began pushing back through the crowd.

"I'm not going either." Several people fell in behind, letting the big woman serve as a battering ram.

"Think I'll wait," Pierre called over his shoulder. "Let the crowd thin out."

"Are you sure?" Meredith wanted to beg him to stay with her. Of course, it was better this way. If it worked out that she could vanish, be lost in this massive explosion, it wouldn't work for Pierre to tell the authorities that she escaped safely with him. She had waited for a chance all these years. Time would tell if this was it.

Their whole world changed New Year's Eve 1991. She and Harvey had been to a party and had too much to drink. He was past being able to drive.

"I'm getting you buckled in, sweetheart. Have a little nappy, and don't get sick on me." She felt confident, fully in charge, even tucked a blanket around him before she pulled away from the curb.

He had passed out immediately, and the last thing Meredith remembered was how sleepy she felt. She tried chewing gum. Then it happened. She drifted off the parkway and hit a tree on the passenger side, Harvey's side. How many times had she wished it had been her legs? How many times had he reminded her that it should have been her legs?

The chatter subsided as they began moving slowly down the stairs. Were they all as frightened as she was? Were their hearts pounding?

They looked calm—helping each other. No one pushed.

The man in front of her grabbed a fire extinguisher. "May come in handy," he said to no one in particular.

"You hear about the ceiling collapsing in the men's room? Whole place was one big inferno," the man behind her said.

No one responded.

The coughing grew worse—hacking and then wheezing—as they moved deeper into the pungent, penetrating cloud. She heard gentle offers to tear up clothing for masks.

At Harvey's insistence, she had taken out two huge life insurance policies to care for him if she died first. Maybe this was it. He could collect. Maybe then he could forgive her. She never touched another drink, and she took care of him each evening as he drank himself into a stupor. She put out his cigarettes. And she usually stayed far enough away that his fist or his cigarette could not reach her. Weather permitting, he drove his cart every day to the golf course, stood long enough to make his shots, and then came home to nurse his bottle. In bad weather, he watched the golf channel and drank beer.

She tied Pierre's t-shirt mask tighter, breathed in the calming maleness of his after-shave.

After the '93 bomb, she began fantasizing her escape—an opportunity to slip away and let Harvey be the very rich widower. At every opportunity, she stuffed hundred-dollar bills through the slit in the lining of her satchel and covered the bottom in a Ziploc bag holding an envelope of color and scissors to convert her sandy, shoulder-length hair into a curly brown boy-cut. She kept track of bus schedules out of the city.

"We have an injured woman. Please let us pass." Two men eased down the stairs, carrying a body whose raw flesh gaped between patches of her clothing. Her breath hissed through slightly parted lips, eyes a dull stare, hair completely gone.

As a path opened, the men kept repeating. "Don't know what happened. An explosion. So many didn't make it. Flames shooting out of doorways." They kept repeating the same thing as they disappeared down the smoky stairs.

"My God," the man's voice broke in a whisper close to her ear.

"Mmhuh." She kept her lips sealed to keep from screaming.

The steady human descent was cradled in murmurs of support, those expressing fatigue being encouraged, helped along. Voices stayed low—an occasional whimper followed by deep-throated sounds of assurance.

She wanted to cover her ears, shut out the sound of creaking steel girders whining, taunting with the threat of snapping, dropping them through floors of rubble.

A cell phone squealed, and a woman called out, "My husband says we've been hit by a small plane."

"Lucky it was small," the man behind her quipped. "If it'd been large, we might have had some damage."

Meredith joined in the burst of gallows laughter—too loud and too forced—but it relieved the tension. She should thank the guy, but if she turned, looked into his face, she'd cry.

As they stepped down, a few people seemed compelled to speak—overwhelmed by the silence or trying to ease the tension? "Could it be terrorists?"

"It's something they'd do. Fly a plane into the World Trade Center."

"Big deal. Scare the hell out of us."

Each time a cell phone rang, the message was the same—both towers hit, both towers burning.

Firemen huffed past, pushed their way up through the crowd, gasping for breath from the weight of the equipment strapped to their backs.

Meredith touched a fireman's shoulder. "Several stayed in our office on twenty-seven."

"We'll send them down. Don't you worry, lady."

She watched each man pass. The grim determination on their faces reminded her of war movies when soldiers charged toward the front line. She imagined that her dad's face must have looked that way in Vietnam—before he dashed into a firefight—carrying no illusions about safety.

"Sort of makes you ashamed," the man behind her said. "We're rushing out of here, and they're plowing straight into all that smoke."

"Yeah," she choked back tears. Was she about to run from the one person who depended on her? Could she disappear, abandon Harvey if terrorists started attacking?

The lights blinked, and blackness distorted her sense of balance. Like a chorus, the stairwell gasped in unison and then fell silent. Only the sound of shuffling feet moving steadily down the stairs and the creaking and popping of the walls kept the darkness from closing in, smothering, cutting off her breath. From above, a deep rumbling shook the stairs. Her ears rang; she gripped the handrail. The steps swayed. Were they coming down like collapsing dominoes? After all this time, were they about to be crushed by falling steel and concrete?

"Take hold of the shoulder in front of you." The voice came from below, echoing out of the blackness, a sound of authority, of reassurance.

The man's big firm hand clutched her shoulder. It felt like a hug. "Thank you," she whimpered as she reached to grip the shoulder in front of her. His shirt felt wet, drenched in sweat. She squeezed tighter to seal the human chain, to let him know he was not alone.

Inching toward the bottom, it felt as if they were concentrating on stepping down in sync like dancers, knees bent, feet light as springs to avoid jostling, to prevent losing touch.

Voices drifted up. "Watch out; it's wet here."

In one step, water began splashing against her pant legs, oozing over the tops of her shoes. It would only take one loose wire dropping into all this slush to electrocute them all. The hand squeezed her shoulder as if he shared the fear—a reminder to pass it on to the sweat-soaked man in front.

Voices rose, swept like a wave up the stairs. "We see light!"

Rounding the next flight, a sheen reflected off the water-soaked walls. The line ahead exited through a door into a huge smoky area. The roar of relieved chatter grew louder as she inched one slow step at a time toward the glare.

"Oh, God," the man behind her moaned. "I never thought we'd make it."

As if stepping unrehearsed onto a stage, the glass-walled mezzanine was a jumble of confusion—the actors did not know their lines. A few tried crowding onto the frozen escalator descending into the lobby. Others stood in a daze, waiting for a director. The chain had broken; the hand on her shoulder let go. Then he moved up beside her—a tall, skinny guy, his bloodshot blue eyes smiled over the top of the handkerchief tied over his nose. She had imagined him short and stocky with stubby strong hands—a take-charge type who protected women and children.

"We better get going," he shrugged like an embarrassed kid. "My name's Marty. Marty Savage."

She nodded, torn between wanting to keep him near, and fearing she could never get away. "I'm Ethel Merman." *Where did that come from?* She smiled at his startled look. "My parents were big fans."

"Exit the lobby, and walk toward Church Street." The authority in the voice on the bullhorn shoved them toward the door.

Bumping forward with the crowd, they stepped outside into a choking gray mist drifting with them into a foreign world of twisted steel, wires, and mounds of paper. A circle of people hovered, forming a coven of horror, staring at a hand splayed palm up on the ground. Turning away opened a kaleidoscope of bodies scorched black and burst open—

"Don't look." Marty grabbed her elbow, shoving her around ripped-apart pieces of office furniture.

Bellowing sounds of human agony mixed with city shrieks of sirens. People milled like sleepwalkers staring upward. Through the swirling grayness, the hole in the sky forced a cascading chorus of disbelief. "It's gone! The South Tower's gone!"

Paralyzed, they clung together gazing up at the black smoke roiling out of their tower. It was impossible to see what floors were involved. She kept hearing Pierre tell his wife that he loved her. Did the firemen persuade him to get out?

Objects were falling down the side of the building. Her heart lurched as an object became a man hurtling toward the ground, his red tie covering his face, his arms and legs flayed out, clawing the air. He slammed into the pavement with such force that his life was transformed into a mound of bloody pulp. Was that her scream? Bile surged into her throat. Forcing it down, she started toward the body.

A policeman stepped in front of the hulk of flesh that had been a man who wore his red tie to work. "Get her out of here." He spoke to Marty. "You may be hit. Move on." Then he raised his voice. "Move on. Go north. Keep going."

Marty said, "Take a breath. Start walking."

She nodded, sucked air through Pierre's t-shirt, and felt Marty's hand pushing her forward.

"You're tougher than that," she whispered, repeating her mom's mantra. Even as her mom was dying, she kept saying, "You may be twelve, but you're tough."

"You can make it. Move, make yourself move."

Marty must have heard her, wondered if she was losing it. "Yeah, you're tough." He stayed right beside her.

Sirens blared; firemen ran with hoses. A woman sat on the curb, blood running down her face, dripping onto her arms and legs. A man knelt before her dabbing at her cuts with his handkerchief.

Meredith clutched her satchel tight and began walking. Lunchtime jogging had saved her. She could move when so many seemed too tired to take another step.

They did not speak, weaving through the crowds standing transfixed, staring in disbelief at the carnage. Occasionally they turned and looked at the black boiling smoke rising from their building. Everything familiar had disappeared. Windows along the street gaped with jagged glass, a soot-stained curtain flapped where a window had been.

Marty grabbed her arm. "It's falling; it's falling! Run! Run, for God's sake!"

Their tower bulged like a giant filling its lungs for one last ferocious blow. They ran with the crowd, not daring to look back.

Meredith felt the shove against her shoulder as a huge man, gasping, lurched past. Within a few feet, he barreled into a tiny woman, slamming her into the curb. As she struggled to stand, the crowd surged around her.

In one movement, Marty bent, scooped his arm around the woman's shoulder.

Meredith shoved her satchel to her right side, slipped her left arm around the tiny waist. They lifted the woman between them, beginning a steady jog—right, left, right, left.

She concentrated on breathing, keeping the rhythm, not looking at Marty, feeling the pace that formed them into one motion.

The woman's very young, black face contorted in pain; tears streaked her ash-caked cheeks. "My leg," she whimpered before her head dropped forward.

People pushed past. Soot rained down. Shouts and screams

drowned by the booming, ripping sound of steel and blown-out glass as the giant tried to suck them into its death struggle.

"Breathe deep and run; breathe deep and run," she panted as she concentrated on staying in step with Marty.

A policeman directed the crowd, urging everyone to keep running. "It's only a few blocks up Greenwich to the triage center. Can you manage her that far?"

"Sure," they spoke together.

Marty looked at her, and his eyes, from above the handkerchief, crinkled into a smile. He was covered in ash, his hair an indistinguishable mat of gray, his lashes powdery.

As they approached the triage unit, medical personnel converged on them, lifting the woman onto a gurney.

Marty turned to Meredith, pulled off his filthy handkerchief to wipe his face. "You were great. I couldn't have made it alone."

This is it. He can't identify me. She lowered her eyes to confirm the t-shirt was gray with soot. "I've got to keep going."

"Wait. We've been through too much for you to leave like this..." He extended his hand.

She let him grip her, then pulled back. "I must go."

He touched her arm with the tips of his fingers. "Shouldn't you catch your breath? It's been a hell of a morning."

"You kept me sane." She leaned close, willing him to understand. "But I've got to go."

"Sure." He squinted as if trying to see behind her soot-crusted mask.

It seemed crazy to shake his hand after they had almost died together. She squeezed his arm. "I'll always remember you." She couldn't look into his face again, or she might not be able to go. This was it, the chance she had waited for. Taking longer strides than usual, she moved quickly into the stream of gray figures hurrying to get somewhere. Most of them looked as if they didn't know where.

Chapter Two

She was running from Harvey. Frantic. Heaving herself forward, forcing her legs to keep moving, feeling her power slipping. He was gaining on her. She could hear him breathing. She made herself turn and look back, stare him in the face.

The priest smiled as though they were in the midst of a friendly conversation. "What do you plan to teach in Mexico?" He sounded casual—no hint that he had noticed her nightmare.

She used the tissue wadded in her fist to dab at the sweat on her upper lip. "I've been teaching English as a Second Language. I want to try my hand in Mexico." Another lie. She'd taken the classes, been certified. Then she crippled her husband and forgot about all those people she'd planned to help. She had barely been able to help herself.

"The Lord must have meant me to be on this bus." He ducked his head, but only for a second. "Forgive me for being so forward. We operate a community center. It's part of the county health department. One of our clients' biggest problems is poor English skills."

The staccato of flashing headlights turned him into a surreal figure. His eyes, deep pools reflecting in the darkness, gazed at her with unblinking intensity. Had he really crossed himself?

"I hadn't thought...of...of staying in Texas." The truth made her throat tighten—she couldn't stay in the states. No identification. No social security for someone named Shannon Staples.

"The Lord works in mysterious ways." He folded his arms across his chest and settled back with an air of confidence.

She would find another seat when they transferred in Atlanta, if not before. In the meantime, she willed herself to relax. She leaned against the metal-cool window, arranged her arm carefully to ease the steady ache that made it feel like one solid burn instead of separate cigarette stabbings.

The bus hummed along the interstate; the other passengers had settled for the night. The countryside streaked past—darkened blurs of houses like sleeping hulks pocked by an occasional TV glowing white. She imagined couples huddled together before the screen, watching the towers fall over and over again.

Or were they making love? More and more, she found herself wondering about people in the office and even those she met when she jogged at lunch. She never gave it a thought before the accident. It would have seemed perverted back then. Celibacy changes perspective. She felt her face flushing as she wondered about the priest. Did he have any idea of what real passion could do for a relationship? She turned just enough to see his head thrown back against the seat, a soft snore escaping parted lips. In the dim light, his face appeared pale beneath a black mop of hair that would curl if it got much longer. Lashes were thick too. Not bad-looking, could even be handsome.

The few men she had known loved sex, the pure raw act of just doing it as often and for as long as possible. She could not imagine even one of them giving it up unless it was snatched away. For the longest time, those thoughts made her accept any punishment Harvey handed out. The pain on his face when she found him desperately trying to get a hard-on—sweat dripping off his chin, his hands working vigorously—still opened a chasm in her gut. She had knelt reflexively, an automatic response born of the old times. Her last memory of the event was the blinding white pain of his fist knocking her backward across the bedroom. When she woke, blood oozed from her mouth, and he was gone. He had rolled his wheelchair out to his cart and driven to the golf course where he was always welcomed with cheers.

The bus pulled into Richmond at 4:40 in the morning—right on time for its one-hour layover. The priest—what was his name—Jacque Richelieu roused quickly and stepped into the aisle, allowing Meredith to slip past him and lead the way toward the front of the bus. She hadn't realized he was so tall. He bent forward to keep from bumping his head.

Glancing back, she said, "You must be miserable trying to fold in beside me." *Perfect excuse!* "You need a seat to yourself."

"I'm okay as long as I stick my legs in the aisle."

The tiny diner next to the station smelled of rancid grease and fried bacon. Yellow and white booths, matching chrome tables, and hanging baskets of plastic ivy dangled under bare fluorescent lights. The glare hurt her eyes and roused the raw, sleep-induced slime in her mouth. The pain in her arm had become a steady throb, pulsing with each heartbeat. Cool air coiled around her at the same time that sweat made her blouse cling damp against her skin. Aware she needed to sit before her legs gave way, she slipped onto a bench with her back to the imploding towers on the television suspended from the ceiling at the front of the diner. Her eyes trailed to the line for the restroom snaking around the tables. She cradled her arm and submitted to waiting for the crowd to clear out.

"May I join you?" The priest bowed his head.

Oh, no! "It's so crowded; we may need to make room." How could she make it clear that she was being a good passenger, not necessarily a new friend?

"Your arm. Have you injured yourself?" He reached across the table.

She looked down at the spots of blood seeping together along the sleeve of her white blouse. *Is he trying to adopt me?* "I plan to change the bandages after breakfast."

He leaned forward with an engaging smile. "I should have told

14

you I'm a physician. I'll get my bag off the bus. I always carry antibiotics."

"I have antibiotic cream and bandages in my satchel." She could hear her mom's voice saying *Don't look a gift horse in the mouth*. "You're very kind." Why did she want to cry? She concentrated on the menu to keep from seeing the doctor's probing eyes.

As soon as they ordered coffee and scrambled eggs, he uncurled from the booth and hurried out to ask the driver to let him board. When he returned and set his little black bag on the booth, Meredith laughed.

Embarrassed, she said, "Your bag looks like the one that belonged to Marcus Welby, MD. Remember that TV program?"

He lifted the bag gently onto the table. "You're not the only one to notice. It belonged to my father. I call it my inheritance."

Don't be catty. "Actually, it brings back memories of all those nights my mom and I watched that show. Dad disapproved of sentimentalizing medicine.

Jacque Richelieu's grin spread wide, making his eyes crinkle. He dropped the bag gingerly on the seat. "My father was quite old when that program ran, but he hated it. He would have agreed with your father."

"My dad was a military man...rarely explained his reasons." *Why did I blurt that?* She could hear him saying she didn't have to tell everything she knew.

"Did your family follow him from base to base?"

"It was just me and Mom. We moved all over the world."

"What an education. I've always thought military families had wonderful opportunities. You experience so many cultures."

"Now you sound like Dad. He was a linguist. After the war, he was a liaison officer, sort of a PR man whose job was to keep the locals happy about the base being in their midst. So, we lived off-base. I went to the local schools, which meant I learned the local language."

"So, you lived in Spain?"

"Our last base was Fort Buchanan in Puerto Rico." *I'm sucked in already. Chatting with this guy when I meant to keep him at bay.* Her coffee tasted strong and burned as she swallowed. The stimulation kicked in almost immediately—a surge of energy verging on nausea fought the fatigue pulling at her whole body.

He looked around. "Everyone's been seated. Gives me space to dress your arm at the table. It's better than the bus."

Meredith nodded, resigned. She almost said, "Yes, Dad." He had always taken charge, knew what was needed. Languages were his forte, history his romance, and fine dining the engine that drove him. Her mom had never fit that storyline. The day before she died, her claw-like fingers gripped Meredith's hand. She whispered, "I tried to hear those foreign words, but they ran together like syrup."

When the waitress cleared their table, the doctor lifted a thermos, asked her to fill it with coffee and to include an extra Styrofoam cup for Meredith. "I'm going to wash my hands, have a look at that arm."

Watching him—lean, muscular, and confident—stride toward the men's room, she felt a slow panic. Was she being taken over? She needed help, but not a parent. Pancreatic cancer had eaten her dad in three months. As if on schedule, he attended all her college graduation exercises, got his affairs in order, moved her into an apartment, and then went into hospice care. It was all tidy, like their lives—no questions, no stopping to wonder what to do next. Then he was gone, his body whisked away like dust on fine furniture.

Harvey had swooped in soon afterward. It felt so right to let him take charge. Then after the accident, she couldn't leave. How could a cripple who could do so little for himself have so much power?

The doctor laid out supplies and began rolling up her sleeve. He slipped on gloves, removed the bandages, and shook his head. "Cigarette burns often get infected. I'll put some antibiotic ointment on them, but you need to take a round of antibiotics as well."

"We don't have time—"

"I have samples." He tossed several packets on the table. "And we need several bottles of water to keep you hydrated."

"I have a bottle—"

"I'll get a few more." He was out of the booth and plunking quarters in a machine near the restrooms before Meredith could utter another word. A man in charge.

The bus looked full again. Either no one had gotten off, or if they had, someone had boarded to take their place. She whistled a silent breath of resignation. There was nothing to do but sit next to the priest-doctor at least until the layover at noon in Charlotte.

Show some courtesy. "I appreciate your help. My arm feels better." She knew she was opening herself to questions. Should she tell part of the truth? How could the woman at the Women's Center and now this doctor be so quick to recognize cigarette burns?

She had spotted the sign welcoming women at the side of a church near Thirty-third Street. She went down the concrete steps and pushed open the door into the little basement room crowded with racks of clothing that smelled like sweaty bodies. She smiled at the tiny little woman peering over the top of her glasses at an old television showing the towers falling. "Do you have a place where I can shower?"

"Oh, my dear! You've come from the towers. You're the first to get here."

"I need to buy a couple of shirts and pants." Meredith squeezed past piles of clothing that needed washing.

"It's an awful thing. Were you up in the tower?"

"On the street. I was on my way out of town." Part true.

"I fear so many didn't get out of those towers. I don't guess you knew anyone who worked there?" She removed her glasses and let her eyes trail over Meredith, keen as an x-ray.

"No." She shook her head.

Apparently satisfied, the woman motioned Meredith through a back door into a well-lit bathroom, complete with a vanity and mirror. "Take your time. I'll look for something that will fit." She smiled at the little dressing table. "We have an assortment of makeup in that top drawer that our guests are welcome to use."

Meredith peeled off her suitcoat and blouse, looked around for a broom to sweep up the ash cascading all around her. Even her bra emptied sweat-soaked goo. The shower burned her face and caused her arm to start bleeding again.

She wrapped herself in a towel and was seated before the little dressing table trying to cut her hair when the woman tapped on the door and peeked in. "I have some undies for you... Oh, my dear. Let me help you. I had my own shop for twenty years. You can't chop off that gorgeous mane willy-nilly." She stared at the blood oozing through the tissue Meredith had used to cover the burns. "We need to take care of that arm. I'll get fresh bandages." She was out the door and back wearing a full white coat and carrying a tray that looked equipped for surgery.

"You're well prepared." Meredith watched her examining the burns.

She brushed at the air. "Lots of our ladies need patching up. We see cigarette burns on women and children all the time. We'll send you off with some antibiotic ointment."

"You've done a good job with that bandage. It looks like it will stay awhile."

"That's why I'm here, sweet girl. Kicks my old butt out of bed every morning knowing I'll be helping another woman or two that day. Now, let's get that hair done up."

"I've been wanting a pixie."

"We can do that. But you'll be curly."

"I think curls will look good dyed this medium cool brown, don't you?" Meredith lifted the package of dye out of her satchel.

"We'll make you a new woman."

Wasn't she going to ask any questions? How did the woman know that she wasn't a killer on the run?

She watched in the mirror as her shoulder-length hair fell, and remembered their early days when Harvey loved to run his fingers through what he called his "hand massage." He said it soothed him to stroke thick hair—better than his old teddy bear. He never touched it again after the crash. He came out of the coma a different person, not only a paraplegic. He became a raging bundle of hate, for their friends who he said pitied him, for the doctors who tried to help him, and most of all for her.

When the haircut was done, she did look like a new woman. An almost forty-year-old with dark brown hair that curled like it belonged on a twenty-something.

The woman stood with hands on her hips beaming in the mirror at her work. "One more thing, sweet girl." She dug in her pocket. We give all our ladies a resource packet." She dangled the drawstring of a tiny sack sewn of heart-covered cotton. "It's for emergencies..."

Don't laugh. She's sincere. "Well, thank you." Then she peeked in the sack and laughed. "I really don't need rubbers."

"We all feel that way." She squeezed Meredith's shoulder. "But, honey, we never know when we'll be caught off-guard."

"I'll save them." Meredith laughed, "just in case..." When the woman, beaming with satisfaction, hurried out of the room, Meredith removed her gold ear studs—the last gift from her mom—and slipped them into the little bag with two foil-wrapped rubbers. Her wedding band and engagement ring were the final symbols of her past. The resource packet made a perfect repository. She snickered at the absurdity as she stuffed the drawstring bag in the bottom of her satchel.

Still reeking with the smell of chemical dye, Meredith returned to the front of the little store and found a youngish blonde staring at the television. She had laid out two almost-new shirts and slacks.

"So, did you see the towers fall?" She popped her gum, eyes glassy with excitement.

"Not really. I only heard it."

"How'd you get so dirty? Beulah said you were solid white dust."

"Debris. It rained down on everyone within blocks."

"Ooh, must have been terrifying."

"Yes." Meredith looked around the shelves lining the brick walls. Hats and shoes and stacks of underwear filled every space. "Do you have a small travel bag?"

Beulah shook her head, and the girl appeared to get the message to shut up. "You'll need a toothbrush and a hairbrush for that pixie."

"I don't know how to thank you."

"I've been there, sweet girl. I got away too."

By the time she paid, she'd received instructions on how to catch the bus at the Lincoln Tunnel that would take her to Newark.

The bus picked up speed, moved onto the interstate as the sun peeked into the opposite side of the coach. Road-weary passengers pulled

down the shades and settled for more sleep.

The man smiled. "I hope this trip gets you away from that abuser. It's not the first time, judging from those scars."

"I thought priests preached forgiveness." The words spilled out before she thought of how it sounded.

"You can forgive without staying around for more...abuse." He half-smiled, looked embarrassed. "I bought a *Times*. You want to see part of it?" He extended the front page.

An olive branch? "You read the front part. I'll take the World or Business section."

His eyes welled with tears. "I can't read about the attacks yet. Television is enough for now."

The poor guy's hurting. "You must see a lot of misery."

"Misery is unique. Suffering has no twins. It's new every time."

She nodded, amazed to hear this man, who ministered with such gentleness, find it too much to read about the assault.

She scanned the pages for names of victims—friends in her old office on the floors below. No names were listed. Had the firemen gotten there in time? How about the burned woman? Was she writhing in agony in some hospital wishing she could die?

There were lists of numbers to call for victim information. The date at the top of the page—Wednesday, September 12—jolted her. Jerry would be expecting her today at 4:30 for what she called her "sanity check." He had stopped being a physician so long ago that it felt like going home every Wednesday afternoon. Shirley always locked the office door and ordered in supper for the three of them before Meredith caught her train. It felt cruel to let those dear people think she was dead. One phone call would ease their minds. But that would involve them in her fraud. They would be frantic when she didn't appear, keep trying to reach her cell phone. Finally, give up and call Harvey. Probably say it was her annual checkup. How would Harvey respond? Was he searching for her or hoping she was dead, maybe wishing she had suffered.

"Are you okay? You're shaking." His voice startled her.

"You're right. The news is upsetting." She had made Harvey's life horrid. Now he wouldn't have to watch her walk and hate her for it; watch her go to work and resent her freedom.

To make Harvey's days more bearable, they had moved out of

the city, picked a condo on his old golf course in Katonah, and she began the one-hour train ride to work. She had his special bed with overhead bars for lifting himself into his wheelchair set up in the bedroom. She took the converted study at the end of the hall. Life was never the same.

Chapter Three

As the bus turned into the Atlanta station, he pointed out the window. "We don't leave until 7:15. How about walking to that restaurant across the street? Looks like it'll have more than breakfast."

"Sure." *Jacque Richelieu? Father Richelieu? He said to call him Rich.* She felt him take her arm when they stepped off the bus, guide her past rows of people queued in long lines—all one canvass—waiting to board separate buses.

Here I go again. Submitting with only a nod. The roar of homebound traffic tossed her back to the city—canyoned between buildings and exhaust-spewing from hissing buses. They darted across a street to beat the flashing light, and she realized she was laughing.

Rich leaned in to shout, "It's not relaxing, but at least we're moving."

"It feels good." She meant it.

The hostess hurried them across the brightly-lit café to a booth on the far side of the room, away from a table of men drinking beer and offering opinions about the towers that kept falling on the overhead television. The screen switched to dark smoke billowing out of the Pentagon and then to a video of a black cloud rising from the field in Pennsylvania where Flight 93 had crashed. After they were left to scan the menu, Meredith whispered, "I think your collar got us this remote table. I'm eternally grateful."

He grunted. "I hate the thing choking me, but it pays off sometimes."

A priest who hates his collar? "That's honest," she said.

He shrugged, and they both ordered cornbread with vegetables that were hot, greasy, and overcooked.

When they left the café, the sun had slipped from view, cooling the air and washing a soft glow on the buildings. With traffic reduced to a trickle, she enjoyed the stroll. When she became aware she had taken his arm, it felt awkward to let go.

The Greyhound that would take them overnight to Shreveport was as crowded as the one before. The dynamics had changed. She no longer thought of finding a separate seat. They settled near the middle of the bus. Rolling her jacket into a pillow against the window, she drifted toward sleep wondering if he could smell the chemicals in her hair dye. Her jacket reeked of it.

The rising Thursday morning sun shaped pine trees into long shadows beside the expressway as they pulled into Shreveport for another transfer. Rich grabbed coffee, rolls, and the local paper while she and a dozen women slipped past each other in the urine-scented ladies' room.

Back on the bus, he tucked paper napkins into his collar and across his lap, "We could pretend this is a picnic."

He's not thinking this is a date? "This cinnamon roll is super."

"If you hang around our community center for a while, I'll treat you to one of my famous breakfasts. I'm known far and wide for my culinary skills." He grinned sideways. "In truth, I'm only good at cinnamon rolls. Mine are better than these."

"You've about sold me." She unfolded the newspaper, and her body jerked. The photograph was titled *Falling Man*—a straight arrow careening down the side of the North Tower. He appeared

MYRA HARGRAVE MCILVAIN

poised to accept his fate—a defiant prisoner baring his chest at the firing squad. She crumpled the paper and squeezed her eyes shut, unable to erase the image of the man with the red tie flaying as he plummeted to the pavement.

Rich touched her trembling hand. "Why don't you set the paper aside for a while?"

"I need to see it." She picked up the wrinkled page and gazed at the image of a truck parked outside Bellevue Hospital covered with photographs of the missing. Was Harvey among those waiting for word? Did the horror of her being incinerated rouse any feelings? If she had gone home instead of running away, would it have been different? Would he have realized that he missed the good days--the fun and the passion? The bus ground forward, taking her farther away from ever knowing what might have been. She folded the paper. "That's enough."

They rode without speaking through the thick pine woods until just after noon when the forests opened to Houston's skyline sparkling in the distance. Rich spoke softly. "Would you get sandwiches while I change clothes? There won't be time at our last layover in Harlingen."

At first, she wasn't sure it was him striding back across the lobby. The deep blue of the knit shirt erased the pallor, gave his face a healthy glow. Before she thought about how it sounded, she blurted, "I like that shirt."

"Ha. It's my regular garb. I only wear the collar for special occasions. Didn't have time to change before I left Baltimore. It was my brother's funeral. He was a bishop, and I was expected to look like a priest."

I've been whining, and he's never mentioned his own pain. "I'm sorry about your brother." She folded her hands together to keep from taking his.

"He's been out of my life for years. I've held onto the memory of riding everywhere on his handlebars. He was my hero. He never came home after seminary. It was like he'd died."

"That would be hard for a child to accept."

His smile did not hide the sadness in his eyes. "I tried to be like him. But I was the black sheep. I really wanted medicine." He sighed. "So here I am, a doctor priest doing what suits me."

24

"Is that so bad?"

He chuckled as they headed out to the bus. "Not for me. I can't wait to get home."

"Yikes, how old is that bus?" Meredith stared at the faded maroon exterior and the step stool positioned beneath the door.

"Welcome to Valley Transit. You'll often be reminded that the squeaky wheel gets the grease, and nobody squeaks in the Valley. I constantly push against quiet acceptance that allows junk like this to stay in business."

The sun disappeared when they climbed into the low-roofed interior that had been sprayed with a sweetened deodorizer. Their seats were three rows back from the front, and they both rocked forward each time the driver applied the squawking brakes.

Meredith pressed her forehead against the cool glass trying to absorb the events of the past three days. She had watched the security of her executive office in the towering behemoth collapse into rubble, seen the cruelty and kindness of strangers, and abandoned her husband. Now she rode beside a man who didn't seem like a priest on a rattling bus that reeked of unwashed bodies, including hers. The landscape changed quickly from coastal plains to fields of cotton next to rows of rusty-colored sorghum stretching to meet the sky.

While they hustled to their last bus in Harlingen, Rich pulled out his cell phone and arranged for someone named Arlene to pick them up at the Brownsville bus station.

As soon as the bus reached the highway, darkness turned groves of trees into ominous rows of silent statues. "Are those orange trees?" Meredith whispered.

"Orange and grapefruit. They're picking now. It'll continue until April. One reason I need to get back, the migrant workers will be lined up at the center waiting for flu shots and immunizations for their kids. Maude is our public health nurse. She'll move them right through the process, but she's rough around the edges."

Wonder what that means? "So, your center's out in the country?"

"Edge of Brownsville. Tucked along the Rio Grande and a resaca—a dry riverbed left behind after floods, centuries ago, changed the river's course. They're used for irrigation. We have bountiful orange groves, head-high sugarcane, and a great garden thanks to our resaca."

When they stepped off the bus into the steamy night air, a tall woman waved over the waiting crowd. Her dark hair was pulled back from her face so tightly that she appeared to be all bone encasing large brown eyes. "Hey, FR."

Did she call him FR? The woman pushed through the Hispanics waiting for their families and threw tattooed arms around the good priest.

"Arlene, I want you to meet Shannon. She's agreed to teach our English classes."

It was a beat before Meredith gathered herself, absorbed the new name—Shannon.

He grinned and looked sideways at Meredith. "Well, I mean, she's giving us a try. So, we've got to be on our toes to keep her from running off to Mexico."

The grin spread across very crooked teeth. "Mighty glad to meet you, Miss Shannon."

"If you call me Shannon, I'll call you Arlene. Okay?"

"You bet." Up close, the hue from her deep rose t-shirt gave her face a soft glow.

Arlene and the priest argued over who'd pull his tattered luggage. When Rich won, Arlene grabbed for the little cloth bag Meredith had gotten from the women's center. "You travel light for such a pretty young thing. I filled the truck with groceries, but there oughta be room for your little dab of luggage in the back." Arlene pointed at an old red pickup with a crumpled right fender.

Mark one on the plus side for friendliness. Meredith laughed, held onto her satchel and tossed her bag in the back with Rich's suitcase.

"Will you stop at the post office?" Rich said. "We should have a pile of mail."

Meredith sat in the middle and gripped the edge of the seat as Arlene ground the gears forward with a lurch. "Hold onto your hat. I never got used to a clutch." She cackled deep in her cigarette throat.

At the post office, they sat in the truck watching the doctor enter the dimly lit building. "You're gonna like it here. He's the easiest man in the world to work for."

"He's been very kind to me."

"Wait'll you see him in shorts. Them legs are cuter than Ben Affleck's." Arlene slapped her palm on the steering wheel for emphasis.

"Shorts?" Meredith tried to keep the surprise out of her voice.

"Yep. He coaches the basketball teams. And he jogs every morning." Arlene cackled again. "I make it a point to get to the garden. Gives me a good look. Don't get me wrong, I've got Frank, but a girl can always look."

I'm not the only one who has trouble seeing him as a priest. Meredith covered her mouth and snorted as she watched the object of their interest approach the truck with his well-muscled arms wrapped around a bundle of mail.

When they turned off the highway, the headlights flashed on a white caliche road. "We've entered what's left of the Gallego's Spanish land grant. The family saved these Sabal Palms lining the road into their compound." The ancient trees led to a tall fence overgrown in flaming red Turk's Cap. "Señor Gaspar Gallego, his two sons, and their wives live behind that wall."

"Yeah. So rich they smell good." Arlene hunched over the steering wheel and peered through the cast iron gate for a glimpse of lights in a big house sitting back in the shadows.

"The Gallegos finance our center. We're legally part of Cameron County's health department. We'd never make it without the Gallegos and a few other contributors. You'll meet Don Gaspar in the morning. His sons are lawyers and rarely come around."

"They own a bunch of banks and buildings in Brownsville and Matamoros. Plus, the migrants' houses." Arlene pointed ahead. "Yonder is our abode."

Tall poles suspended night lights playing over Bougainvillea clustered around low concrete block buildings. An orange grove edged one side and bent around toward the back of the property.

Arlene pulled up to one of the largest buildings where a dimly lit kitchen sprawled beyond the windows. "Help me unload all this crap. I'll sort it in the morning. I got everything from toilet paper to tea bags for Lupe." She glanced at Meredith. "Lupe runs the clothing and food store. She and her boy Max..." Arlene cut her eyes at the priest, "...that's Maximillian. They stay in the rooms next to yours."

"You'll meet them in the morning," Rich grabbed a load of groceries and appeared not to notice Arlene's little slight about the son's name. "Come see your room." He nodded toward a hall that led from the kitchen. "These two doors on the right are communal bathrooms. The first two bedrooms on the left belong to Lupe and then Max. Yours is here at the very end."

He pushed open the door to a wave of heat and lunged to snap on the window unit. "We keep it off until someone needs the space." He stood in the middle of the room and gazed about as if he was seeing it for the first time. He shrugged and pointed at a single bed pushed up against the wall and piled with throw pillows to look like a couch. A maple chest dominated one wall, and a desk and reading lamp sat next to a second window. "I asked Arlene to make sure the bed had fresh sheets." His voice sought approval.

"It's perfect. That bed's the most inviting thing I've seen in days." She laughed, and Rich relaxed and laughed too.

"Oh...and all the rooms have adjoining doors. I don't suppose they've ever been opened." He touched a door centering one wall, rubbed his hand over a sliding brass latch that looked stuck in place.

"It'll be perfect." She drew a blank on what else to say that would convey approval.

"I live in the duplex beyond the garden. Arlene has the other side." He inched toward the door. "I can feel the AC working. I'll let you get to bed."

"Not until I try one of those bathrooms."

"They only have showers."

"Great. I'm not a bathtub person. I hate the thought of sitting in my own dirty water." She saw his slight smile. *Why did you say that, big mouth?* "I'll be up early to explore," she said.

"Remove your bandage, wash the area carefully." He backed out the door.

She hurried to the bathroom, letting her clothing drop in a stiff heap on the floor. The shower was a fiberglass cubicle tucked behind a yellow plastic curtain that felt crisp with age. The pointy brass spigot beat hot water against her face, massaged her body. She watched the hair dye streak the bottom of the shower and wondered how long she could go without another treatment.

When she finally stretched out on the bed, the mattress felt firm, better than she expected. She tossed for a while, listening to the on and off clunking of the AC, her mind wandering to Harvey. Was he passed out? Had he drunk himself into oblivion? Had he dropped his cigarette, set the condo on fire? When she flopped the pillow over her head to drown out the AC, she remembered how hard it had been to move from the twenty-four-hour noise of the city to the deadly quiet condo on the golf course. They had turned on the TV in the alcove that separated their bedrooms and been lulled to sleep by its constant noise and flashes of light bouncing off the walls. Gradually, they lowered the volume until they were weaned from the sound. The pillow muffled the jarring clunks of the AC and finally lulled her to sleep.

She woke, stiff as an icicle, the spread and sheet pulled tight over her ears. The bedside clock showed five—six at home. When is daylight in this part of the world? She pulled the curtain aside and stared into the gauzy glow spreading from a high pole at the rear of the buildings. He was jogging—long, lean strides toward the orange grove on the edge of the property. She turned away, feeling like a peeping Tom. Arlene was right about his legs.

She dressed in her extra pair of slacks, shirt, and underwear from the women's center. Arlene already had coffee going in an industrial-sized pot and was cracking eggs and chopping onions at a furious pace. "How was your night? Did that AC freeze your ass?"

"You bet. Should I turn it off?" This was not the time to mention Rich's legs.

"Naw. It may be September, but it'll be a scorcher. You have to stay on top of the thing. It's like taking pain pills. You can't let it get ahead of you, or you go through hell until it's performing again." She waved her spatula. "Pour some coffee. By the time I get done with breakfast, FR and Lupe'll be in here." She motioned to a skinny old man hunched on a chair by the back door. "Meet Señor Gaspar Gallego."

The old man showed a toothless smile and lifted his coffee cup.

"*Buenos días.*" Meredith saluted with her cup and tried to keep the surprise out of her voice as she greeted the wealthy owner who looked more like a shriveled janitor.

He broke into rapid Spanish, asking where she was from. What she was doing here. When she responded, he showed a pink–gum grin. Looking up mischievously at Arlene, he said, "*Su español es excelente.*"

Arlene cackled, "You bet she's good. Rich hires the best."

"So, everybody eats here?" Meredith settled on the end of a long bench, set her cup on the red and white oilcloth table cover.

"Yeah. We're open to anyone who needs a meal." She turned toward the door. "Well, look who's here. This is Lupe, keeper of the store and mother of Maximillian."

Meredith turned to the sweet smile of a rotund angel. "*Encantada de conocerte.*" Standing seemed appropriate. Then she stepped forward and took the crusty-hard hand.

"*Igualmente, Señorita.*" Lupe ducked her head and shifted to English. "Welcome to our community center. We hope you like it here."

"Wow, your English is good." Meredith liked holding Lupe's hand.

"My Maximillian taught me. He goes to college."

"I look forward to meeting him."

Arlene remained silent, clearly not chiming in with praise for Lupe's smart kid.

"After breakfast, may I look at your clothing store? I need to buy some things."

Lupe sipped her coffee and eyed Meredith over the top of her cup. She forgot her English. "We don't get many skinny clothes. I tell the rich ladies our women eat beans and rice. Makes big middles." She laughed deep in her heavy breasts and patted her ample stomach. "I put back things nobody wants. Maybe they not too big for you."

Rich burst in the door, his hair still wet from the shower. He wore another blue—powder blue—shirt making his face glow with good health. "Hope I'm not late." He stopped. "Super. You've met the crew." He grabbed a handful of oranges from a crate on the end of the long counter, tossed one to Don Gaspar, who caught it with one swift hand. The priest began slicing oranges into quarters. "These are early Navels. They'll be really sweet by December." He filled a large aluminum bowl, placed it on the table. He poured a cup of coffee and flopped onto the bench across from Meredith. "I'll show you around after breakfast. Then I've got to get to clinic. They're lined up already."

"I can show her," Lupe laid her hand on Meredith's shoulder. "She needs clothes. Besides, you got two ladies crying yesterday."

"What's wrong?" The doctor held his cup midway to his mouth.

"Maude got after them."

He grimaced. "Poor things, squeezed between Maude and their husbands. I'll talk to her." He shook his head and gulped the last of his coffee.

"Everybody, eat now." Arlene backed away from the enormous black stove and pointed a long wooden spoon toward plates stacked on the counter next to troughs of tableware and a package of paper napkins.

Meredith remembered that Maude was the nurse and wondered how she made women cry. She picked up her plate and stared at the mound of eggs, stack of tortillas, and pot of black beans. "It smells wonderful."

"It looks like a lot, but Arlene keeps it hot for people who show up for clinic or come by the store. Be sure to sample her hot sauce. Carefully. Once you get used to the heat, you can't eat a meal without it." All the time he talked, Rich filled his plate with every item on the stove.

Arlene did not sit. She stood at the end of the table munching eggs folded into a tortilla. Don Gaspar filled his plate, went back to his station beside the door. Soon, he shuffled outside and climbed onto a tractor-size green lawnmower.

"Does Don Gaspar mow the grass?" Meredith stared after the little man.

Rich's gaze followed. "That's his transportation. He mows, but a gardener keeps the grounds."

Meredith ate two oranges after her eggs. "This is the best breakfast I've had in forever."

"Arlene makes every meal taste like the best." Lupe eyed Arlene until she saw her toothy smile, then she pushed back from the bench. "Come see our store."

The sprawling room, packed tight with rows of clothing, smelled musty like the women's center. Canned goods and boxes of dry foods filled shelves built between the windows.

Lupe dug under the counter and pulled out a stack of pants and shirts. "You need eights?"

"No, no. Look for tens."

Lupe looked up and down her body, shook her head, and kept pulling out wrinkled clothing. "These been here a long time."

"I'll take it all to a washeteria with my dirty clothes."

"We got washers and dryers in the activity building. Cost a quarter. Father Rich say that pays for soap and electricity. You gotta get there early to beat the workers."

Meredith held up a black suede jacket with string ties across the bust and at the wrist.

Lupe shrugged. "Rich ladies buy stuff they never wear."

"I can use these denim pants." She tossed aside a sequined halter that tied in the back. A white scooped-neck dress boasted foot-long fringe around the bottom. She slapped on a fedora with a patterned black and white band that made them laugh. Finally, they uncovered two pairs of jeans and two shirts.

Meredith looked at her loot. "Doesn't anyone wear Calvin Klein cotton briefs?" She held up six panties embroidered with words like *Queen* and *Diesel.*

Lupe cranked the handle on the ancient adding machine. "Maybe they keep the Calvin Kleins." She shook her head. "This comes to eight dollar. We give you a discount."

"Oh, no, no! I can pay. It's in my room. But do you have change for a hundred?"

"That's all I got in my register. We can ask Maximillian. He always has cash."

"Did I hear my name?" He was barely taller than Meredith and smelled as good as the men's department at Nordstrom's. His black hair matched the muscle shirt that looked painted on over well-defined pecs.

Lupe swung onto his oiled bicep and gazed up into a face fully aware of its beauty. In English she said, "Miss Shannon come here to teach English."

"*Came* here." He corrected without looking at Lupe.

You little twerp. Don't insult your mother. Meredith smiled but did not offer her hand.

"Did I hear you need change?" He pulled a roll of bills from his pocket.

"For a hundred, please."

He flipped off five bills, held them close to his pecs. "I usually charge an exchange fee."

"Whatever. I'll get my money." She pushed past him and headed down the hall. She heard Lupe whispering not to charge the sweet *Señorita.*

She pulled her satchel from under her bed, slipped her fingers into the slit in the lining that bulged with bills. She needed to dig it all out this evening. Count how much she had actually stuffed into the opening over the years.

Maximillian took the hundred, held it up to the light like he knew how to distinguish a counterfeit, and then handed her the bills. "I won't charge you. Anybody working here for peanuts can't pay my rates. Besides, maybe you can pound some English into my mother."

Meredith clutched the money. "Actually, Lupe's English is quite good."

"Her grammar stinks." He shrugged, looked from beneath droopy eyelids at Meredith. "You may call me Max."

"Okay. Call me, Shannon." She turned, scooped up the clothes. "Could I drop these in the washing machine before we take the tour?"

"Oh, yes." Lupe patted Max's oiled arm like it was a treasure. She trotted ahead along the caliche path to the activity building. "Maximillian gets cross sometimes because he works so hard. College in day and a security man at the Piedras Negras Restaurant in Matamoros."

Meredith felt sorry for the woman. "What does he plan after he graduates?"

"A businessman." She waved her hand. "He already knows business."

I bet he does. Meredith followed Lupe into the building. Two boys about five-years-old bounced basketballs. "What a super gym! Do you have a lot of spectators on those bleachers?"

"Always. Father Rich has volunteers come every day after school." She pointed to a corkboard where a long sheet held two names beside each date, including several names listed on weekends. "We got two girl and two boy teams." She lifted her chin. "The girls are best. Come see where you teach."

The classroom was a smaller space, separated from the gym by restrooms. Shelves lined with books and magazines angled back from windows looking out on the driveway. A set of old World Book Encyclopedias lined the bottom of one shelf. Chalkboards on rollers occupied a corner, and several desks were wedged between lounge chairs. A large pot of blazing red bougainvillea thrived in front of a window. And a locked wooden box had a sign in English and Spanish pasted on top, KEY AT THE CLINIC.

Lupe waved her hand. "We had to lock the computers because no one was looking after them. Lots of kids come after school, but they have to check in with Miss Maude."

"Maybe I can hang around enough to keep them unlocked."

"Sure would be good. My Maximillian hated to ask for the key..." She looked around the room, then spread her arms, "Father Rich says this is our library. We have parties and meetings here.

"It's lovely. And so tidy." Meredith ran her hand along the back of an over-stuffed chair and ottoman. "I could spend hours reading in this room."

"I dust and water the plants. Don Gaspar cleans the floors."

"Why does he do so much work? Surely he could hire help."

Lupe brushed at the air. "He retired. His sons and their wives work now."

Meredith held her tongue to keep from asking since when was mowing a massive lawn and cleaning floors not work?

"Here's our washroom." Lupe opened a door into bedlam. The washers and dryers churned out heat, and a young Mexican girl shuttled between four squealing preschoolers and several piles of dirty laundry. "Maria, this is our English teacher." Lupe spoke in Spanish, spreading her arms toward Meredith—the grand prize.

Maria stepped over a mound of laundry and clutched Meredith's hand. "I will come to class. My children will be quiet. Okay?" Her face, still young and beautiful, did not fit the heavy body bulging with another baby.

"Of course. They can learn English too." She looked at the dirty faces, eyes wide, questioning the stranger, and she wondered how this bunch could be tamed.

"One washer is almost done. I put yours in next." Maria reached for Meredith's bundle.

"Oh, no. I'll come back tonight."

Maria held onto the bundle. "I can help."

"It's not necessary. I'll read tonight while my clothes wash."

Maria looked around at the movement swarming the room. "That sounds nice."

"Tell your friends to come at nine tomorrow. Help decide the best time for classes."

Maria held her palms together, prayer-style over her lips. "Gracias, *Señorita*. The pickers too?"

Pickers? Orange pickers? The migrants? "Of course. Welcome everyone."

"Come see the clinic." Lupe tugged at Meredith, waved good-bye to the harried mother.

The clinic was a long concrete-block building with large windows edged by Oleanders—brilliant with a mixture of red and pink blossoms. Meredith could see the doctor, still wearing his blue shirt, bent over a child on an examining table. The waiting room buzzed with chatting women and children looking at books and playing with an assortment of blocks, wooden wagons, trucks, and baby dolls.

A woman, almost as tall as the door with hair as yellow as a crayon, looked into the room and waved to Lupe. "Follow me." She marched ahead without speaking. Her old-time white nurse uniform was starched as stiff as her back. "Here." She shoved open the office door.

The room looked nothing like Meredith expected. It resembled a cozy study. Shelves bulged with books turned every direction. A burly brown sofa faced an over-stuffed chair with faded arms. A spotting scope atop a tripod aimed toward a thicket of palm trees and a field of sugarcane beyond. The desk, invisible beneath stacks of folders and scattered pens, sat sideways to the sitting area. She'd expected it to resemble her dad's study that looked like he'd organized it with a T-square.

Lupe folded her hands like a supplicant and looked up at the woman. "Miss Maude, this is Miss Shannon, our English teacher."

It sounded like *harrumph,* and her stomach shook as she said it. "So, you'll teach English?" She spoke in rapid Spanish.

"*Sí,*" Meredith smiled, waited for the next burst that appeared to be coming.

"I'm getting immunizations up-to-date. Have you had a flu shot?" Maude folded arms that looked like they belonged on a wrestler—including black hairs—across a bulging middle.

"I'll get it when you have time."

"Today's as good as any."

Rich burst into the room and looked at Meredith. "How's your arm?"

She brushed the air. "The infection's gone. You fixed me up."

"You and Maude have met?" He clasped both hands behind his back and rocked up on his toes, apparently waiting for Maude to respond.

"If she had an infection, she better wait a few days for her flu shot."

Rich seemed not to hear. He bound to his desk, rummaged through several drawers. "I'll give you the form for payroll. You'll be on our books. The health department's too complicated."

Payroll? A cold surge gripped her. Of course, he'd want her social security number. She had allowed herself to forget that little matter.

He bent toward her, frowning. "Unless you've changed your mind?"

"No. I'd like to stay—"

"I don't need it until next week. We pay on Fridays..." He bent closer, searching her face.

"I'll take the form. You need to get back to your patients."

He straightened up. "Maybe tonight I can show you around?"

"Tonight's good." She turned, hoping he didn't notice how hard her heart was pounding.

Chapter Four

On the walk back to the main building, Meredith tried to listen and nod as Lupe chattered, pointed to the tree-sized Bougainvilleas turning the drab concrete-block buildings into showcases of color. Bending low to avoid a hummingbird zipping past, Lupe said, "This is the prettiest place I've ever lived—flowers and birds everywhere. Father Rich knows all the birds. If you get up before daylight, you can jog with him. He goes through the orange grove and along the river."

Jogging would clear my head. Help me figure my way out of this mess. She stepped in the door and was relieved to see a woman waiting at the far end of the hall in Lupe's store.

"Here I am!" Lupe hustled toward her customer.

Meredith shoved open her door and fell across her bed, still clutching the laundry. What was she thinking? She couldn't stay here. She let herself succumb to Rich, imagine she could live in his secure little world. Would she ever stop falling into her old habit—depending on a man to save her ass? She had to get to Mexico. Forget the crazy notion that a runaway—a perpetrator of insurance fraud—could escape to a remote retreat and live happily ever after.

She raised up to the smell of fresh coffee. Did Arlene stay in the kitchen all day? A slug of caffeine should help. She raked the brush over her hair to relax the tight curls and followed the aroma. She heard Arlene's deep rattling cough and the slam of the back door. The lights were out in the cool, cleanser-fresh kitchen. She carried the coffee to the end of the table near an old TV flashing pictures of President Bush standing on the rubble of the World Trade Center, his arm around a fireman, shouting into a bullhorn. "...the people who knocked these buildings down will hear from all of us soon..." She hunched over the steaming cup. She had run from the man she crippled, turned her back on grieving people, and started over with lies. Grabbing a paper towel from the stand in the middle of the table, she blew her nose and noticed Arlene slumped on a bench in the yard, her back against a palm tree. The old hippie blew smoke rings like a defiant teenager and flicked ashes into a can cupped in one hand. When the cigarette burned to her fingers, she ground out the butt and headed back toward the kitchen. The suffocating stench of ashes clouded in with her. "Well, look here. If it's not the last rose of summer. Has this place already got to you?" She slumped on the bench, squeezed Meredith's hand.

Shaking her head and blowing her nose again, she said, "This place is super. But I can't stay."

"What's chasing you off, girl?" Arlene's hand squeezed tighter.

Meredith looked into questioning eyes swimming in a mist of green. "I don't have a social security card."

Arlene's gaze narrowed—calculator shrewd. "I bet we can fix that." She sucked in a breath that made her voice rattle. "My Frank knows folks on both sides of the river. He'll be here tonight." She looked at the big clock over the back door. "I gotta get lunch heating. You settle down. We'll figure it out." She stood and then bent close. "Does FR know?"

"FR?"

Arlene shrugged and grimaced. "Father Rich. I feel like a pervert calling him father when all I see is a hunk of man."

Meredith laughed. "No, I can't tell FR.

"Good. He doesn't dress like a priest, but he's got a lot of churchy notions about doing stuff by the book."

Meredith returned to the library for a closer look at what occupied its shelves. Ignoring the women's voices and giggling children next door in the laundry room, she fingered through the stack of well-worn Spanish-language newspapers from Matamoros and rows of children's books in Spanish and a few in English. *Ferdinand the Bull* was the most used. She flipped through the copy of *Del Amor y Otros Demonios* and noticed no names were written on the checkout card of the tale about a nineteenth-century girl dying from the bite of a rabid dog. Must have been a contribution from the dear priest who did a lot more reading than the residents around here. Aside from the romance novels, which were worn and marked in the best places, the adult's most popular—if wear meant anything—was *Don Quixote*.

She covered her mouth and froze when she spotted the *Times* headline, "Memorial Services for Victims." Now, they were suffering through funerals. She unfolded the paper, her heart racing, and scanned the alphabetical list. Pierre Abbe was the second one. She began running her finger along the column, wincing each time she saw another name—friends she had worked with for years—gone. Crushing the paper against her face, she remembered Pierre looking at his phone like he was seeing his wife. Had the fires reached their floor and burned all those who stayed behind? Had they tried to leave at the last minute and cried out in terror? Crushed alive? Trembling, she wondered if her tears were from grief or shame? She had escaped, and she had run from it all. She shoved the paper on the shelf without reading the remaining names.

She jerked to attention and forced a smile when three women—carrying baskets of clean clothing—followed their preschoolers into the library. She introduced herself in Spanish and explained her presence. "Father Rich said several people in the community want to learn English." She tried to read what was going on behind those sweet smiles. "You can help your kids with schoolwork if you speak English. And a lot of businesses want folks who speak Spanish and English." She waved toward the shiny computers sitting in the box. "You can even practice typing on those computers..."

"Beats ironing," a woman said.

The other two laughed. "And cleaning houses."

She thought two of the women perked up at the idea of learning English. As they chatted among themselves, walking back to their car with books for the children and romance novels for themselves, Meredith watched their animated hand gestures. How was she going to get a bunch of women who had known each other all their lives to morph into an English class? Would an English-speaking coffee klatch work?

She decided to make signs saying *CAFÉ KLATCH Y CONVERSACIÓN EN INGLÉS* and post them in the laundry room and on the door of Lupe's store. She sat down at one of the computers and began designing. If school kids came to use the computers, maybe she could connect with their parents through them. Enticing adults was going to be a challenge.

Her signs increased in number until she'd put them on every door throughout the compound. She posted the last one on the kitchen door and grinned at Arlene, who was coming in from a cigarette break. "I figured I'd get better attendance if I call the English lessons something besides classes."

"You bet." People around here are big on school for kids. They don't think of themselves as doing any learning." Arlene eyed the sign. "Why don't you add cookies? I believe you get to the brain through the stomach."

"Ha! I love it! Do you mind if I make some this afternoon?"

"No, no! I got a freezer full. You got to be prepared around this joint. We get last-minute things going all the time."

"You are a darling. May I bake them now?"

"Go on. Take care your class. I'll throw them in while I cook my meatballs and spaghetti."

After lunch, Meredith went back to the library to create bold-colored sign-strips that read *Y GALLETAS*. She finished updating all her signs and met Lupe at the kitchen door.

"You hear about the collapse of the Queen Isabella Causeway?"

Terrorist attack! She grabbed for Lupe's hands. "Where's that?"

"It's the bridge to South Padre Island. Thirteen have been rescued, but four have been killed. They're diving for more."

Arlene waved at the TV. "I turned on my programs and saw it. They've photographed license plates of five vehicles. They're in fifty feet of water."

"What caused it?" She could barely speak.

"Four barges rammed it in the middle of the night. Knocked out three sections in the highest part of the bridge. Poor jerks had no idea. Drove right up to the top of the span and fell in..." Arlene turned back to the stove. "Makes you sick. Heads are going to roll for that tug captain. Can't imagine how he shoved those barges into that thing..."

"It's not even been on CNN," Lupe said. "All they talk about is those planes crashing..."

Meredith felt weak with relief. "We're so far from the East Coast—"

"Yep. Backwater place that nobody notices...but just the same...people died." Arlene slammed out the door for a smoke.

The fresh-baked cookies and Arlene's meatballs and spaghetti smelled wonderful, but Meredith had no appetite. All the talk of more deaths and the roiling stress of trying to figure a way to stay here turned her stomach into a tight knot. When they finished the dishes, she told Arlene that she'd be in the laundry room. She had to believe that Frank would come through.

Rich had gobbled his food and hurried to the gym. "It's the girl's practice night. I'll have to chase the boys off the court." He laughed. "They'll hang around to jeer, which they've never figured out makes the girls work harder." As he hurried out the door, he called, "come see the practice. I think you'll enjoy it."

Meredith found two middle-school girls using the computers. "We're doing social studies," one explained in Spanish.

"Did you see the coffee klatch posters? You think your mothers would be interested?"

"We saw. But they work." Both girls went back to the keyboards.

"We'll have night...get-togethers, if we have enough interest."

"Sure. We'll tell them," spoken in English before they turned away.

After the girls left, she paced the floor while her laundry

finished. She kept looking at the door, watching for Arlene. She settled in a lounge chair and tried to focus on the paper when Arlene appeared with a man who had to be six and a half feet tall. His face looked like carved mahogany—sharp cheekbones and a nose that ran straight from his forehead. As soon as Arlene introduced him, he drew himself up and said, "It's actually Francisco, for Francisco de Goya. Papa was a painter, wanted that for me." He grinned—a pause for effect. "And that is what I am. A house painter."

Meredith laughed and understood his appeal—grandiose and self-deprecating all at once—a perfect fit for Arlene.

He lowered his voice, looked around as if the walls might be listening. "So, you need a social security card?"

She nodded. "Is it possible?"

"Anything's possible. I know a woman who is first-rate. Never know her work's fake." He raised both eyebrows. "But she's expensive."

Meredith's mouth became so dry she could barely mumble, "How much?"

"Five hundred." He held up a hand as if to stop any protest. "She charges three hundred down. If you're satisfied, you pay the balance."

Meredith blew out a breath before she realized she'd been holding it. "I can do that." She looked from one conspirator to the other. "It's in my room. Should I get it now?"

He nodded. "Probably best to meet in the kitchen."

Relief made her steps feel like she was floating as she rushed to her room. She pulled her satchel from under her bed and slipped her fingers into the ever-enlarging slit. The lining bulged like an overstuffed mattress. *She must take time to count her money.* "Tonight, for sure," she promised as she locked the door behind her.

In one quick motion, Frank folded and slipped the bills into the pocket of his black leather vest. "I'll return after Sunday mass."

Mass? Will he confess? Meredith smiled and stammered, "I don't want to get you in trouble."

When he waved his bony hand, she noticed he had long fingernails. How could he paint houses?

"See you in the morning, sweetie. Frank's taking me dancing." Arlene placed a quick kiss on Meredith's cheek, grabbed her man by the arm, and they were out the door.

He ushered his lady onto the seat of an old white van. Across its side in beautiful black calligraphy was scrawled *Francisco, Painter*.

She watched them drive away. Relief that her troubles were about to end left her exhausted. Seeing FR coach the girls would have to wait for another time. She crawled into bed without noticing the clunking of the AC.

The sound of voices in the next room woke her. The clock showed five.

"I've worried all night." Lupe's whisper carried through the thin wall.

"It's not easy to cross. Long lines of drunks trying to prove their citizenship. Don't wake me for breakfast. But save me some."

Worrying about him romping around all night must drive Lupe crazy. Before she dressed, Meredith beat her jogging shoes together over her trash can. Her throat constricted. How long would it take to be rid of the ashes?

When she rounded the side of the building, Rich came toward her in the hazy light.

"You're up early." He fell into step, an easy pace.

"I'm still on Eastern Time."

"Slender as you are, I should have known you're a jogger."

Weird, he noticed my size. "I've done it for years." When they moved into the darkness of the orange grove, the memory of the last time she jogged made her breath come short. She sucked in deep gulps of air. This time she wasn't running for her life. She focused on breathing, feeling her energy return as they emerged from the trees onto a rutted path next to a lazy Rio Grande. "My goodness, the river's so narrow. I imagined it a formidable expanse that brave Mexicans dare to cross to find liberty."

"Ha!" Rich threw his head back. "They mostly wade across. Unless they step in a sinkhole. All they want is work. Nowadays, it's a narrow stream. We've had a ten-year drought. Last spring, the river actually dried up at Boca Chica. Not a drop flowed into the Gulf."

Meredith looked ahead at the trail, parallel ruts separated by ankle-high weeds, winding out of sight.

"I heard Max talking to Lupe this morning. He had to wait in line forever to come back across."

"Max makes problems for himself even when there aren't any."

She looked at him, wondering what he meant, waiting for him to continue.

"The attacks destroyed hope for workers to move back and forth across the border. For a time, Vincente Fox and Bush appeared to be simpatico."

"I'd forgotten that President Fox visited Bush last week. It seems like years ago."

"It was eons in terms of the divide created by those planes. The attacks shut the border."

"Do many illegals cross along here?"

"Yep. Our center opened originally to help migrants working on area farms. Now our clients are both legal and those hiding in open sight." He suddenly raised his arm, "Look at the barn owl in the top of that tall Mexican fan palm."

"I see it," she lied. Then she saw the bird's big white breast and wondered why she'd been dishonest in the first place.

The bird sighting didn't slow his pace. "We've been fortunate, stayed out of trouble with the border patrol. Primarily, we have workers who come to pick oranges and grapefruit. You notice Maude was pushing flu shots? We encourage immunizations. Try to get the kids into school while they're here. When illegals show up, we feed them, give them clean clothing, and send them on their way. We're left alone because we don't harbor the poor souls."

The trail twisted into a sharp bend. "There're so many turns it's hard to see where we're going." She gazed at head-high sugarcane forming long green rows that stretched back from the river.

"The Rio Grande has changed course so many times that some of the land like ours juts over toward Mexico, then along here the river makes another turn and bends back on the Texas side. Farmers use this little trail to move their equipment." He shrugged. "Of course, the border patrol uses it too."

A narrow bridge rose ahead. "This canal irrigates the Gallegos' sugarcane field. The old Spanish land grants were laid out in *porciones* fronting one-mile sections along the river and stretching back several miles for cattle grazing. This bridge marks the edge of the Gallegos' property. It's where I turn back for a roundtrip run of three miles."

The sun, almost above the horizon, brought the scrubby trees on the far bank into sharper focus. A breeze brushed the sweat on her face.

"Oops! Look here!" Rich bent into the weeds and scooped a plastic bag from the water. It was stuffed with jeans, a wallet, and a plaid shirt. He held it out, dripping water that had started seeping into it. "I hate to find these." His eyes probed along the bank. "It's not been long since whoever was carrying this bag lost it in the river."

"You think the person is around here?"

He kept staring at the shoreline. "I'm afraid this will end with a floater."

"A floater?"

"A drowning victim whose body finally floats to the surface." He turned toward her, his face twisted in pain. "It happens so often. They come up here from villages or farms. Never learned to swim. Then they try crossing, to find work. To keep from looking like drowned rats, they strip to underwear and ferry their belongings in bags above their heads. It's so easy to step in a hole and go under."

"Why don't we watch? Maybe we'll see him along here." She shuddered, "or God forbid, see his body."

Rich turned back to the river. "Once they go under, the body doesn't surface for twenty-four to forty-eight hours, depending on the warmth of the water." He reached for her arm. "This bag—still intact—is a sign the poor fellow hasn't been gone for long. He'll float on down the river for some distance before coming up. And you don't want to see his body once it surfaces."

"What will you do with that bag?" She walked alongside him, feeling like she might vomit, aware that he was leading her.

"I'll call the border patrol. Maybe they'll be able to match the body with this stuff. Usually, it's impossible."

They parted ways at the edge of the orange grove. She hurriedly showered, and when she stepped back into the hall, she stopped short, startled by Max sporting a very brief jockstrap. Instead of flexing his muscles like the bodybuilders she'd seen on covers of newsstand magazines, he grunted, "I see ol' Rich found another floater."

Did he watch us coming through the orange grove? "He only found the belongings..."

"Be glad." He smirked. "They swell up. Turtles eat their lips and eyelids."

She wanted to tell him to shut up. Instead, she stared, paralyzed.

"Our county can't afford a coroner, so the funeral home's paid $500 to take the corpse. They smell so putrid that they're thrown in a cooler. Hauled off in a rust-specked old trailer."

"Hush that talk!" Lupe stood at the door of her room. "He just wanting to be a smarty. We're decent. We bury those poor souls."

"Yep," he started into the bathroom. "We plant them fast as we can in *El Jardin*, a paupers' plot behind a barbed-wire fence." He slammed the door.

Lupe reached for Meredith's arm. "Maximillian knows that stuff because he worked a little bit for the funeral home..."

And the little turd relished in horrifying this city girl. She brushed it away. "It's okay, Lupe. He's very descriptive. Gave me a good education."

After breakfast, Meredith hauled a coffee pot and Arlene's cookies to the library. She kept glancing out the window to see if anyone would show up. Right on time, two dust-covered cars clunked into the parking lot carrying Maria and her swarm of well-scrubbed children and three other Hispanic women and their kids. The three she'd met yesterday did not show. She ignored the nagging thought that she'd not done a good sales job. She shouldn't have described it as an English class.

Maria explained that two of them were wives of the migrant workers picking oranges. Half an hour passed as the women chatted about the causeway wreck while they helped Meredith match books with the older children and divide blocks and small cars among the toddlers.

Besides guiding the conversations in English, she decided that some of that cache cushioning her satchel needed to go for easy-to-clean toys and more books. Finally, squirming babies latched onto large brown breasts, and the mothers' attention turned to how they could learn English by discussing what was on their minds. As they talked about the accident and how many had died, Meredith reminded them of how to say their ideas in English. Several of the children abandoned their books and began mimicking the English words. The time spread into two hours and took on the air of a summer camp. Only thing lacking was teaching them to sing *Kumbaya.*

During the early afternoon, barefoot children and women wearing dusty flip-flops came into the library carrying plastic bags stuffed with clothing from Lupe's store. *Don't think about the clothing in that plastic bag this morning.* As they searched the shelves for books and magazines, Meredith's spirits lifted. With a fake social security card and a little toughening in regard to the border problems, she could make a home teaching English. Still, waiting for Francisco to come through, and trying not to think of the man who had tried to keep his clothing dry, made the day drag.

The same middle school girls showed up after supper to work on their social studies. They reported, in Spanish, that their mothers were not interested in learning English. She smiled to herself as she noted that their class reports on computer screens were written in English.

By the time she crawled into bed, she was so stressed that she tossed all night.

Glad to see five o'clock, she dressed, wishing she had asked Rich if he jogged on Sunday. When she rounded the building, she looked across the garden at the duplex. Both sides were dark. Frank's van was parked against Arlene's front steps.

Has he already picked up the card? She increased her pace through the still dark grove. Maybe Rich had started running earlier, and she could catch him at the river. The air lay still, almost suffocating in the grove. When she burst into the open, the priest was nowhere in sight. A great blue heron stood on pencil legs in the edge of the water, and then it lifted itself in a lazy swish of wings to the far side of the river.

As she ran, her eyes searched the riverbank. What would she do if she discovered a body? Would she smell it before she came upon the badly decomposed remains? She forgot to look up into the trees for the barn owl.

Breathing hard, she made her final dash through the orange grove. Frank's van was gone. Perhaps he was getting the card. Closer to the main building, she smelled cinnamon rolls and laughed to herself. Dear FR had made his famous treat.

Eager to get a quick shower and enjoy the special breakfast, she burst into the hall and reached her key toward the lock. The door pushed open. Startled, she pulled her key against her chest. She never forgot to lock a door. Her dad had pounded that into her head wherever they lived in the world, "We may be among allies, but sometimes people steal. We can't afford to leave a door unlocked and cause an international incident."

She froze. The room was dark. Heart pounding, she reached inside and flipped the switch for the overhead light. Bedlam. The drawers of the little chest hung open, her bra looked naked splayed across the tile floor. Her satchel sat open on the bed next to its black silk lining. She dropped to the bed, clutched the smooth leather, and stared into the hollow where stitching joined the sides to its broad bare bottom. She flung it aside, looked under the bed, and then realized that the window was open, the curtain fanning in the breeze.

She sat on the bed staring at the satchel, the vessel that had been her security—empty and ripped apart.

Chapter Five

Meredith sat on her bed, her fingers digging into the leather of the empty satchel. Without money, without her social security card, she couldn't stay here. But how could she get away? Her quick decisions, nimble lies, uncanny good fortune at being alive—had left her empty, nowhere to turn.

The knock on her door caused it to swing open to Arlene, gazing at the mess. "What the hell happened?" She was across the room, tossing the satchel aside, bundling Meredith into her arms.

She leaned into the bony shoulder. "It's all gone. I can't pay Frank. I can't stay. And I don't have a way to leave."

"No, no, no! Hush that talk. We'll figure this out." She rocked Meredith like a colicky baby. "First thing, I'm picking up this crap." She scooped up the bra, shut the drawers, and arranged the scattered English class papers back in the folder. "We need to tell FR. He sent me to see about you... And there he is."

The priest stood in the open doorway, his hand tracing the broken lock, his face aghast as he stared at the satchel on Meredith's disheveled bed. "You've been robbed?"

I've got to tell the truth. She nodded, her mouth drawn tight.

His eyes darted to the still-bolted door into Max's room and then back to the damaged lock. "We should never have put in such flimsy hardware."

"Yep. You can open these doors with a credit card." Arlene flopped back onto the bed, folded her arm around Meredith's shoulders.

Father Rich paced about the room. "They must have gone out the window. We better get the sheriff."

"No. That might stir up trouble for the center." She couldn't look at his face. If she did, she'd have to admit her real reason was fear of getting caught.

"I'll ask Frank and Max to look around. Whoever it was may still be out there. Maybe they left tracks under the window."

Meredith lifted her head as he hurried away. She wondered if he actually believed the thief was a stranger.

"You're legal now," Arlene whispered. "Frank's back with your card."

"But I can't pay. I don't have a penny."

"Not to worry. Frank's good for it." Her toothy grin spread across her face. "And your credit's good with him."

Or he'll break my leg? Meredith forced a smile.

Rich returned with a steaming cup of coffee and a warm cinnamon roll. "This is my prescription for now. Frank and Max are looking around. We'll get a locksmith in here tomorrow. Make all our doors more secure. Meantime, I'm putting a bolt on the inside and a strap lock on the outside."

Meredith moved by rote through the day while everyone zipped around, trying to make life right again. Frank brushed aside Meredith's effort to thank him. "I'll pay you back as quickly as I can," she said.

"At your salary? We should live so long. Don't get all sideways. Do what you can."

Is he so easy-going because he's the thief? Meredith nodded, unable to speak. If he did it, she didn't want him to see her cry.

Whatever the truth, she'd pay him back or bust.

At supper, Lupe stood at the end of the table holding an envelope against her breasts. She cleared her voice and in English she said, "We take up money for Shannon. A little till your pay." She scurried to the end of the table and bowed holding the offering with great reverence.

Meredith had controlled her tears all day, but that envelope and the message it offered brought a snorting sob as she leaned into Lupe's embrace. There were thirty, one-dollar bills with a note from Arlene saying they hoped it would last until payday.

That night as she crossed the hall from the bathroom, Lupe stood outside her door. "My Maximillian gave the most. Ten dollar."

Guilt payment? Meredith bent to hug Lupe. "That was so generous. I know you're proud of him."

Lupe nodded, folded her fingers in prayer fashion at her waist, and hurried down the hall.

She thinks he's the thief. Meredith watched Lupe wipe at her eyes as she closed the door to her room.

True to his word, Rich had the locksmith out. And Meredith forced herself to stay present to the three women who came to coffee and the stumbling conversation about how to talk to their children's teachers.

At lunch, after everyone left the dining hall, Meredith asked Arlene how to find the community grocery.

"Wait till I've got supper going, and I'll drive you." Wiry little muscles moved tattoos on Arlene's skinny arms. A trickle of sweat creased her hairline as she kneaded a roll of dough.

"I need to get back before school's out. I expect some kids to come for the computers and a few women to show up during basketball practice."

"Go through the orange grove behind FR's and my house. They're picking Navels right now, but you won't be in the way. That's the kid's trail. It's a lot safer and closer than going out to the highway. After you cross the bridge over the resaca, you can't miss the store. It's a couple of blocks north of where the trail passes between a row of houses."

It felt good to walk fast, feel sweat trickling down her back, concentrate on movement to relieve the tension. The rows of trees hung thick with oranges, scenting the air with their heady citrus aroma. Men in loose-fitting clothes wore hats with rags tucked in back like curtains covering their necks. She wondered which men were husbands of the women in her classes. She tried not to stare as they moved like machines—skittered up ladders, grasped fruit in each hand, filled a bag on their shoulders, scooted down, dumped the oranges in crates—and started over again. No one saw her, or if they did, they weren't about to miss a beat in their rhythm. She wondered how much they earned for each pick.

The trail moved between a line of flat-roofed stuccoed houses colored in faded pastels. Spindly mesquites offered yellow–flowered shade. Dogs barked and came to investigate. She waved at small, half-dressed children who stared at her from behind wire fences draped with wash. When she turned onto the caliche-covered street, she spotted the two-story, wood-fronted store. One ancient pickup nosed the screened double doors.

"*Hola*," the woman behind the counter called as Meredith hesitated at the entrance, adjusting to the dim interior.

"Aw, your *pan dulce* smells wonderful," Meredith called out in Spanish and gazed at the counter stacked with several varieties of Mexican sweet breads. "Are you the baker?"

The woman's silken brown hair was pulled back to frame a once-beautiful face made soft by smile lines. "Ol' man Camacho makes them. He's out back taking a nap. You want him?"

"No, thanks." Meredith nodded toward two wooden tables sitting in front of a line of coffee and soft drink dispensers. "I want to enjoy one of your sweet breads with a cup of coffee."

"You beat the school kids. The ol' man always makes a fresh batch for them and the highway crews. The farmworkers save their money for beer." It sounded like a statement of fact, not judgment. Leaving Meredith to enjoy the treat, the woman busied herself replenishing a barrel of oranges.

When she hooked the plastic shopping basket over her arm and selected the large-size box of Tampax, she was startled at the price. The sticker on the deodorant caused her to start calculating how far her thirty dollars would go. *Get used to this. From now on, you watch prices.* The travel-size shampoo from the women's center was gone, and so was the tiny tube of toothpaste. As the tab mounted, she backtracked for smaller sizes, thinking how stupid she'd been to blow three bucks on the pan dulce and coffee. The total with tax would leave very little until payday.

The old register took forever to clang each number in bold black letters.

$30.08

Meredith's heart pounded, pumping the flush from her throat to her face. "I was sure I added correctly." *You are not a thief. Stop feeling so damn guilty.* "I'll put something back."

"Wait! How short are you?" The words came soft, no indictment.

Her throat tightened when she looked into the brown eyes crinkled into a smile. "I have thirty dollars."

"Aw, forget it." The woman waved the back of a brown hand. "The ol' man cheats ever'body outta that much ever day."

"I don't want to get you fired. I'll get a cheaper toothpaste."

"Fired? Hell, honey, I own this place." Her breasts bulged as she leaned across the counter and spoke in a stage whisper. "Secret is, I married the ol' man because I needed a steady cook."

Meredith laughed and reached for the woman's hand. She seemed too tough to welcome a hug. "I'm Shannon."

"Carmelita." She clasped Meredith's hand with both of hers. I saw you come up the road. You staying around here? You're not part of the migrant crowd?"

Carmelita. Meredith looked at the fleshy rolls beneath the bright orange muumuu and imagined her young—hair flowing down her back—dancing to the staccato rhythm of castanets. "I teach English at the community center. We have morning and afternoon coffee klatches, and we're starting a class tonight."

"You teach reading?" Carmelita switched to English, "Mama taught me to read Spanish before I started school. Never learned to read English."

"I'll teach reading to anyone who's interested."

"Ha. I been selling the *Brownsville Herald* for years. Never read a word of it."

53

"The night class ends a little after eight. You want to come then?"

"I'll see how the ol' man manages the beer crowd for an hour or so. If he doesn't mess up, I may be a regular."

Meredith smiled and swung her plastic sack of treasures as she traced her route back through the little village and the orange grove. She was pulling for ol' man Camacho to do a decent job with the beer drinkers.

A big Suburban pulled up to the door of the library a few minutes before seven. Carmelita swept out in a flowing rose-colored muumuu, her feet adorned in glittering sandals. "Figured I should work on my English, too."

"Doesn't sound like you need help," Meredith laughed as Carmelita circled the room, speaking English as she hugged all three women and kissed more than eight preschoolers and babies. The big beautiful woman received the same quiet deference as Rich. She obviously was more to these women than a local grocer.

The class was the best yet. Even the children looked to Carmelita for approval of their performance. When the last of the group left, Meredith hooked her arm through Carmelita's as they walked back into the library. "I could use you in every class. You inspired them all."

"Thanks for not telling them I can't read." Carmelita ducked her head. "I got kicked out of school at the beginning of second grade."

"Kicked out? I can't imagine you as a rowdy kid."

"The school forbid us to speak Spanish. I hated English. It felt bad in my mouth—harsh and brassy. So, when I came home crying every day, Papa made a stink at the school board. They said I either did it their way or stayed home. He decided my arithmetic was so good that I should learn to run the store."

Meredith touched the soft roundness of Carmelita's shoulder. "You're smart as a whip. You'll be reading in no time." She blinked back tears and turned to the shelf of books she hoped would interest Carmelita. "You want to read romance novels, history of the Rio Grande, the newspaper? We can start anywhere."

"Let's start on the paper. I want to know what it says about the attack on the World Trade Center." She was already pulling the *Times* off the lower shelf.

Meredith clutched her fingers into a fist to still the tremor and heard her dad's voice saying *Suck it up. It'll make you stronger to read all that again.*

"I know *the* and *new.*" Carmelita traced her finger along the banner.

"That's a good start. It's *The New York Times.* That caption under President Bush's photo says, 'His speech showed he was calm and resolute even in face of a continuing threat."

Carmelita's fingers followed the words. "I can read *he, was, and, in, a.*" She shook her head. "That's not much. That's all I learned when we had to read about Dick and Jane and jump."

Meredith laughed. "And you still know those words! Let's get busy and get you reading more interesting stuff."

"Look, this picture was on the news. They're protesting against invading Afghanistan. Let's read this article."

Meredith crawled in bed that night, pulled the curtain back to view a blanket of stars framed in the window. Some force beyond her needed to be thanked.

It felt like she had slept for some time when voices in Max's room—low and urgent—woke her. She looked outside where a dim swatch of light from a pole behind the clinic cast a haze in the darkness. Her clock rolled over to three.

"You can't do this. What about your education—"

"I'll get it. The recruiting officer said it'll be free."

"Don't believe. He just wants you. There's going to be war. He don't care you'll be killed."

"I'm already in danger. The border's shut down. They keep stopping me. I'll be a hell of a lot safer in the army. Besides, I've signed up. I gotta be at the bus station at six. Help me find my sweatpants. Fast."

"I don't know your sweatpants. Talk to Father Rich. He knows best."

"Shit, woman. He's a damn priest."

"How about Miss Shannon. She's smart."

"Smart? She's a dumbass working here for nothing. Besides, where did she come from?"

"You mustn't say that. Have respect."

"Respect? You're so stupid. Always believing the goody gringos. You're gonna be sorry one day that you trusted these people, especially that fake priest. Doesn't even wear a collar."

"Hush up, Maximillian. You're shaming your mama."

"I'm sick of you and this whole place. I got to git if I'm catching that bus. See you sometime." The walls shook as the door slammed shut.

Meredith lay in the dark, listening to Lupe sobbing on the other side of the wall. She felt torn with the need to comfort the woman, yet aware that Lupe would feel ashamed to know she'd been overheard.

Chapter Six

When the clock glowed five, Meredith crawled out of bed, aching with grief for Lupe still crying in the next room. She needed to run, and she wanted to let Rich know what had happened.

He waved at her as she came around the corner of the building. "I hoped you'd be out this morning. I'm bursting with news." Even in the dim light from the pole at the edge of the property, his face looked radiant. "Carmelita gave me a check last night for $500." He grabbed Meredith's shoulders and shook her for emphasis. "For books in the library!"

"Can she afford that?"

"Oh yeah. She's a regular benefactor. But this was out of the blue." He swung into a steady jog. "I could hardly wait to tell you."

"Your good news may soften what I tell you about Max—"

"What's he into now?" The words spewed out, singed with disgust.

Meredith tried to keep her tone neutral as she related what she'd heard. There was no reason to share Max's opinion of the two of them.

"I hate it for Lupe, but it might be best. Sometimes the military's what a kid needs. Max was ten when his dad went to prison. It's not been easy for him."

"I hope you can help her feel better."

"Yeah. I'll meet her after mass. She never misses."

"Where's the church?"

"It's an old chapel in the Gallegos' compound. French priests—Oblate fathers—came to the Valley in the mid-1800s. One was an architect." Rich chuckled, sort of to himself. "I've always imagined that Father Pierre Yves Keralum was a bit of a maverick like me. He was a priest who preferred being an architect. So, he went up and down the Valley on horseback building little Gothic Revival chapels in the midst of the mesquite."

"And, one of his chapels is on the Gallegos' land?"

"You bet. Most of them have deteriorated. Not the Gallegos'. The family has maintained it in pristine condition. Down to the polished pews. You'll have to come see."

"I'd love to."

"Anyway, one of the young priests from Immaculate Conception Cathedral in Brownsville, which Keralum also designed, conducts mass here every Tuesday, Thursday, and Saturday morning. Lupe never misses."

They turned around at the end of their run and started back along the river when they both saw splashing on the Mexican side.

"He's drowning!" Rich whispered and arched into a shallow dive, skimming the water in a few powerful strokes toward what looked like a child, arms thrashing.

Meredith froze, her gaze fixed on three men dissolving into the thicket of trees on the far bank. Rich appeared to ignore them as he cradled the small body and swam easy, his voice a soothing murmur.

Thank God, he won't be a floater. "I think he's running from those men," she whispered as the priest rose out of the water carrying a child in his arms.

"Yep, and he's exhausted. Let's get him to the clinic." Rich was already jogging, the boy clasped in his arms. Small hands gripped the back of the doctor's shirt. "*Estas seguro*," he kept repeating all the way to the clinic. When he laid the boy on the hospital bed, he assured the child again that he was safe.

Rich stroked the wet mat of black hair away from the boy's face. "He's a baby. Scared half to death." He held a glass of water for the boy to sip between sobs. "Ask Arlene for oatmeal and milk. I'll get him cleaned up."

When she returned with a tray, the child was not making a sound as he smeared at tears with his fingers and wiped them on an animal-printed hospital gown.

"*Señorita Shannon. Se llama Javier Escandón. Tiene quatro años,*" Rich said.

"*Hola, Javi.*" She squeezed his hand.

"Men hurt his *mamá*. She told him to swim across the river to America." The doctor shook his head, switched to English. "Sounds like they killed her. And they were after him."

Meredith swallowed bile. "And this baby witnessed all that."

"Whatever happened to her has terrified him." He smiled at Javier. "You've cleaned your bowl. Want more?"

Javier nodded, black eyes tearing again. He wiped his face and then his mouth on the paper napkin. *"Atole?"*

"Ha!" He stroked the child's tangled curls. "I bet we have brown sugar cane and cinnamon sticks. Let's ask *Señorita* Shannon to get us some atole and more breakfast."

When she brought a tray of eggs and biscuits and mugs of atole, she saw the surprise in Rich's raised brows as Javier tucked his napkin into the neck of his gown.

They could hear patients arriving, settling in the waiting room. Right on time—at exactly seven—Maude swept into the room. She stood beside the bed, head tilted back, examining the boy through her bifocals. "Four years old? Has he had his shots?"

Rich kept his hand on the child's shoulder. "Probably not."

"So, he's a wetback...?" Her hand flew to her mouth. "Sorry, it slipped out."

"Not around here, Maude. I mean it." His eyes narrowed, shutter-speed fast before he turned to Meredith. "Will you stay with Javier? I still need to check on Lupe."

Maude started out of the room and stopped, pointed out the window. "Like I figured, the border patrol's already onto him. Look! They've pulled up to the kitchen door."

Rich scrambled out of his mud-soaked jogging shoes and

hurried to his office for a pair of old loafers. "Maude, please take care of the patients who're already lined up." Anger edged his voice. He turned to Meredith, "if Maria's here, ask her to bring her kids and sit with Javier."

"I can stay with him."

"If the border patrol comes in, Maria will look like his mother. If it's Jeff McDade, we're okay. He's our man in the trenches."

As soon as Meredith explained, Maria appeared to know the drill. She quickly gathered a few trucks and Legos and hustled her children to the clinic.

Javier perked up when the kids arrived, but choked into sobs and leaned against Maria as she stroked his cheek. Her children, unimpressed with the new kid, sprawled on their stomachs to roll cars under the hospital bed.

Meredith hurried to her English class reeling with questions of how these people cobbled together the strength to survive. How did they face the gripping terror of a lost child almost drowning and then calmly hide him from the authorities?

She stepped into the library where two women—young and already overweight—corralled squirming children. She laughed and joked in dual English and Spanish as they settled their brood for the class. No one noticed, or maybe cared, that her pants and shirt were stiff with dried sweat and mud. Tolerant was the word she thought of as she watched everyone accept without question the events swirling about them. As they munched cookies and sipped coffee loaded with cream and sugar, she wondered if the snacks were the only attraction. Between bites, maybe they'd absorb a little English.

After class, Meredith looked in on Javier. Her heart lurched at the sight of Rich approaching with a towering man dressed in official-looking green pants and shirt.

Border patrol Jeff McDade's face was chiseled in the image of a young Paul Newman—same penetrating blue eyes. Only this look-alike was a half-foot taller, stooping as he entered the clinic. "Glad to see you, Maria. Is the boy feeling better?" He might be an Anglo, but his Spanish sounded local.

"Almost well." Maria stroked Javier's cheek. Not a guilty bone in her body.

"We'll send out feelers. See if we get a clue on his mother."

After introductions, he reached for Meredith's hand, "I understand you overheard Max and his mama last night."

He's not here to take Javier. Relief made it feel like her knees might buckle. "Would you like to talk in the library?" Did she sound like an innocent bystander?

When they stepped inside, McDade's gaze scanned the room. "Nice setup. I help in the gym, but I've never come in here. Do you have many takers for your classes?"

"Mornings, afternoons, and nights." What if he asked how long she'd been here? She wiped a crease of sweat off her lip.

"So, tell me about Max. Did he tell his mama why he joined the army?"

"Not really. Sounded like restrictions on border crossing made it hard to get to work."

McDade nodded. "Yep. He's been squeezed." He flipped through a little notebook. "You ever see him with a lot of money? On a buying spree, maybe?"

He was the grand donor when I got robbed. "Nothing big. Bodybuilding defined Max."

She went over what she heard, again leaving out Max's opinion of her and the priest.

He flipped his notebook to another page. "Rich said you saw those guys across the river this morning. Did you notice anything about them? Could you identify them?"

She shuddered, was it the memory or relief? "They faded into the trees so fast that it felt creepy. I wouldn't want to meet them."

"Huh. That's wise. There're some bad characters over there."

A couple of women who had arrived with their laundry came into the library. McDade called them by name, took time to chat a minute, and then stood. "Thanks for your help. Looks like you've got a good operation here. If I have other questions, may I come back?"

"Oh, sure. I'm always around." She immediately wished she'd not said that.

"So, you live here?" He smiled with those Paul Newman eyes.

"I have a room." She told herself to stop talking.

"I'll see you then. My boys and I live on the other side of the orange grove." He nodded toward Carmelita's houses.

She decided not to extend the conversation by indicating that

61

she knew Carmelita. He was a hunk, but she didn't need to chat with a lawman.

He said good-bye to both women who giggled like schoolgirls, obviously as charmed as she was. Maybe it was getting away from Harvey that turned her on to every man she saw. She had to get a grip. Entanglements spelled trouble.

McDade waved toward the kitchen and folded himself into a green and white jeep. She realized that the two-toned vehicles she had glimpsed through the trees moving along the river trail were border patrol. It seemed odd that she had never met one when she and Rich were jogging. Did they wait in the trees...watch them go past? She'd have to pay better attention.

He was barely out of sight when Lupe crossed the path to the clinic carrying two large plastic bags. Her eyes were tear-puffed, almost shut.

Meredith entered the clinic as Lupe spread the clothing on Javier's bed. "Father Rich sent these to you." Her teary smile took in everyone as she held out a little cowboy shirt.

Javier's fingers stroked the shirt's snap buttons. He pushed the covers back and began pulling off the hospital gown.

When they gathered for lunch, Rich paced the kitchen. "Maria and the children will eat with us, but she's got to get home before school's out. And *we* need to decide what to do with Javier." He looked around the room like he was searching for an answer. "The kid's got to feel safe until they get an answer about his mother. Jeff doesn't expect it'll be good."

"He can have Maximillian's room..." Lupe buried her face in both hands.

"A room isn't enough." Rich eyed the industrial-size stove and sink and the two long tables stretched under the row of bare fluorescent lights. "He needs a family."

Meredith scooted next to Lupe and squeezed her arms around her while she shook with silent sobs. Finally, Lupe rummaged in her pocket for a wrinkled tissue. "Will you help me clean out Maximillian's room?"

"Of course."

Maria came to the kitchen with all the children who were silenced by the large space. Javier's face was flushed red, and he huddled against Maria. "Miss Maude gave him shots," she whispered.

His big eyes searched, connected first with Rich, and then with Meredith. A slight smile of recognition turned into a broad grin when Arlene placed a plate of tamales, rice, and beans before him. Again, he tucked his paper napkin in his collar and wiped his mouth when he finished.

Rich moved around the table and squatted beside the boy. His voice stayed low, almost a whisper.

The child's face grew solemn, he shook his head and inched closer to Maria, who looked near tears.

Finally, the priest motioned to Meredith. "Let's show him his room. Let him see how his door opens into yours and Lupe's."

She felt like crying with relief. The good priest was probably breaking the law. At least he wasn't sending the child away.

The boy latched onto Maria's hand and followed Rich down the hall. He hung back until Meredith hurried next door and slid the rusty bolt away to open her space. He stepped one foot into her room—his eyes examining. After pacing between all three rooms, he nodded—a four-year-old aware he had nowhere else to go.

His lips trembled when Maria bundled him in her arms and in rapid Spanish explained how she and the children would be coming every day. When she finally turned to leave, Meredith whispered, "Thank you for helping him."

Maria nodded, her face reddening as she hurried her children out the door.

When Javier realized they were emptying the room for him, he bundled some of Max's shirts in his arms and grinned. "They smell good, like my *papá*."

Meredith realized that all the adults froze for a beat. He has a *papá*. Had they killed him? Then Javier moved on, began stretching his new shirts from Lupe's store onto the coat hangers that had belonged to Max.

That afternoon, Maria returned with her older boy, who quickly championed Javier as his own. The child appeared eager to sit on the floor and lean against Maria's son all during the English class. Then he followed the children to the gym to chase basketballs.

Maria stood in the doorway watching, her arms folded across her full belly. "My man says we got too many babies. This one will make six. We don't have no more beds or room at the table." She shook her head. "If that man would let me take Miss Maude's pills, we won't be so crowded." She looked up at Meredith. "You know men? They can't keep they britches zipped. Always ready to make another one."

As though connected by an underground information network, Carmelita and Don Gaspar arrived for supper. The old man honored the occasion by wearing a handsome white Mexican wedding shirt. Carmelita wore a flowing red muumuu and strapped a matching red tank of helium over her shoulder. After introductions, she held out a soft brown bear to Javier, who stood tight against the priest's leg. "You want balloons in your room?"

Javier pulled the bear, which was half his size, against his chest, mouthed "*Gracias, Señora*" without making a sound. He stared at the tank, unsure of what it would do. Carmelita tore into a large sack of balloons, fastened one to a hose, and with a few short puffs of helium, blew it into an image of Mickey Mouse with big round ears.

Javier's eyes danced as he grasped the dangling ribbon. "*Ven aquí.*" He motioned the adults to his room.

Meredith tied Mickey and Minnie Mouse to the foot of his bed. Carmelita continued to blow up Disney characters while Javier bounced about, clutching ribbons for each balloon. Then he stopped and counted, "*uno, dos, tres, cuatro, cinco.*" Naming each of Maria's children, he clutched all five ties and said, "*Les vamos a dar una sorpresa.*"

"They're sleeping now. But you can share in the morning." Rich turned and spoke to the space before him. "He sees beyond himself..."

Don Gaspar's lips pursed, and his gnarly hand caressed the top of Javier's head. "A little child shall lead them..." He bent and kissed the boy's cheek, then took the priest's arm and they walked back to the kitchen.

Meredith had volunteered to give Javier his shower, but she began wondering if she'd lost her mind as she dodged behind the curtain, trying not to get soaked while directing the giggling kid. She had turned the shower into an English lesson, calling out names for body parts. "Soap your face, into your ears, back of your neck." He squealed the names, then curled his skinny butt on the shower drain and scrubbed his feet shouting, "I'm washing my feet."

That was English, plain as day! "Do you speak English?" Why was her heart pounding?

"Yes." He rubbed the cloth between each toe.

"Who taught you?"

"Mamá teaches me." He lifted his head, tears swirling and spilling. "They killed her."

"You saw them hurt her?" Meredith stroked the tiny shoulder.

"Um-hum. She wouldn't let them take me. Then she couldn't move."

Dear God, don't let me cry. "She wanted to protect you."

He stepped out of the shower and pinched his eyes shut. "She said swim to America. But I forgot how. *Papi* saved me."

Papi? Sweet child, are you searching for a daddy? "Father Rich will help take care of you."

"You, too?"

"Yes, me too. But we need a better way to bathe you. I'm soaked." She kissed his forehead and toweled him dry."

When they stepped into the hall, Rich was grinning, holding out a glass. "Milk's supposed to help you sleep."

Meredith pulled at her wet t-shirt hoping her breasts didn't show through. Then she realized the man was focused on the child, following him into the room as he gulped his milk.

"Let's say your prayers." The priest was already kneeling, folding his hands.

Javier, obviously familiar with the routine, dropped to his knees against Rich.

Meredith sank beside them and closed her eyes as Rich's sweet words blessed the boy, asked God to watch over his *mamá* and *papá*, and asked that he be safe for the night. Then he gave thanks that Javier could speak Spanish and English.

She raised her head, but Rich offered no sign that the prayer was intended to let her know he had heard.

Javier crossed himself, not waiting for the priest's example.

"I'll see you in the morning." Rich seemed to see her for the first time. "My goodness, you did get wet." He backed to the door. "I'll leave a light in the bathroom."

With Max gone, he knows we don't need to lock doors. "Good night. And thanks for Javier's milk."

The child shouted, "*Muchas gracias*" and patted the bed for her to lie down—a clear sign someone had been reading to him at bedtime.

She snuggled her shoulder against the hot little body, swept with the fullness that she could have had a child like him. She and Harvey could be in New York getting their boy to sleep. She swallowed hard and began to read *Buenas Noches, Pepe y Mila,* about picking up toys, getting bathed, and going to bed. When Javier began repeating many of the words, she started tracing her finger along each line. Then she read *El Principito* about a pilot who crashed and found a boy who was really a prince from a distant place.

"I'm a *principito* from across the river," Javier pointed. "*Papi* found me."

She needed to tell Rich what Javier was saying. The child was clearly Catholic. No reason for him to confuse the words. "Father Rich is so strong. He carried you to safety." Meredith kissed the boy's forehead. "You call me if you need me. Okay?"

He shoved his face into the bear mumbling "*mamá mamá*" as she turned off the light. She sat on the side of his bed, rubbed his back until she felt his steady breathing.

She found everyone in the kitchen—bent over cups of coffee—their voices low. "I figured he was some peasant's kid who escaped an assault on his mother." Carmelita looked up and waved Meredith to a place next to her. "Shocked he could count. Now Rich says he speaks English. Whatever his background—son of a cartel boss or whatever—he's had a good start.

Chapter Seven

Cartel boss? Meredith froze—waiting—watching the faces as the mention of cartels brought no reaction.

Carmelita looked around the table as she spoke. "Javier's had a good start. While he's here, we need to see to it that he gets into preschool."

"What about Maria's children... and all the others..." Rich turned to Don Gaspar. "We mustn't let Javier slip behind, but this is a wakeup call. All the preschoolers around here deserve the same good start."

"We should talk to my sons." Don Gaspar pushed himself up from the bench, carried his empty cup to the sink, and walked out the door to his waiting tractor.

Rich rose to follow, his step as heavy as Don Gaspar's.

"Wait!" She couldn't let him leave without knowing what the boy was calling him. She reached the door as he turned to face her. Startled by the fatigue lining his face, the almost vacant look in his eyes, she stammered, "He...Javier called you *Papi*."

"Daddy." Rich closed his eyes, rubbed a hand across his face.

"He's lost everything. Searching for a home." A slight smile curled one corner of his mouth. "Makes you want to cry, doesn't it?"

"Yes," she whispered as she watched the priest walk out the door.

"The kid couldn't pick a better daddy." Carmelita came around the table and draped an arm over her shoulder. "I called Frank. He'll produce a birth certificate by morning."

So, Frank is the creator of the needed document? "Can he do it overnight?"

"You bet. We'll help Javier deliver the balloons to his friends. Then off to school, we'll go."

"There are several other children who'll be there in the morning. Do you have enough balloons for all?"

"Sure. I'll bring extra helium, too."

"I agree with Rich. I hate to see Javier go to school, and the others be left behind."

"I bet when Don Gaspar talks to his sons, it won't be long before we figure out a way to get all these younger kids in school. We make sure that while they're here, the older migrant children get on those buses every morning." Carmelita's smile made her face the picture of serenity. "How about you and me getting books for the library after lunch tomorrow?"

Meredith felt a rush of adrenalin. Was it the coffee or seeing power unfold—a few people making a difference. She said, "Rich...told me...about your generous gift—"

Carmelita made a dismissive wave of one hand. "I should've done it long ago."

She watched Carmelita rev the motor of her giant red car, its taillights disappearing into the night. Fatigue folded her into sleep so quickly that her mind had no time to wander.

The shriek jolted her awake. An animal? When it came again, she realized it was Javier and sprinted into his room. He twisted in his bed, pummeling the bear, and wailing a guttural sound.

"Estas bien, Javi." She stroked his face, wiped his snot-covered nose on her t-shirt, and rubbed his back. She kept whispering that he was safe. Finally, his body grew still, and his breathing sounded deep. She crawled back in bed, curled into a ball trying to ease the hurt that she felt for that baby.

The man with the red tie kept falling, flaying his arm, his legs thrashing. She raced to catch him, her heart pounding, her arms outstretched to halt his fall, to cushion him. Then someone snatched her up, shook her until she opened her eyes. She was drenched in sweat. "Javi? What's wrong?"

He pushed his bear into her bed and crawled in. *"Yo quiero a mi mamá. Los hombres vienen a buscarme."* His arms felt like icicles, and his tears wet the shoulder of her t-shirt.

She hugged him against her. "Your *mamá* wanted you safe, *Principito*. Those men are afraid to cross the river." *Dear God, let me be right.* She rocked him until he relaxed.

He thrashed and cried out, the AC clunked, and her mind roamed all the dark alleys of her imagination. The cartels came looking for Javier. Jeff McDade asked about her past. Rich discovered her social security card was a fake. Frank was the thief and maybe a gangster. Or a cartel member?

Finally, the blessed morning light roused Javier. Rubbing his eyes, he sat up, pulled his bear against himself. *"Esos hombres me asustaron."*

Meredith stroked his cheek. "Those men aren't going to scare you anymore."

"Will they let my *mamá* come?"

He cannot see me cry. "She sent you here so we could take care of you."

Javier nodded, crawled out of bed, and trotted to the bathroom. She slipped on clean pants and shirt, her mind searching for ways to make that baby believe her. Maybe convince herself.

When they walked into the kitchen, Rich met them with a grin, "You two slept in this morning?"

She raised both eyebrows. "Javier, Brown Bear, and I don't fit too well on my little bed."

He scooted onto the bench next to the little boy. "You're combed and cleaned up. After you share the balloons with your friends, it'll be time to go to your new school."

Javier nodded, kept eyes on his plate of *huevos y pan dulce.* "Is *Doña* Carmelita taking me?"

"I thought I'd go too," Rich said.

"I'll come back here?" His eyes were huge, black, and

questioning.

"Absolutely. You'll have fun in school. Then tell us all about it." Rich's smile was big, but his eyes looked sad enough to cry.

The class turned to joy-filled bedlam as Javier shared his balloons as fast as Carmelita could blow them up. Meredith changed her lesson plan to naming colors. Finally, they tied the strings to each child's wrist and turned them loose in the gym. Patients from the clinic joined the line of youngsters waiting for Carmelita to fill the balloons. The underground network kicked in, sending migrants and other residents of Carmelita's neighborhood in old cars and on foot to grab a balloon and spill outside to watch the Disney figures dance in the late-morning sunlight.

"Looks like preschool will start another day." Rich tied balloon strings to wrists while Carmelita worked the helium tank.

She looked up, sweat running down the side of her soft brown cheek. "Book-shopping will have to wait, too."

Arlene used all the leftover ham for sandwiches and then resorted to peanut butter and jelly as the balloon-play continued past lunchtime.

Meredith relaxed as she watched Javier romp with as much abandon as any of the children. That night during his shower, he bubbled with English names of body parts and seemed to expect Rich as he arrived with his glass of milk. When they finished his bedtime prayer, he remained on his knees and turned to Meredith, his brows creased. "You didn't cross yourself?"

The truth. "I'm not Catholic, Javi."

"*Papi* is Catholic."

"Not everyone is a Catholic." She looked at Rich, who stayed on his knees, showed no notice of his new name, and made no effort to help her.

"Who's not a Catholic?" Concern clouded the boy's face.

"I'm not sure—"

"*Doña* Maude isn't a Catholic—" The priest was saving her.

"She gave me shots." Javier climbed slowly on the bed. "Okay. You can read to me."

Meredith lay beside the little boy wondering what must be going through his head.

As always, Rich sat next to the boy for breakfast. "You know J*avi*, this school has lots of children who speak Spanish. But most of the time, you will be using English."

He nodded—unconcerned—took another bite of egg. "My school too. We like Spanish best, but our teachers say English is important. *Mamá* says English is a necessity."

"Aw, yes. Your *mamá* is very wise."

"I know..." He wiped his mouth and laid his fork across his plate. "I miss her."

Rich used one arm to hug the child against him while they both finished their coffee/milk in silence.

When Carmelita arrived, Javier skipped out to her SUV. Despite the smooth surface, Meredith feared undercurrents could be building. Were they causing more trauma by sending him to another strange place? She watched the clock as the morning coffee klatch droned on, everyone laughing as they struggled to express themselves in English. Finally, Carmelita's big vehicle pulled near the building. Rich got out, looked toward the library, and offered a thumbs-up before striding to the clinic.

As soon as the class ended, Meredith rushed to meet Carmelita for the planned book-shopping trip. "How did he do? Did he seem frightened?"

"It worked out. His teacher's a young thing. She greeted him in Spanish. Showed him around the school. Introduced him to kids and adults who spoke in English and Spanish. And you know what? Javier did too!"

"His mother deserves the credit. Yet, he was so dirty and ragged when Rich pulled him out of the water..." She shuddered. "He kept saying the men hurt his *mamá*."

"She could've been some rich lady, kidnapped by the cartel. Or, she could be a member who did 'em wrong—"

"That gives me the creeps. And they're right across the river?"

"Yep. Couple of years ago, a guy named Osiel Cárdenas Guillén assassinated his best friend and took control of the Gulf Cartel. He recruited a bunch of army deserters to protect him against other cartels and the Mexican military."

"So, they do whatever they want?"

"Pretty much. The new bunch, *Los Zetas,* joined with the Gulf. Call themselves *La Compañía.* Besides kidnapping, they tax people, operate a protection racket, extort businesses. They'll do whatever it takes to move tons of Colombian cocaine across the river."

"Can we do anything?"

"Last summer the U.S. sanctioned Cárdenas and some other international criminals. Froze all their assets in the U.S. Then outlawed doing business with them."

As they drove into Brownsville, Meredith stared at the scene before them—a mass of recreational vehicles clogged parking lots and eased onto streets at a snail's pace. "Where did all those motorhomes come from?"

"Cha Ching!" Carmelita cackled. "We call them Winter Texans. The Valley's bread and butter. They swarm in about October and stay until the snows melt."

Meredith tried to read a license plate. "What states do they come from?"

"Mostly west of the Mississippi."

Stop scaring yourself. You don't know anyone with an RV. "I guess Florida gets the folks from the northeast?"

"Yeah," Carmelita laughed. "They're nice people. Love our climate and our prices. Never fail to ask for a better deal, even for groceries."

"Do you give senior discounts?"

Carmelita pursed her lips. "Nope. I figure they can afford those fancy rigs, they don't need my help."

"All these people coming down for the winter...they must feel safe..."

Carmelita wheeled into a shopping center parking lot. "We keep hoping things will improve. When Florida cracked down on the cartels in the '80s, they came here. If we get tough enough, maybe they'll go somewhere else." She parked in front of a giant bookstore. Her great breasts heaved, and she looked at Meredith. "Doing this gives me goosebumps. I never figured I'd shop in a bookstore."

Meredith reached for her hand, still clutching the steering wheel. "Give yourself credit. You've been ready to read for a long time. You only needed a push. Look at all the books you suggested for the library." She opened the folder where she'd listed the titles proposed by members of the coffee klatches.

"Okay. Let's go blow our loot."

Meredith eyed the people in the parking lot and the shoppers in the store—ordinary humans preoccupied with their lives—no one looked like a drug dealer. But they could be carrying cocaine, planning to meet the next person in the drug chain. She shuddered and forced herself to focus on book buying.

When they loaded the last box into the car, Carmelita laughed. "Didn't take us long to spend every dime." She steered the SUV into traffic. "There's a children's store downtown. I want to get some kid stuff—toys and sheets—make Javier's room look like it belongs to a boy."

"Brownsville's such a small place, why so many banks along here—"

"We're on Elizabeth Street. Rich Mexicans love our reliable banks. The peso's unstable. So, they put their money up here. Look ahead. Don Gaspar's sons are married to two women who run those banks across the street from each other. They're from really rich families in Northern Mexico."

"Do they have children?"

"Oh, no. They're all business. You'll see them at Thanksgiving, Christmas."

"You think they work with the cartels?"

"Naw." Carmelita laughed. "Cartels launder money through a few big-city Texas banks. But these down here have stayed clean."

"It's scary to think that only a river divides us."

Carmelita sighed. "Brownsville was just named an All-American City for 2001. Those thugs across over there have a Golden Rule. 'Don't kill Americans. It brings too much heat.'"

"You think Javier's family is mixed up in something? You think those men will come after him? I've been reassuring him, but I need some assurance myself."

"I believe he's okay." She pulled into a parking space and left the motor running. "We can talk to Jeff McDade about it. He'll make you feel better."

"You don't think he'll turn Javier into authorities if his mother doesn't show up?" Meredith felt hot all over. Ashamed to be worried that McDade might discover her secret.

When Meredith and Carmelita picked up Javier at his new school, his teacher slipped them a note and then said, "Javier is one of my big boys. He can count to 100. And he knows his colors." She raised an eyebrow as she laid her hand onto Javier's shoulder. "In English and Spanish—"

Meredith took Javier's hand, praying he liked his teacher as much as she did. She read the note: *Javier cried a little after you left him. Then he settled down.* Meredith passed the note to Carmelita.

He climbed onto a junior size seat Carmelita had strapped in the back. "Did *Mamá* come?" The words sounded soft, unsure.

"She can't come, *Principito*. Remember, she sent you here to be safe."

He nodded and watched the scenery pass without another word. As soon as the car stopped, he unbuckled his seat and leaped into Rich's arms. When they entered the kitchen, his eyes searched every corner before he settled for two of Arlene's oatmeal cookies and a glass of milk.

"*La maestra es muy bonita.*" He lifted his eyes and said in English, "My *mamá* teaches me better."

That night, Meredith was better prepared for the bedtime ritual. She had bought a large plastic tub that fit in the bottom of the shower and a long hose she attached to the spigot. Rich waited in the hall with the glass of milk. He lingered after the prayer, and Meredith wondered if he wanted to read the bedtime books.

Javier answered her question with a quick *buenas noches* to the priest and patted the bed for Meredith. Despite the assortment of new books from Carmelita, he wanted to hear the same bedtime stories.

When her clock rolled to five, she jerked awake. Javier was not snuggled against her. She jumped up and peeked into his room. His empty bed shoved a jolt of fear into her throat. She tiptoed to Lupe's door and saw them both curled around Brown Bear.

Is that a twinge of jealousy? She shook her head in disgust for being so petty. She should be glad to have a chance to jog before getting him ready for school.

Rich and Carmelita met with the family at Don Gaspar's big house to discuss the possibility of opening a preschool at the center. Meredith waited until past midnight for him to return with some news. Finally, she crawled into bed, telling herself that something must be developing or they would have ended the meeting.

The next morning, Rich waved as she jogged toward him. "I was hoping to meet you."

She swung in beside him.

"It's all business—no jumping into stuff. They want statistics. We'll ask Maria to get women to count the preschool kids living in Carmelita's houses. Including the migrant apartments."

"I can help."

"We'll need you, for sure. They want to know the cost of teacher pay, supplies, equipment. The Gallego brothers will look into construction. We've got to have an experienced teacher who can help design and set up the place." He touched her shoulder as they reached the bridge and turned around. "It'll take a long time. Thanks to Javier, it's going to happen."

Even after his hand slipped away and they began jogging again, she could feel the pressure. "I can cry when I think of how much joy that little boy has brought."

"Me, too. He's filling an empty spot."

She wished for the courage to ask what he meant.

At five Saturday morning, Meredith's eyes popped open. Javier was not snuggled against her. It should have been her night. He'd been sleeping back and forth between her and Lupe for the past two weeks. She hopped out of bed, dressed quickly, telling herself that it was a good sign—he'd slept in his own bed. Her heart lurched when she saw the blanket thrown back and his bear alone on the pillow. In

75

two strides, she entered Lupe's darkened room. The woman lay on her side, her arms extended as if welcoming a small body.

Had he gone to Rich? He shadowed the man, constantly reached for his hand. She ran around the back of the building. Frank's truck nosed the steps on Arlene's side of the dark duplex. Her breath came hard; throat swelled with fear. She banged on Rich's door, waited, and started to knock again. Arlene's door opened, and Frank's head stuck out, exposing a bare torso. "Doc's at the clinic. Some kid broke his arm."

She turned, shouting over her shoulder that Javier was missing. Lights were on in the clinic, and she could see some adults and the doctor bent over a child. No sign of Javier.

The darkness in the orange grove closed around her, adding to the terror of what might be ahead. He seemed to have settled down. His teacher said he'd stopped crying. Had he been hiding his misery? She burst into the open; the breeze off the river hit the sweat on her body, forcing a shudder. Weeds edged the brooding water—barely moving—harboring its tales of hope and fear.

She squinted. For an instant, she thought it was a great blue hunched on the edge of the bank. Then she saw him huddled in the tall grass, his arms clasping his knees. She tried to quiet her breath, not scare the child. He lifted his head, stared at her like she was a stranger.

"Javi, I've been worried." She scooted down beside him, folded his icy arms against her.

"I want *Mamá.*" His cheeks were wet, and his nose ran onto his lip. "She's gone forever."

Meredith pulled up the hem of her t-shirt and wiped his nose. "She's safe in heaven, *Principito*. And you're safe here."

Gasping for breath, Frank flopped down beside them and reached across the child to include Meredith in his hug. "You scared crap out of us, Javier."

She directed her eyes to the child, hoping Frank would get her message—ease off on the talk.

Frank moved his arm to encircle the boy. "Long time ago, I was scared and lonely when I lost my *papá* and *mamá*. You know what I did?"

Javier raised his head. Waited.

He said they wanted him to be a painter. Named him for Francisco de Goya. Meredith stared at Frank, trying to make her gaze curb his yen to be flamboyant.

The man lifted his free arm, waved his hand as though he were painting the streaks of hazy clouds edged pink by the rising sun. "I went to bed every night looking at the stars because I knew that two of those tiny sparkles were *Mamá* and *Papá*. Couldn't tell which ones because there were so many up there watching over their kids. Made me feel safe, always put me right to sleep. Like a lullaby."

"Heaven's up there." Javier gazed at the sky. "I'll look for them."

"Now that you've got a plan, how about breakfast?" Frank was already standing, and the boy hopped up beside him.

Meredith patted Frank's back. "*Muchas gracias, amigo.*" She meant it, even if he had made up the whole thing.

They'd finished eating when Rich hurried into the dining room.

"Here, Papi. Come sit with us," Javier called.

The priest headed in their direction without commenting on his new title. "They've started burning off the sugarcane. Do you want to watch?"

Javier jumped up, rushed ahead of Rich. "Don't let them burn our house!"

He scooped the child into his arms and hurried around the clinic to the edge of the field. "They're being careful. See how the men use flame throwers to set fire in just the right places. They burn only the cane."

Javier covered his ears to block the roaring sound of leaves sucked into the blaze as it swept across the field. When the flames subsided, smoke rose from the scarred earth leaving charred stalks all the way to the horizon.

"See! It's stopped at the canal." Rich pointed into the hazy distance.

Javier nodded, kept staring at the field.

"Monday, they'll be in here cutting the stalks and hauling them off to make sugar.

"They burned *mi abuelo's* cane." Javier looked back at the smoldering field and then turned away.

"Your grandpa has a big farm?" Rich kept his voice low.

"He went to heaven when they burned his house."

Rich stroked the boy's back as he carried him to the kitchen. "I know that makes you sad."

"And I cry."

"It makes me cry too."

Javier kissed Rich's cheek. "You'll feel better soon."

Meredith wanted to hug both of them.

Worried about Javier's reaction to the sugarcane burning, she kept her eye on him as several women arrived with their children for the Saturday morning coffee and cookie class. When activity in the gym picked up, he joined in the play. No hint of trauma. That night, when they finished reading, he said, "Open my curtains. *Mamá* and *Papá* can watch me."

Meredith's throat swelled as she thought of what the child must have witnessed. She waited until she was sure he was asleep before going to the kitchen.

The regulars were huddled around the table watching President Bush announce military strikes against al Qaeda training camps and Taliban military installations in Afghanistan. She poured her coffee, eyes glued to the screen as it shifted to hazy images of long rocket streaks and puffs of white anti-aircraft responses from the ground. Lupe held her head, elbows on the table.

Meredith slid onto the bench, scooted against Lupe, and wrapped her arm around the woman who flinched with each explosion. "Remember, Maximillian's still training at Fort Hood."

"He'll be there soon." Lupe's tears wet Meredith's shoulder.

Arlene leaned against Frank, whose eyes looked watery in the light of each blast. He stroked her back with the same gentleness he had offered the boy.

Rich's arms sprawled across the table as though his body weighed too much to hold itself up. Did he wish for the comfort of touching someone? Did he tire of always being the consoler? He stood suddenly and headed for the door. "I wonder if we'll blow up the whole country to destroy a few terrorist camps and capture bin Laden." He did not wait for a response, waved a dismissive motion, and walked out the door.

Chapter Eight

Meredith joined Maria's team as they walked the neighborhood and counted an encouraging number of three-and four-year-olds for the preschool. Maria kept the list of eligible children, and Meredith tracked adults interested in conversational English and reading classes.

On the first morning, Maria pointed out Jeff McDade's house, a white wood structure that dominated the block. It looked like a cottage in a home and garden magazine—sparkling white with green shutters, grass trimmed to the edge of flower beds that were a riot of colorful hibiscus. Tree-size bougainvilleas crowned the house in pinks and reds. The other homes along the street appeared worn out, and the yards sprawled into dusty kid playgrounds.

"I would expect Jeff's house to be as neat as he is." Meredith stood in the middle of the street, absorbing the image. "That's the way Dad kept our houses at each deployment."

Maria folded her arms over her bulky middle. "Everybody loves Mister Jeff. We don't care if he's squeaky clean because he takes care of us. When bad stuff happens, he fixes it."

"It was the same with my dad. He was loved wherever we lived." As they moved on down the street, counting children, she kept thinking about Jeff, wondering if his home life—in its perfect setting—was as strained as hers had been.

When they finished the count, the Gallegos Foundation held another meeting. Meredith waited up, hoping to hear the news. Rich's old truck rattled to a stop by the kitchen door instead of moving under the shed beside his house.

He pushed the door open. "I saw you waiting." He smiled thanks as she handed him hot coffee. "The Gallego boys started to back-pedal. They didn't like the idea of losing half the class of forty when the migrants leave in April."

"That leaves twenty, for God's sake!"

He nodded, "I talked long and hard. Argued that six or seven months of preschool—same as the older kids get in public school—will change lives."

She wanted to reach across the table, hold his hands, and comfort him. Instead, she held his eyes with hers. "Your argument's good. You'll make them see—"

His face softened. "Sorry, I'm dumping on you. Carmelita saved the night. She pointed out that twenty children would require at least two teachers. Plus helpers. While the workers are here, we'll need four teachers. That got their attention."

She softened her voice to a whisper, spread her hands across the table. "Remember, Don Gaspar's here every day. Javier will remind him how much a child learns at that age."

He clasped both her hands. "I'm glad you waited for me." He pulled back, blew out his breath, and stood.

She held her hands against her breast and watched him hurry out the door.

For Thanksgiving, Javier brought home a big paper turkey he had colored. They hung it on the dining room wall at the end of the tables. Carmelita brought her ol' man and a roaster pan brimming with hot tamales. Meredith was surprised to see the ol' man wasn't old at all, just sagging around his middle from eating too much of his own *panes dulces*. Maria and her family provided mounds of roasted sweet potatoes, and Don Gaspar and his sons and their beautiful wives dropped by with four pecan pies.

A white four-door pickup—washed like new—stopped near the kitchen. Jeff McDade and identical twins who Meredith had seen playing basketball with the elementary kids, climbed down from the high cab. Jeff lifted a smoked turkey from the passenger door.

"I'd like you to meet Patrick and Carson." Jeff beamed at his sons who were smaller versions of their father, including their perfectly combed sandy hair and luminous blue eyes.

Javier called, "*Mamita*, sit with us," as he crawled onto a bench next to Rich.

Mamita? Meredith caught the flash of anxiety on Rich's face. Had they been expecting miracles? The boy had been sleeping through the night, appeared to be less needy. She settled next to him and then tensed again when Jeff and his sons scooted onto the facing bench.

Father Rich offered a quick blessing and then said, "Jeff and his sons smoke the best turkey in the Valley."

"It's delicious. How do you smoke it?" She would never smoke a turkey, but it was something to say.

"Built it out of an old oil drum."

"They haul it everywhere. Jeff cooks for border patrol get-togethers." Rich grabbed a hot tortilla from a basket passing along the table and slathered butter on it for Javier.

Spanish and English flowed, blending like the mixture of Mexican and Anglo foods— turkey and tamales, hot sopapillas and pecan pies. The afternoon mellowed with beer and margaritas. Frank settled in the corner of the room, strummed flamenco chords on his guitar.

Someone flipped on the news to President Bush addressing troops and their families at Fort Campbell, Kentucky. He looked confident as he said, "Afghanistan is just the beginning of the war against terror. There are other terrorists who threaten America and our friends, and there are other nations willing to sponsor them." Lupe edged in between Carmelita and Meredith as the president went on to say, "we aren't going to be secure until all the threats are defeated."

"War forever," Lupe whispered. "Maximillian will be gone soon."

"We've got war at home, too." Carmelita spoke softly. "I read in the newspaper that we've arrested almost twelve hundred people since 9/11. We're holding them in jail because they're from the Middle East or South Asia."

Meredith caught herself before she blurted out congratulations to Carmelita for reading the paper. "I saw that article. It scared me."

Carmelita's smile was radiant, a woman who had joined the literate. She raised her voice, "How about it, Jeff? Have you fellows arrested a lot of Middle Easterners?"

He set his beer can down and smiled at the faces turned toward him. "No. Not a one." He grinned, "But we're keeping an eye out."

The buzz of conversation picked up, and everyone moved outside, where Rich brought out a kickball. The sun slipped past the palms separating the complex from the scorched sugarcane field. Most of the adults settled on folding chairs. Jeff pulled his next to Meredith. "Would you and Javier go for pizza and roller-skating with me and my boys tomorrow night?" He shrugged. "The pizza's okay. I mainly watch to make sure the boys don't break their necks."

Me and Javier? Stay calm. "Sounds like fun." Did she appear to mean it, or could he tell she was nervous? So far, he wasn't asking questions. Sitting around, watching kids skate could open the door. "I haven't skated in years." She grinned. "I'll try if you promise not to laugh."

"It's a deal." His blue eyes looked as inviting as a pool waiting for a skinny-dipper.

Rich ambled over, sweating from a round of kickball with the kids who were Javier's age. He had opened a can of beer and held it against his forehead. "May I bring beers to you two?"

Jeff 's nod toward her was a question. She shook her head. "Thanks, I don't drink." She could hear her dad saying no explanation was necessary. She still felt naked.

Jeff shook his head, and Rich melted into his chair without a comment.

A cold beer sounded good, but what if she really couldn't hold her liquor? Harvey swore that she didn't go to sleep at the wheel, that she was in an alcoholic blackout—like her mother. She had been a fool to tell him about the times at the officers' club when she supervised her mother's highball glass, asked the bartenders to refill with mostly water. Now, her eyes roamed the crowd of ordinary people enjoying themselves. She had found a place where she fit. She'd be a fool to gamble.

Finally, Jeff stood, said he needed to get the boys home. Asked if it was okay to pick her up tomorrow at five.

"Sure...great... I know Javier will love it." She remembered to smile. "I will, too."

Watching Jeff head to his truck, Rich said, "He's a nice fellow, Shannon."

"I know. But I'm scared he'll decide to report Javier." That was part true.

Rich sighed, looked toward the boy chasing after a ball. "Jeff's tough on criminals. I've never known him to go after lost souls desperate for a better life."

If he believed that, Meredith wondered, why did he look so sad?

Javier appeared again, clutched her hand in his sweaty palm, and grinned at Rich. He had been doing that all afternoon. Was he making sure they didn't disappear?

At bedtime, he ran ahead to the bathroom, dropping his dirty clothes in a box, and waiting for Meredith to adjust the water. He had mastered washing himself in the little tub, turned it into a singsong English recitation of his body parts.

When they all three knelt for his bedtime prayer, he grabbed both their hands. "Thank you, God, for *Papi* and *Mamita*."

Meredith's heart lurched, forcing a silent gasp of pain. Was this baby trying to create a new family?

As she opened Javier's curtains, she looked back at Rich, still leaning over the boy. When their eyes met, he frowned and shook his head.

"Good night, sweet boy." He kissed Javier's forehead and rushed out.

"So, Jeff's coming in the back door? Using the kids as a ploy to get you on a date?" Sweat ran down the back of Arlene's neck as she scrubbed a gallon-size pot, and handed it to Meredith to rinse and dry.

"Jeff's being nice. He's helping Javier get adjusted."

"Hell, woman. Men who look like Jeff aren't into adjusting kids."

"You're scaring me."

"I'll scare you some more. Are you on the pill?"

Meredith felt the jolt of reality. She'd not had sex since the crash. Her prescription expired years ago.

Arlene tossed the pot scrubber in the sink, wiped her face on her sleeve. "Don't say it. Your face tells it all." She blew out her breath, leaned close. "Talk to Maude. She'll be thrilled. She pushes birth control on all the women around here. Upsets their husbands and the priest when he hears about it."

"What does Rich say?" She tried to keep the surprise out of her voice.

"For a man of the cloth, FR's cool. It's the parish priest who keeps everybody in line."

"I can't do that. First off, I don't plan to need the pill." She giggled. "Besides, it feels like Maude runs the morality police."

"Okay. I'll have Frank get you some rubbers. At least you'll have protection... just in case."

Rubbers? If I hadn't been robbed, I'd still have my rescue packet from the women's center. "We're going to eat pizza with three little boys. You make it sound like an orgy."

"It's a start. Come on to my place. I've got some jeans that look a lot better than those tacky things you're wearing from Lupe's store."

Meredith was surprised to see her butt fit in Arlene's skinny-girl jeans. She didn't fill the cotton sweater like its owner, but its rich blue added color to her cheeks. And she caught the admiration in Rich's eyes when she and Javier came to the kitchen to wait for Jeff and the boys.

Meredith watched Javier climb into the backseat of the giant truck and was glad that she had on jeans. She would need to heist a straight skirt to her hips to get her foot high enough to step into that cab.

Jeff touched her elbow until she was seated. His eyes worked like magnets when he grinned. "I know this thing's a monster. But it pulls our boat and all our camping gear."

"It's as high as a bus. We can see everything from up here." She waved at Rich, watching from the kitchen door.

At the rink, Patrick and Carson—experienced skaters—helped Javier lace his shoes and anchored him as they moved onto the floor. He wobbled, and his ankles bowed during a complete circle of the giant room. Then he grinned at Meredith and pushed his feet in a skating motion.

"He's getting the hang of it." Jeff reached for Meredith's hand. "Let's skate along with them."

She wobbled for the first few gliding motions. His firm hold helped her relax and the old balance and physical memory began to return.

"Look at me, *Mamita*!" Javier skated past, the wobbling almost gone and assurance shaping his movement.

"*Mamita*?" Jeff cocked his head, half-smiled.

"He's adopted Rich and me." She shrugged, hoping that would be enough.

After a few circles of the rink, Jeff suggested they order a drink and watch the boys who had not slowed for a minute.

"My skating muscles have atrophied." Meredith laughed as she stepped off the rink and flopped onto the nearest bench. Jeff returned their skates and went for drinks.

"So, tell me how you ended up down here?" He set her soda on a paper napkin and relaxed onto the padded bench next to her.

Don't tell it all. "I thought Mexico would be a good place for a new start. I met Rich on the bus. He convinced me to give the center a try." She grinned. "I liked it and decided it could be my new start."

His touch felt light on her ring finger. "It's not been long since you stopped wearing something on that hand."

He's a cop all right. She pulled her hand to her lap. "You could say I'm escaping an old relationship."

"*I* could say that. What do *you* say?" He hit his forehead with the butt of his hand. "Damn. I sound like a border patrol agent." He bent close. "Sorry, Shannon. I've got the cool of a prairie dog. When I'm interested in someone, instead of asking, I interrogate."

"That's okay. I'm still sensitive." She may have shut him down for now, but he was not going to let up. "How about you and the boys? I didn't look at your ring finger."

He leaned back, sipped his beer. "Fair enough. It's been a long time since I wore a ring. My wife died when the boys were born. We've been on our own ever since."

"I'm sorry. That's hard—two little ones all by yourself..." *Is that all? What can I say now?*

"Naw, I don't mean it to sound bad. I've had help all along. My mother lived with us while the boys were babies. After she died, we moved out to Carmelita's place. The boys have a slew of *mamás* all over the place." He leaned his shoulder against hers. "For instance, if you go to dinner with me next weekend, I have a host of ladies who'll be glad to keep the boys."

"I don't know, Jeff. I'm not sure I'm ready for going out. I feel guilty to be doing this tonight." She stopped, looked at his eyes gazing at her. "Truthfully, I came to give Javier a chance to be with your boys, learn to skate..." She watched him pull back like a man who realized he'd been intruding.

He sucked in a breath. "Well, maybe we can be parent friends."

For the rest of the evening, he treated her like a parent friend. It felt lonely—two people connected by the children they watched.

When they got back, he stepped into the kitchen carrying the sleeping Javier. "Hey, Rich, we've got a worn-out kid."

Rich had been alone—watching television—something she'd never known him to do. He reached for Javier. "I'll take him."

"I'll say good-night to you, folks. I've got two sleeping kids to get home. Shannon can tell you how much fun they had." He seemed to salute her before he hurried out the door.

Rich's eyes followed Jeff. Then he looked at Meredith, a question on his face. "Will you turn back Javier's bed?"

The boy roused just enough to say, "Goodnight, *Papi*."

After she got ready for bed, she slipped down the hall and found that Rich had turned off the television and gone to his apartment. Was he waiting for Javier to get home or for her?

Chapter Nine

Don Gaspar and his sons delivered Christmas trees for all the buildings in the center. Javier and the other children danced on their toes as Jeff McDade and several men set up each tree. It had been two weeks since she'd seen him. He waved and strolled across the gym. "You want to help decorate this big tree?"

She hesitated a moment. "My class is about to start. When it's over, I'll check to see if you're still here."

He nodded and turned to the children who were trailing him. Over his shoulder, he called, "maybe later."

She didn't go to the gym because the kids who came to class with their mothers wanted to decorate the library tree. The nostalgia felt palatable as the women labored in English to recount family holiday customs. She remembered her mom fingering the treasured ornaments as she retold how each one was handed down in the family.

The decorating lasted until bedtime when the entire center had been turned into a holiday party place—lights, colored paper swags, icicles cut from aluminum foil, and children's painted Christmas balls. Rich and several neighborhood men hauled out a life-size crèche, complete with floodlights, and assembled it on the front lawn.

Javier, like all the other kids, was giddy with excitement and wanted to hear four Christmas books before bedtime.

Meredith had drifted into deep, exhausted sleep when the crash of thunder and flares of lightning lit her room. Rain pounded the roof, shook the building. She pulled the bedspread up to her ears and then thought of Javier probably folded into a cold knot on top of his spread. The floor felt like ice to her bare feet as she hurried to cover him. A flash of lightning lit his empty bed. Heart racing, hoping he had crawled in with Lupe, she met the startled woman rushing into the room carrying an extra cover.

"He's gone!" She grabbed Lupe's blanket. "He's out there in his pajamas. I'm going to the river. Get Father Rich." She shoved her feet in shoes, realized she didn't own a coat. *How stupid, not to know this place would eventually get cold.* She pulled her spread off the bed and wrapped it over her head. The wind hit with staggering force. Rain turned the path into a trough of water that splashed up her pant legs. The orange grove loomed black, and then lightning turned the trail white, lit the trees—limbs thrashing—pelting fruit as hard as hailstones. The flashes faded, wiped out the path. Disoriented, her foot caught in a tangle of branches, and she fell on her shoulder—still clutching the blanket. The next flash opened the tunnel of whipping trees as she crawled to her feet. The river lay beyond strobing white waves in the persistent flares. She stared into the darkness, frozen in place, waiting for the next burst to expose the riverbank. Then she saw him, folded over like an injured animal.

Please, God, help me. She fell to her knees, pulled the wet boy into her arms, wrapping him in Lupe's blanket, rubbing his icy arms, stroking his shivering body.

"They're gone," he sobbed, and buried his face in her wet t-shirt.

"Who's gone, *Javi?*"

"*Mamá* and *Papá*. They stopped watching me."

"Ohh! *Javi*." Her heart ached as she looked into the pounding rain blackening the sky. "They're still up there. The clouds covered them. Like a blanket keeping them warm. When the storm passes, we'll see them again. Watching over you."

The flashlight glared, blinded her in its blue light. Rich, breathing hard, knelt, and wrapped them inside his coat. "Thank God. Oh, thank God," he whispered against her cheek. He lifted them both, holding her against him for an instant. "You're soaking wet. Wrap in the blanket. I'll fold him inside my coat."

Frank bounded out of the trees and tossed his poncho over her, pulling her to his heaving body. "Come on. We'll get you warmed up. Arlene's making hot chocolate and coffee."

Rich hurried ahead, swaying with the boy, making soothing sounds. She leaned—drained of strength—against Frank who practically carried her back to the warmth of Arlene's kitchen. A bevy of hands and towels rubbed her and Javier dry. She collapsed on a bench, held the hot cup between her palms, and felt dulled with doubt. How could this child ever get over his trauma? And who was this man Frank who showed every sign of kindness and at the same time knew all the ins and outs of illicit deeds?

Rich, still clutching Javier, settled beside her. The child sipped hot chocolate, his big frightened eyes absorbing the priest's gentle assurances.

Lupe rushed in with dry socks and a red coat for Javier. He zipped it to the top and snapped the hood over his wet head. She held out a bulky down jacket for Meredith. "It's the smallest we have. It'll warm you up."

"It feels soft and comforting." Meredith stuffed her hands into the pockets, and the racking chills subsided.

"Let's get to sleep before morning comes." Rich didn't wait for a response. He carried Javier toward his room.

"I want *Mamita's* bed." He reached over the priest's shoulder to Meredith.

"I'll get dry blankets." Lupe hurried back to the store.

"Remember what I told you." Rich tucked the boy into her bed. "We'll see the stars again when the clouds go away."

Javier stretched out his arms. "Sleep with us, Papi."

"It's *Señorita* Shannon's bed." He kept his eyes on Javier.

"She'll let you. Give him room, *Mamita*." The boy scooted against the wall, patted the bed.

"We can't do that, Javier. He's not my husband." She wanted to add, but I wish.

Rich stroked Javier's hair out of his face. "I'll see you in the morning, dear boy." He left without looking at her.

She spooned her body around the child as he muttered, "Why don't you and Papi get married?"

She kept her voice steady and whispered. "Priests don't get married, Javi."

If the boy heard, he did not respond.

She awoke sweating. Her clock showed five, and the rain persisted. Javier felt like a hot rock, his breathing labored. She dressed in pants and a shirt. Her shoes were soaked with mud. Socks would have to do.

Rich and Frank were already eating.

"Where're your shoes?" Arlene stood at the end of the table, the steam from her mug coiling around her face.

"Nothing's dry. Would you check on Javier? I'm certain he has fever." She accepted Arlene's offer of coffee and followed Rich to her room.

"He needs to be in the clinic." He wrapped the listless boy in the blanket.

Once in the clinic, Javier whimpered a little while the doctor poked and prodded, but he didn't come fully awake.

"It looks like strep throat. His tonsils are lousy. Both ears inflamed. Temp of 103. We'll run a culture. Meantime we'll get medicine in him and get his temperature down." He lifted his eyes to Meredith. "How about you? You're still running around in socks."

"Only a little sore throat." She waved her cup. "The hot coffee helps."

"Let me look." He reached for his light and tongue depressor, motioning her to a chair—taking charge the way he had done on the bus. "You and Javier have matching throats and ears. Your chest is rattling, and your temp is 102." His eyes searched her face, his hand on her shoulder made her melt. "I think you should crawl in this other bed next to Javier and let me watch both of you."

"I hate to miss the class—"

"You *may* teach them a little English. For sure, you'll give them a sore throat."

She and Javier slept most of the day, interrupted only by the good news that Maria had another healthy boy last night. "It's a good thing the midwife didn't need to call the doc," Maude said. "They'd have had a hell of a time finding him down by the river."

Arlene brought trays of soup and juices and the news that Maria and the new baby were in super condition.

She roused in the night to see Rich beside her bed. "What're you doing here?" Her throat was so sore, she could barely whisper.

"I have the sofa in my office."

She didn't have the energy to argue. She closed her eyes, dreamed he had pulled the beds together, and crawled in with them. No one paid attention to him being there. She woke to Lupe standing over her, and felt embarrassed, as if she needed to explain the dream.

"I tried to dry your muddy shoes, but they're curling up." Her smile made her look like an angel. "I found these sneakers and dry socks. Father Rich said, you got to get well before you get up."

Javier's fever broke and he perked up by nightfall. He asked Rich to move their beds together. "I want to hold *Mamita's* hand." He stretched his arm through the metal rail.

"That's a good idea," Rich said.

"*Mamita* said priests don't get married. Will you stop being a priest?"

"Aww," he sounded pained. "I promised to be a priest, Javier. When we make promises, it's very important to keep them. Otherwise, our word's no good."

Javier held tight to her hand. "I wish you didn't make a promise."

Rich avoided her eyes, tucked the blanket around the boy, kissed his forehead, and hurried toward his office.

Javier bounced back within days and romped through the events leading up to Christmas. The children caroled for the Christmas Eve pageant. Maria placed her new baby boy in the manger. She looked radiant as the Virgin Mary draped in the blue bedsheet, gazing at her child.

Meredith went through the motions, sang, celebrated, and enjoyed the small gifts of love, but she moved with a slower, wearied pace. Rich seemed extra busy in the clinic with all the cases of strep throat and flu. He moved in and out of the excitement all during the holidays. On the few mornings when she mustered the energy to jog, he didn't show. She couldn't say he avoided her; he acknowledged her presence, but there was a difference, a remoteness that felt like abandonment.

If it hadn't been for Carmelita, Meredith would not have known about the search for a teacher that can help with the preschool building plans. Carmelita always stayed after class and lifted Meredith's spirits by devouring the Brownsville paper and then poring over the *Times* as soon as it arrived.

One morning in early March, they sprawled after class in the big chairs and sipped coffee. Meredith said, "You've been fooling yourself. All you needed was a little confidence to start reading."

"Yeah, I knew words like sugar, toilet paper, things we stock in the store. Truth is…I didn't marry the ol' man for his cooking. When Papá died, I was desperate for someone who could read. You can't order stuff. Can't run a store without reading—"

Harvey filled the void for me. Until he didn't. Meredith looked at the lovely round face, so open, and before she thought, she said, "How has that been—needing him more than you wanted him?"

Carmelita's eyes roamed off to a private space. "We got it worked out. The store's our connection." She smiled. "You're the only person who talks about what I'm finding in the news. When I told the ol' man that the battle of Tora Bora had ended the war, he grunted. Said he'd believe it when boys like Max come home. My neighbors didn't even care about that young man on the airplane with the bomb in his shoe. They said they'd not be flying anyway." She heaved a big sigh. "Being able to read has narrowed my circle of friends."

"At least we have each other." Meredith had to look away. She'd missed a chance to tell Carmelita her secret. Maybe someday.

Although March brought the heavenly scent of orange blossoms—white flowers clustered around the ready-to-pick Valencias—the atmosphere grew tense. TV and newspapers touted the threat from Iraq. Reports increased linking Saddam Hussein to the September 11 attack, claiming he was a growing threat to the region. After Max's deployment to Afghanistan, CNN drew Lupe like a magnet to its spiraling images of war. Even Arlene gave up her daily soap operas and game shows in deference to Lupe's clamoring need to know.

Despite the national news, the rich orange blossom fragrance that spread everywhere had invigorated Meredith, encouraged her to get back to the trail. To keep from waking Javier, she dressed quietly and ran into Lupe in the hallway.

"I been walking ever morning to chapel with Father Rich," Lupe whispered. "He's so sad."

Meredith clasped the woman's rough hands. "What's happened?"

Lupe shrugged. "He been to chapel ever day. Even when there's no Mass. Me too. Since my Maximillian went to war." She lifted questioning eyes. "Sometimes I see tears. Then I leave fast, so he won't know I been looking..."

So that's why he's not been on the trail. She watched the little woman hurry up the hall and wished she had an excuse to join her.

The white blooms seemed to light the trail through the grove. Large crates lined the path ready for the workers at daybreak to continue harvesting the juicy little Valencias.

She felt as empty as the path that stretched along the river. Had he really stopped jogging? Had their mornings together come to an end? Beyond the orange grove, the stunted pieces of newly planted sugarcane looked as bleak as she felt.

She turned around at the bridge, and looked back at the trail that the sun was beginning to define. The gulf breeze skimmed the river, cooling the sweat that tingled her face and clung to her clothing.

Movement drew her attention to the sunlit weeds, golden along the bank. Had she heard a sound, a voice? She stopped, scanned the edge of the river where the water sloshed into a tangle of brush. A head raised up. Frightened eyes stared from swollen slits.

"Please," it was a whisper. "Please, *Señorita*." A woman raised a hand like a wave.

Meredith squatted, gripped the tiny woman under her arms, and tried to pull her onto the bank. The cry of pain made her stop. She was naked; her hands crossed her breasts in a covering motion. "Don't be afraid." Meredith switched to Spanish. "I'm going to help you."

The woman whispered—again—a plea that slipped unformed from lips so badly bruised and split that trickles of blood oozed between her teeth.

Meredith looked across the river. Were they watching? The trees on the Mexican side formed a thicket so dense that the morning sun did not penetrate.

"My son..." The words, barely audible, were in English.

Meredith stroked the black hair away from her swollen cheek. "I'm going to yell for help. *Auxilio. Ayudame.*"

She kept screaming until two of the workers appeared out of the orange grove, bent as if they were unsure what they were seeing. *"La profesora."*

They ran toward her. When they saw the woman, both men stopped, pulled off their shirts. *"Dios mío!"* They crossed themselves and knelt—a gentleness reserved for the sacraments—to wrap the woman.

Every man who emerged from the trees crossed himself. Their eyes shifted to the far side of the river. They whispered, *"La Compañía.* Turn your back. Don't show your face."

They formed a gurney of shirts, lifted her, and followed Meredith's lead to the clinic. She couldn't hear what they were whispering. Someone had run ahead to get Rich, who entered the clinic just as they lowered her onto a bed.

"Dios mío!" He whispered as he bent over the woman. Maude pulled the curtains around the patient. Within minutes, she handed the migrants' shirts to Meredith.

The men stood outside—a silent vigil—watching, waiting. They passed the shirts among themselves and held them against their chests as though the cloth felt too much like shrouds to be worn again.

"Shannon?" Rich held the door open. His face was ashen. "She's Javier's mother—"

"Are you sure? I couldn't understand her—"

"Her name's Aleta. I've called an ambulance. She needs blood. She's torn all to pieces. More repair than I can do here. She must have fought like a wild animal. Blood and torn flesh are caked under her nails. Broken ribs. He reached toward her. "Help me tell him—"

She gripped his hand. Was it to comfort him or steady herself?

Chapter Ten

Javier was eating breakfast. He had dressed for school and tried to comb his hair. "I did it by myself." He bowed out his chest to show his shirt.

Rich scooped the boy into his arms. "You look terrific." He sank on the bench as if his legs could not hold him. "We have good news for you. Javier...your *mamá* is safe—"

"Where?" The boy whirled, his eyes scouring the room.

"She's in the clinic. But...Javier, she's hurt. She needs to go to the hospital."

"I'll help her!" He scrambled to the floor and ran down the hall.

Rich leaped from the bench, his eyes wild. "God, help us do this right!" He scooped Javier into his arms as the boy reached the clinic. "You must be gentle. I'll lift you up to her."

"*Mamá!*" It was a guttural scream. His arms flayed, his body writhed as he fought to get to the woman.

How can he recognize her? Her face looked contorted in bloody welts. An IV probed one arm; an oxygen tube creased the space between bulging lips and a smashed nose.

Rich eased the child onto the bed, holding him tight to keep from crushing the woman. Her eyes *teared*. She wheezed his name.

"You're safe now. I'll take care of you." Javier used his index finger to stroke her chest. "You're safe, *Mamá*."

"Your *mamá* needs to go in an ambulance. To a big hospital. Where they can get her well."

The siren was faint. Probably turning off the highway. Javier's brows knitted into a deep frown. His eyes grew huge as the flashing lights approached. Jeff McDade's green and white jeep pulled up beside the ambulance. Two men converged on the clinic door pushing a padded stretcher.

Rich circled the child in his arms while the EMS lifted his mother onto the gurney and began strapping wide belts around her. Outside, they watched her loaded into the massive vehicle. A crowd swarmed calling out words of comfort.

"I'll get my books. I can read to her." Javier began to scramble, trying to get out of Rich's grip.

"We can't go with her, Javier. She going to a hospital in Corpus Christi."

"No!" The boy jerked. "I'm going with her." He began to hit Rich in the face. He pounded his shoulders. Screamed to be let down. He thrashed his feet— kicked tennis shoes against Rich's side. Then a mighty thud landed in Rich's crotch, and he crumpled.

Frank materialized out of the crowd, grabbed the boy, and whirled him about, staring into his face. "Javier! Listen to me! Stop screaming! I am taking you to the hospital! Now. In my van."

The ambulance began to move, the siren started its whine. Javier opened his mouth and howled like an injured animal.

"Javier!" Frank's voice stayed firm. His hands gripped the boy's shoulders. "We're going now. Get your clothes! Go now!"

Javier shook, sucked in another sob, and turned to Meredith. "Help me?"

"Yes, sweetheart. I'll help." She grabbed his hand, and they ran together toward his room.

"I'll take my books." His breath came in short bursts like he'd been racing. He jumped to reach his shirts on hangers in his closet.

"I'll get your clothes. And your toothbrush." She wanted to gather him in her arms, tell him it would be okay, but he didn't need it from her.

They stuffed his things in Meredith's bag from the women's center, and he ran to the kitchen. Arlene had packed sandwiches and scooped some bottles of water into a grocery bag.

Frank stepped in the door. "Go pee. And we're off."

"I don't need to."

"Go anyway. We got a full tank of gas. We're not stopping."

Javier ran down the hall and returned, still pulling up his short school pants.

The crowd—it seemed like everyone who had ever been to the center—watched in silence as Frank's old white van stirred caliche dust until it turned from view onto the highway.

Rich, still moving slowly, led the way back into the kitchen. He accepted the glass of iced tea from Arlene. "I've never seen such pure animal rage in a child. No wonder she sent him to the river. He would have fought to the death for her."

Whatever his background, Frank knew how to connect with humans in need. Meredith looked around the table. The faces looked slack—exhausted.

Jeff reached out, clasped her hand. "The workers told me you found her. They're worried about you going alone on that trail. I am too." He looked around. "You need to jog around here. Maybe up to the highway and back."

"You think the cartel is across the river?"

"They're thick over there. They know better than to cross. But you don't need to taunt them."

"He's right," Rich whispered.

She nodded and looked away to keep from asking him to jog with her. This time she had to take care of herself. Not depend on a man.

The women in the afternoon class were as distraught as Meredith. The entire lesson became a conversation in English, then Spanish about Javier, his mother, and the cartels watching from across the river. The women were about to leave, helping pick up the toys and books when Rich stepped in the door.

"The surgeon in Corpus called. She's patched up." He stuffed hands in his pockets, shook his head, and chuckled. "And Javier's settled down. The doctor said he's in the waiting room, holding his books. Planning to read to her."

The tension melted in weepy laughter. They filed out, each woman clasped Rich's hand in silent support. When the last one left, Meredith said, "Arlene keeps a bottle of bourbon in her pantry. How about a drink?"

His shoulders dropped. "That's a capital idea." A frown, "But you won't join me?"

I wish I could tell you. "I need a slug of Arlene's coffee." She resisted taking his hand as they walked across the lawn to the kitchen.

"Frank just called," Arlene shouted as they stepped in the door. "Aleta's gonna be okay. And that kid has captured the entire staff. Three nurses proposed marriage." She cackled. "Javier told them, he'd have to ask his *mamá.*"

The community was abuzz with excitement over the little boy whose mother had miraculously risen out of the river—a symbol of hope that all was going to be right with the world. The coffee klatches drew more participants than ever. Even the number of kids increased who came after school to use the computers. Surely, they seemed to believe, this holy ground would bless all who walked here.

Sarita, a high school freshman who had the bearing of an Aztec goddess, had been using the computers a couple of times a week. After Aleta surfaced, she was one of the kids who began coming daily. On that first afternoon, she had fixed her hazel-blue eyes on Meredith. "It's like God blessed this place." She shoved silken black hair off her shoulder. "I've been finishing my term paper on the computer. Now, I want to do all my homework here...be touched by what's happening."

Meredith mumbled through her best line of encouragement. "It's a great study hall. I'll move the bulletin boards to cordon off an area for you."

"You're so kind," she cooed and settled dreamily before the computer.

A couple of other students came and left before the extra-long conversation—concern and curiosity—about Javier and his mother finally ground to an end. When the last car pulled away, Sarita peeked around the bulletin board. "That was such an inspiring class. I love the way you kept encouraging each lady to speak in English."

"You're welcome to join us." *I bet you wouldn't in a million years.*

"Oh, I couldn't. I'm so busy. I expect to be in advance placement soon." She clapped her hands. "And there's my ride! See you tomorrow."

To Meredith's surprise, the girl appeared the following day, right after supper. The group had been talking about Javier and his mother over the steady clatter of the printer when a car pulled up, sat with headlights glaring through the window. Then the lights flashed.

There was a rustle behind the bulletin board. "That's my ride. And I'm still printing my term paper." Sarita stuck her head out, took in the room with her smile. "Miss Shannon, would you save it for me?" She was already throwing a book bag over her head and rushing to the door. "And I'd love for you to read it."

I'm not editing term papers. "Sure." Meredith watched her dash in front of the car lights. The wheels threw caliche as it skidded away.

All eyes turned back to Meredith. One woman said, "I wonder if Jessie knows who is giving that child a ride?"

"I don't know for sure...but I'd be willing to guess."

Aleta's medical progress no longer held the group's focus, and Meredith was glad when they called it an evening. She was certain that Sarita's mother would know before bedtime just who was giving her daughter a ride.

The printer had mercifully stopped before the class ended. Meredith stacked the girl's printed pages, and her eye caught the title, "Oblate Fathers in the U.S." Remembering that Rich had mentioned the Oblates building churches in the Valley, she became absorbed in the paper. Her excitement mounted as she read. She was eager to let Sarita know how well she'd done.

Arlene and Lupe weren't the least interested in talking about a Sarita's term paper, and Rich stayed so busy that she didn't get to tell him. The next day, she hurried to finish supper and met Sarita at the door of the library.

"Did you read it?" The girl was extraordinarily beautiful, and her body language was very sensual, yet she seemed as open as a child."

"You've done a masterful job. I learned so much, and you've documented it so well."

"Thank Father Rich for that. I used his books."

Something else I did not know. "Really?"

"Sure. He loans to everybody." She stomped one foot and looked stern. "But you better not be late getting the books back to him."

Meredith laughed. "What does he do?"

"First, he takes down all your info. He knows where to reach you if you're late. We see his old red truck at school. We know he's after somebody."

"Wow! What do the teacher's think of that?"

"Hey! They love him. If our librarian doesn't have stuff, she sends us to him."

"I've seen books in his office—"

"They're in his house. A guy told me it looks like a book morgue...solid walls of old dead books."

"Are you planning on college? Working toward a scholarship?"

"I'll be a sophomore next year. If I keep my grades up, my advisor said I can get in any school I want."

"I'll be rooting for you. What're you doing this summer?"

"Reading for sure. And I'm job hunting."

Meredith went to bed, adding another plus to life in her growing community.

Late Friday evening, Frank's big van pulled up to the kitchen door. Javier, a triumphant smile on his face, jumped out of the back where his mother had ridden on an air mattress. He stood like the man in charge, took her arm as she walked slowly into the kitchen.

Frank ambled behind the procession, running his hand through disheveled hair and rolling his eyes. "Javier's going to need new books. He's read them all, at least twenty times."

Aleta, still horribly bruised, stretched out a tiny hand. "Frank's exhausted. They stayed in my room all week."

"It was cheap." Frank grinned. "We each had a recliner. They brought us food that was a lot tastier than the liquids Aleta got."

"*Mamá* can sleep in my bed. Mister Frank said I can use his air mattress." Javier rubbed his cheek against Aleta's shoulder. "When she's well, I'll sleep with her."

"How about getting to bed now? It's way past time," Meredith said.

Javier looked at her for the first time. "*Mamá* can bathe me now—"

"Oh, yes..." Meredith's voice broke. She rushed ahead to open the door to Javier's room.

"Papi, don't forget my prayers." Javier knelt, looked up at Meredith. "You, too..." He frowned, appeared confused.

She stroked his back and knelt. "You want to call me Shannon?"

For the first time since Javier arrived, Meredith closed the door between their rooms. She crawled in bed and buried her face in her pillow, ashamed for anyone to hear her cry. He needed his real mother. No more pretending that she had a son.

The next morning, her eyes popped open at five. Telling herself it was a sign her body demanded care, she jogged the caliche road to and from the highway until she counted three miles.

The regular breakfast crew was drinking coffee when Aleta walked in, her hand on the arm of her son, who moved with the grace of a gentleman escort. Meredith was struck by the reality that Javier had come from a world very different from this no-frills community center.

Lupe's face became a rosy picture of delight as she stared at Aleta. "That big man's shirt from the store looks perfect on you." The tiny woman was wrapped in folds of indigo silk, tied at the waist with a piece of drapery cord.

"Thanks to Lupe, I don't have to wear the hospital gown today." Her voice sounded strong despite her swollen face distorted by bruises fading to a sickly green."

After breakfast, instead of Don Gaspar leaving on his big green mower, he bowed to Aleta and asked where she was from.

"Monterrey and Veracruz. Until recent times, we lived on my family's sugarcane plantation." She cut her eyes toward Javier. "It's not been good. The Gulf Cartel has taken control—"

Don Gaspar nodded. "My son's' wives had to leave... You're from Veracruz? They will want to meet you. Talk of home..."

That afternoon, Meredith stopped by the kitchen. Arlene was lolled back in an enormous leather recliner.

"Looky what Carmelita and her ol' man brought over. It's mostly for Aleta." She sat the chair up and motioned for Meredith to come close. "Don Gaspar and Aleta had an interesting visit after you left. Seems she went to the same wonderful, fabulous, sensational, perfect private school as the ol' man's daughters-in-law. He's sending them over tonight." Arlene leaned the chair back. "So, la-de-da, we're entertaining the bigshots. You want to know the truth? I wouldn't know them if I ran over them with Rich's old truck."

"Aleta doesn't seem like a fancy-pants..."

"We'll see. When all the squealing and hollering gets going, I'm out of here. One more thing... Jeff came by, talked to her. Real low. They think I'm stone-cold deaf and can't hear what they're whispering. She needs to apply for asylum at the INS office in Harlingen."

"That's scary. Can she get it?"

"Jeff sounds okay. She's got good reasons to stay. He thinks one of those cartel gangs may try to grab her again. Appears something happened to her husband. She was vague about his Monterrey connections. I figure it's some kind of funny business. He sent her and the kid to her family on the coast. Her grandfather disappeared. Then they set the place on fire."

"That's awful. Have you told Rich?"

"He's been at the clinic all day. But that's not all. She got away. Made it almost to Matamoros before they caught her. They're angling for a big ransom. After she told Javier to swim the river, they gang-raped her for punishment. She asked Jeff to get her a gun."

Meredith rubbed her arms, feeling a foreboding chill. "Is he going to?"

Arlene shrugged, went into a coughing fit. "I gotta have a cigarette." She stood. In between bouts of coughing she said, "Jeff's going to talk to Gaspar. Ask him to move her and Javier into his big house. He's got a man who's sort of a guard, lives on the grounds."

"I bet I've seen him. He watched me for so long the first time I jogged up the road that I got the creeps."

"That's him. Soon shoot you as look at you..."

"I can't wait to hear what Rich thinks of all this."

"Ha. You'll never know what FR thinks about anybody. He does not gossip. Even a little." Arlene sucked in the smoke and then looked back at Meredith. "Funniest thing. Frank insists that Javier can actually read. Do you believe that?"

"He knows a ton of words. And he knows the stories word-for-word. When he gets started, I'm not sure what he's memorized and what he's reading. I'm going to tidy up the library. Maybe the Gallego women will want to see our setup. I'll be back in time to help with supper."

On her way to the library, Meredith glanced toward the clinic. Rich was examining a little girl sitting on a tall table. His face was so close it looked like he was telling her a secret. She was smiling, trusting the good man. A wave of sadness caved through her chest. She wished they could talk. Wished he'd tell her if he missed Javier, if he felt like part of himself had been amputated?

She stepped into the library and smiled to herself. Sarita had lifted her spirits. The well-worn books, wrinkled newspapers, and dog-eared magazines were proof that people —adults and children— were using the place. And the computers were busy every night. She could hear her dad saying it was time she got off the pity-pot.

When she returned to the kitchen, she inhaled the delicious aroma. Rich looked up from a huge kettle, but his smile did not hide the hollow look in his eyes. "This pot roast is chock-full of vegetables from Arlene's garden. Have a taste. I've been thinking about it all afternoon."

"You look like you've been missing him, too?" *I can't believe I blurted that out.* She looked away, embarrassed.

Air escaped his lips. "Yes. Staying busy helps. At bedtime...not so much."

To keep from wrapping him in her arms, Meredith began slicing tomatoes, fully aware that he was watching her. What was he thinking? Did he want to talk?

Supper had just ended when Don Gaspar arrived with his beautiful daughters-in-law—they could be twins. They wore wrap-around sunglasses and similar versions of black pants and handkerchief tops designed in metallic patterns. Meredith identified them as the donors of the high-fashion clothing that Lupe stuffed under the counter. They held no resemblance to the bankers she knew in New York, who slouched in sweatpants after hours.

"Aleta! It's really you!" They grabbed her from each side, knelt, and kissed her cheeks. One of them removed her sunglasses and her mascaraed eyes addressed the room. "We were classmates in Veracruz." She turned back to Aleta. "Then she ran off to the university in Mexico City."

At break-neck pace, the conversation darted to Aleta's brilliant son who had inspired their husbands to build a preschool. Meredith perked up, felt the urge to raise her hand, ask when they planned to start construction, but interrupting the show didn't seem appropriate.

They trailed Aleta and Javier to their bedroom, chattering about moving them into the big house. "You'll be more comfortable. And *Papá* needs the company."

Arlene stood, eyelids lowered. "Hey Shannon, all that news calls for a cigarette. You wanna join me?"

"Sure. I have a few minutes before the ladies arrive for class." She preferred listening to Rich and Don Gaspar talk about contractor bids, but they were not including her in their conversation.

Arlene took a deep drag on her cigarette. Smoke billowed out with her words, "That's the other side. Aleta seems different, but they're her breed. Really rich."

"You think she'll move in with Don Gaspar?" Meredith wanted to cry.

"Yep. Soon as she doesn't need help getting Javier fed and off to school."

"It feels like everything's up-side-down. Javier's practically gone. Rich doesn't jog anymore..."

"He's a mystery. Frank says he's not like any priest he's ever known. All this going to pray every morning is new. Even Lupe thinks it's weird."

Meredith decided not to reveal what Rich had told her about his brother influencing him to join the priesthood. She wondered why he had shared it with her.

She was a little disappointed when Serita stopped showing up. But school was almost out, and she was probably job-hunting at fast-food joints.

On Monday morning, Carmelita came to take Javier to preschool. "You look handsome this morning. Your friends will be glad you're back."

He nodded, his face grave. "I think they missed me." He kissed his mother several times on each cheek. "Don't worry. You're safe here. I'll be back at 3:30."

"I'll watch for you. Maybe you can read to me when you get home."

"I promise." He reached for Carmelita's hand and did not look back.

Meredith sighed, "I worried he'd not want to leave you."

Aleta's eyes followed her child until the SUV disappeared. "He's a brave *niño*. There have been so many changes..." Her gaze shifted to Meredith. "In that regard, I wanted to speak to you. He's confused...sometimes calls you *mamá* and *mamita*." Her smile looked weak, strained. "He corrects himself. I've told him he can have two *mamás*. But Javier isn't easily fooled. He's grasping for his former life and not wanting to give up this one." She reached for Meredith's hand. "Please understand. This life's been good to him. But he hesitates to say Shannon." She squeezed as though begging. "I wonder if you mind my calling you *Tita* Shannon? I... I think it might help him. I've been saying *Tía Lupe* and *Tía* Arlene. It's not appropriate for a child to address an adult by a given name."

Stop nodding like one of those silly bobbleheads on a spring. She returned Aleta's squeeze. "I'll help in any way." Her lips trembled, and her eyes filled with hot tears. "I've never been an auntie. Sounds good."

"You were a wonderful *mamá* for Javier." She pulled Meredith into a hug, buried her face against her chest.

She speaks the truth. Suck it up. Meredith realized she was nodding again as she extracted herself from Aleta's grip. "I've got to get the library ready for class." Clinching her teeth to get control, she fled across the lawn, remembering that Arlene had said Aleta did not fit the mold. She might dress in the outrageous clothing donated by the Gallego women, but she was a gentle soul.

She told herself it was for the best when Aleta and Javier moved into the grand old house. Despite their new life of luxury, mother and son squeezed onto the tractor and rode to meals. Arlene was quick to say, "She hangs around long enough to help with dishes."

"*Abuelo* Gaspar goes to bed right after dinner," Aleta explained when she started staying to watch the after-supper war news with Lupe.

One night when Meredith returned from her class, she found Lupe looking more forlorn than ever. "Aleta's getting scared as me about the terrorist. Tonight, when Vice President Chaney said they're going to attack us again, Aleta exploded. She hit the table with her fist and yelled 'I hope Mexico never sends troops. We have too much war.' She's ashamed of Mexico. Like me."

Barely a week later, the conversation class had gone on extra-long, and fatigue pulled at Meredith's body. When she entered the kitchen, a news reporter was speaking breathlessly about the closing ceremony for the Ground Zero cleanup. She sat at the far end of the table from the TV. The scene was a replay of the morning ceremony. A fire bell rang, symbolizing the time of the collapse of the North Tower. Her chest felt full, tightness pulled at her throat.

The CNN voice went on in a solemn tone explaining the honor guard of police, firefighters, and others. They walked up a ramp where a stretcher bore an American flag, symbolizing the victims who were killed but never found. The stretcher was moved to a waiting ambulance. *Everyone thinks I'm part of that symbol. Is Harvey watching? Jerry and Betty are there, for sure.* The shaking started in her shoulders and took control of her arms. She wanted to leave but dared not stand for fear she'd fall.

A pair of buglers began to play *Taps*, followed by a flyover of NYPD helicopters. She hadn't noticed Rich come around the table, but she felt the pressure of his hand on her shoulder. "Let's go outside." It was a soft whisper.

She leaned on him, needed the strength that he offered. Arlene's smoking bench provided a place to settle. She accepted his handkerchief and realized tears were dripping onto her shirt.

His voice sounded far away. "When you feel like talking, I'm here." He loosened his grip, and she was sorry.

I want to tell you right now. Tell you everything. "Maybe someday."

He pulled in a deep breath. "After witnessing terrible things, it takes a long time to heal."

Lies are burying me. "You've taken good care of me. I'm better now." She stood, hurried back to the kitchen to keep from throwing her arms around him.

Chapter Eleven

Proof that work was starting on the preschool came when Don Gaspar arrived at dawn one morning in early June and began plowing a new garden behind the building.

Arlene leaned on the door to Lupe's store blowing her nose on the hem of her apron. Her voice sounded raspy. "I never had a garden until I came here. I thought I'd lost it. All the talk of building a school...not a soul admitted that the damn thing would sit right on top of my gorgeous tomatoes."

"Don Gaspar understood." Meredith turned her head, tried to avoid the smoke from Arlene's fresh-lit cigarette. "When he gets it laid out, I'll help you move the plants."

"I've been planting since February. I don't think they'll survive a move." The cigarette calmed her cough. "I wonder how deep the roots go."

Don Gaspar finally killed the loud put-put of his tractor and beamed at his beautiful rows of rich soil. "We'll move the plants after breakfast."

Meredith was returning from her morning class when she saw Arlene on her knees, palms down like she was crawling between the garden rows.

Aleta was crumpled in the dirt beside her. "She almost fainted. *Abuelo's* gone to get a chair."

The tractor's puttering engine announced its arrival carrying a black wrought iron bench in its bucket.

"I ran out of steam," Arlene whispered as they lifted her to the seat. She fumbled in her pocket, cupped a pack of cigarettes in her hand. "These things are probably killing me."

"I think you're right, sweet girl." Meredith stroked Arlene's shoulder as she struck a match and inhaled deeply.

They had started moving the plants following Arlene's direction when Aleta, carefully balancing a tomato plant that was already producing tiny blooms, whispered, "I hope this works. It'll be awful if we kill Arlene's garden."

"I'm afraid that's what we're doing."

"I heard you two." Arlene leaned—elbows on her knees— offering a toothy grin. "I know we'll lose a lot. I'm blown away by you guys willing to try."

When Rich came to lunch, Arlene allowed him to get his stethoscope and listen to her chest. He stood back and shook his head. "The good part is, you don't have the energy to go outside to smoke."

"And I'd love a cigarette."

"And I'd love to get you into town for a chest X-Ray. You think Frank could drive you?"

Arlene shrugged. "I'll ask him tonight." Dark circles rimmed her eyes. "You really think I should?"

"You bet. I'll call the hospital. Get it set up."

Rich looked from Meredith to Aleta. "The board planned for an extra cook when the preschool gets built. Might as well start looking now."

That's the first time you've included me. Meredith nodded. "So, Arlene's kitchen will be part of the school?"

He smiled at Arlene. "Yep. Our chef agreed we could use her kitchen so long as she serves as head cook."

"Now, he's sending me off to the hospital. Do a bunch of tests to keep me out..." She began a fit of coughing and forgot her complaints.

June's heat wrapped everything in a shroud of humidity. The days slowed and tore Meredith into a juggernaut of joy and sorrow. The school's outline sprawled from the kitchen wall almost to the duplex and out toward the new garden. She delighted in seeing Javier romp with excitement when his *maestra* agreed to take charge of the design and to stay on as lead teacher.

On the other hand, Arlene needed an assistant chef immediately. "I flunked the breathing test. My good lung's not good enough. So, they can't operate. I'll try the radiation if it doesn't burn me up. I don't intend to spend my last days scalded like an old dog."

Carmelita, who always knew what to do, arrived the next morning with Maria in tow. Her baby slept in a sling crisscrossing his mama's middle. "We always planned to hire a kitchen helper. Now's the time to get it done."

Arlene, still refusing to sit when everyone was eating, leaned against the table. "So, Maria's a prospect?"

"Looking at me shows I can cook." Maria held out her arms as proof that size spoke for culinary skill. She blinked, bit at her lip. "That man got himself a skinny *amante*."

"Well damn his hide. Keeps you knocked up with six kids in a row. Then he screws around." Arlene blew out her breath. "Makes me so mad I could smoke."

"No! No!" Maria waved her hands. "Don't go back to no cigarettes. The don's son is helping. He say that man got to pay so we can stay in our house. He can't be honky-tonking ever night."

"You're hired! We'll make beautiful music together." Arlene sank into the recliner. "Matter of fact, I could use your help today."

112

By the end of July, stakes cordoned off the perimeter, and the school took shape, while Arlene and her garden withered. Compost, water, and gentle coaxing could not stop its decline, and radiation could not restore Arlene.

The ten o'clock news drew Meredith, Rich, and Lupe to the kitchen. They hunched together, staring at the images, listening to words of certainty from each side. Inspectors claimed there was no evidence of Iraq having weapons of mass destruction. The Senate Judiciary Committee claimed there were reports of Iraq having ten tons of uranium and one ton of slightly enriched uranium.

Lupe pressed her fingertips to her lips. "Who do we believe?"

Rich sighed, leaned on the table, his fingers massaging his temples. "For centuries those religious groups have warred among themselves. We better have a plan for stability before we barge in there. All hell's going to break loose when there's nobody to keep them apart."

Lupe's questions were interrupted by Frank pushing a cart into the kitchen. "Gaspar said I could paint a mural for Arlene. I got her to bed, gave her some morphine. It'll keep her a few hours. I'd like to work a while. Then hang a drape over it."

"We'll leave you to your task." Rich stood. "There's been enough bad news for tonight."

"It's a gift for Arlene. But I want to surprise everybody."

"I'll read for a while. I can hear if she needs something."

"I appreciate it, Doc. I know she keeps you awake at night. The walls are thin as...I almost said toilet paper—"

"Ha! You'd be right." Rich sort of saluted in Meredith's direction then turned to leave.

"Anybody want to accompany me to the library? I'm going to wash a load and read for a while." Why did she even imagine that Rich would come for a while?

As she headed to the laundry room, she could hear Frank's radio blaring at full volume— Willie Nelson and Lee Ann Womack singing, *Mendocino County Line*.

She had folded her wash in a basket and started back into the library when she clearly saw a man move from a crouched position under the window. Startled, her body tingled, alert. She switched off the laundry room light and reached inside the library door to douse the bright overheads. She was locked in—a lifelong habit. Still, she had to be sure. Her hand gripped the cool laundry room knob, and it held. Growing accustomed to the darkness, she eased across the library, scanned the uncovered windows that formed the wall facing the main building. Kitchen lights outlined a patch that faded into the darkened front yard. Had she locked the door to their rooms? Her arms had been full of laundry.

If she opened the door and yelled, Frank might not hear over the sound of his radio. The clunk of the window AC made her jump. If she turned it off, maybe she could hear movement on the driveway. Or tell if Frank's radio was still playing. But the heat would make the room insufferable, and she couldn't turn it back on. Whoever it was, knew she was in there. He'd been watching her, expecting her to leave after she turned off the lights. The longer she delayed, the clearer it would be that she saw him. It felt like she and the man were communicating.

Shivering, she sank into an overstuffed chair, pulled her feet up, and wrapped her arms around her knees. Gazing into the darkness made her eyes burn. The shape of the man moved along the edge of the kitchen light, disappeared up the road toward the highway.

She waited as time ticked slowly. She needed to pee, but if she slipped into the restroom, he might return without her knowing. After an agonizing wait—how long—he was back, came toward her, and then cut between the buildings. The night light on the high pole behind the clinic shaped him in clothes that shined. Moisture from crossing the river?

Then he melted into the black tunnel of the orange grove. Did he go back across the river? A flash of light cut through the trees—a rhythmic flare as it moved along the riverbank. It had to be the border patrol. They'd never see him crouching in the woods, waiting for them to pass.

He might be lurking in the grove, waiting for her to come out. She moved the big chair next to the window, *scooched* her knees up close to keep warm, and drifted to sleep.

Creeping morning light woke her with a start. Stiff from sleeping in a cold knot, she hurried across the lawn to the kitchen, hoping to find Rich. Instead, Maria hustled about preparing breakfast while her children paced up and down looking at the huge curtain that covered the entire wall. "When we got here, Frank was leaving. That man worked till dawn."

I need to report the events of last night. "He can't hold up to all-nighters."

"That's what I told him." Maria's face crumbled. "He loves his woman. He says he got to hurry with the mural. That new teacher wants him to paint pictures on the walls in the school."

Here comes Lupe, but Rich's not with her. She looked back at Maria, who was saying, "He brings Arlene to help with lunch. She can't hardly stand no time at all. Breaks my heart."

Lupe hurried in the door. "Something's wrong with Aleta. She came to chapel crying. Still wearing a bathrobe. She's talking to Father Rich."

Meredith helped prepare breakfast, tried to keep her mind on the chatter, the speculation about what could be wrong with Aleta, and what Frank was painting behind that curtain. When she spotted Rich coming down the road, she poured him a cup of coffee and met him outside the kitchen door.

"I need to talk to you."

"Trouble?" He motioned her to Arlene's bench.

While she related the evening's events, he nodded, sipped his coffee. Finally, he leaned back, gulped the last drop, and said, "He was looking for Aleta. Word got out that she was here."

"Is he trying to take her?"

"I'm not sure. I called Jeff. He's waiting to come until Javier leaves for school. Aleta's so upset, it's hard to make sense of what she's saying. After she talks to Jeff, you might want to hang around in case she needs you."

"You think she'll talk to me?"

"If she talks to anyone, it'll be you. She believes you gave Javier the mothering he needed."

Meredith gripped her middle, feeling she might break wide open. "I'm glad to know that."

As if nothing had happened, Aleta and Javier arrived for breakfast on the big green tractor. She looked smaller somehow, more birdlike than ever, and her hands trembled when she cut up oranges and steamed the tortillas. Javier appeared unaware of any problem, bounding about the kitchen as curious as the other children about what was behind Frank's curtain.

Like clockwork, Javier departed for school, and Jeff showed up. He and Aleta were still sitting outside on the bench talking when Meredith started her class. She kept glancing out the window, seeing Aleta's animated hand movements that looked near hysterics. When the women began leaving the library, Aleta looked over, stood quickly, and offered her hand to Jeff.

If she wants to talk, she knows where to find me. Meredith had started organizing the room for the afternoon session when Aleta stepped in the door. "Welcome to our library."

"May I visit?"

"You look near tears." Meredith motioned her to one of the comfy chairs.

"I've cried too much. Now, I need strength." She melted against the soft cushions. "A man came last night. He had a note saying it was safe to come home. It was signed by my husband." She lifted pleading black eyes.

"Safe? How can he say that?" Meredith covered her mouth. "I don't mean to blame your husband."

"Leonardo is an educated man. He did not write that primitive note."

"So, it's a trick?" Meredith glanced out the window into the bright morning sun. Fear tingling goosebumps on her arms.

"Monterrey is so rich. The *las maña* want control. My husband led the resistance in San Pedro. It's always been a safe suburb, across the Santa Catarina River from the old town. He received threats." She seemed unaware of the constant movement of her fingers. "He sent Javier and me to safety at my family hacienda in Veracruz. My *abuelo disappeared,* and they took Javier and me." Her eyes turned to huge black pools. She leaned forward. "I miss my husband. I miss our life...I fear he's joined them. Given up everything for our ransom."

"Is your land worth enough to pay off a ransom?"

She slumped, looked whipped. "My *bisabuelo* started a sugarcane plantation in the early days. During the Revolution, our land was a battleground. It was divided into *ejidos,* ten-acre farms." Aleta sat up straight. "When my *abuelo* was a young man, he took charge. The farmers loved him. *"*

I bet they did. That revolution was against the land barons and the church that supported them. "So, your grandfather was good to the farmers?"

"Oh, yes. When they had troubles, he bought the land from them and gave them jobs. The hacienda and the sugar mill thrived again. Now, it's been stolen."

"You can't get it back?"

"Only when law returns to my country. Last year, even soldiers joined El Mata Amigos' Gulf cartel."

"The friend killer?"

She looked near hysterics, clawing fingers across her scalp and through thick, tousled hair. "A man named *Osiel Cádenas Guillén* killed his friend to get control of the cartel. Now, he may control my husband." Her hands stopped moving as she clutched the top of her head. "I can't decide what's best. If my husband is alive, Javier needs his papá." She turned pleading eyes to Meredith. "I miss the school my friends and I ran for our children. But I've loved helping Javier's teacher select curriculum and books for the new school—"

My chance to be honest. Meredith leaned forward, clasped Aleta's hands. "I escaped a bad life. This place feels like a safe harbor."

Aleta sucked in and then blew out her breath. She sat still, staring at Meredith. Then she wiped tears with the back of her hand and stood almost at attention. "Okay, *mi tita.* I knew you'd know what to do. I must hurry to help Maria get lunch."

I didn't mean to decide for her. Meredith felt her own breath coming in surprised gasps as she watched Aleta walk across the front lawn in her clunky jogging shoes, swishing her colorful Gypsy skirt.

After lunch, Meredith hurried to see Arlene. She looked forward to their short visits. Even as her body shut down, Arlene felt alive and warm. Meredith had few long-time friends. Moving so often from base to base, it had seemed useless to get attached. Then after crippling Harvey, the few friends they shared drifted away. She had clung to Jerry and Shirley, but running away had ended their weekly visits. Finding Arlene had been special. She touched Meredith in a raw, untamed way that drew her in.

When Arlene stopped coming to the kitchen to help with meals, she'd insisted that Meredith go through her closet. "You need my tight-ass jeans. Regular clothes hurt my skin. Frank's got me all these frilly, soft nightgowns. I want to see you wearing my things. So, let's dig 'em out."

Meredith had accepted a few at a time. Eventually, the closet was almost empty.

When she walked in the door, Arlene said, "Those jeans look better on you than they ever did on me. You don't fill the shirt so good, but the color's nice."

"Were you watching me walk over here?"

Frank had installed a glass door so that Arlene could see through the living room and out the front of the little house. He had said, "It doesn't match Doc's door, but she can see the comings and goings from her bed."

"I saw a bunch of women and kids leave the library this morning. Is the AC bringing them to your classes?" Her face was the same white as the mound of pillows behind her.

Meredith laughed. "Yeah. Carmelita's little houses must be hotter than hell." She cupped Arlene's ice-cold hand. "It's surprising how many school-age kids are coming. They're smart, but their English is lousy. I hope it'll help them thrive in school."

"Getting the mothers speaking English will go a long way."

"Carmelita came to the rescue. She's bought all kinds of games and books. That's pulling them in."

"Frank raises the shades before he leaves. I watch them walking along the trail." She squeezed Meredith's hand. "How's it going in the kitchen?"

She wants the truth about her domain. "You'll be proud. Maria constantly quotes you, 'Arlene says to do it this way...' She's taken Aleta under her wing. Turned that little rich girl into a first-rate tortilla maker. She can pat those things out almost as fast as you."

"Does she paint her fingernails?"

"Only her toenails. I admit the kitchen is no longer the serene culinary Den of Arlene. Kids are all over, rolling cars under the table, peeing on the toilet seat. Maria stays cool, cooking away with her baby strapped to her back. He likes the steady rocking."

"Frank said the health department decreed a commercial dishwasher."

"It'll be delivered tomorrow."

"My dishes never made anybody sick...they're always scared kids might catch something." Her head slumped, and she whispered, "Would you roll me to the garden tomorrow?"

"Absolutely!" Meredith arranged the pillows, then kissed the clammy forehead, and hurried out the door.

The next morning, she pushed Arlene's wheelchair across the yard. "We've planted a lot of the fall garden. We'll have celery, snap beans, broccoli—"

"I recognize them." Her breath came in short gasps. "I gotta quit."

Meredith was helping her into bed, when Rich tapped on the door. "Looks like you could use a hospital bed. It'd be a lot easier to get in and out—"

"Nooo! I quit cigarettes. I'm not giving up Frank."

"Good for you." Rich's grin didn't hide an embarrassed duck of his head. "Frank said the same thing. But he wanted me to ask, just in case."

Here we stand. Two lonely celibates listening to a dying woman claim her bed partner. Apparently, Rich felt as awkward as she did. He chatted a few minutes and then scooted out the door.

They watched him stroll back toward the main building. Arlene said, "Too bad that man can't have a woman." She turned glassy eyes toward Meredith. "Why don't you seduce him? Do you both a lot of good."

"Crazy woman! That morphine's gone to your head." Meredith laughed and then couldn't stop tears.

"Yep. I figured as much." She curled cold fingers around Meredith's hand and grew silent.

Meredith looked at the shriveled body, so still. Why hadn't she told the truth? Now, it was too late. Arlene had moved into that private space where death had become her companion. Even her words came from inside, looking out at those who did not know their time.

The next week, Frank spread the word that he was unveiling the mural on Thursday night. The kitchen had filled when he arrived pushing the wheelchair that seemed to swallow Arlene. She looked like a frail wisp of blue in her lovely soft robe. Frank looked almost as thin as his woman. His eyes–deep cavities—gazed at his love as he pulled the cord, letting the drape fall away. "This mural is for my woman." The crowd gasped as they were thrust into Arlene's garden—row upon row of lush tomatoes, beans climbing a stark white trellis, melons peeking from beneath vines, squashes of every color and shape sprawled on the rich black soil. Toward the end of one row, a skinny woman bent—spade in hand—tending her lovely plants.

"That's Tía Arlene," Javier's voice broke the awed silence. He scooted on his knees up to the scene, stared into the garden, his hand raised as if to wave. Applause filled the room.

"So that's why you've been sneaking out at night." She pulled his hand against her face, kissed his fingers.

Gradually, the slow march to the end pulled them into a silent vigil as Arlene's breath came in short, gasping gulps. The days dragged; her hands clawed at her chest as she sucked for air. Rich administered more and more morphine to quiet her desperate, silent pleas. Frank did not move from her bedside, held her in his arms, wetting her hair with his tears. His sweet voice crooned Willie Nelson songs against his lover's cheek.

On that final morning, the intervals grew longer between her breaths. Frank stretched out beside her, pulled her into his embrace. "I'm holding you, baby. I'm holding you."

Meredith let go of Arlene's hand and lifted it to Frank's shoulder as the blessed sound of silence—the end of her torture—finally came.

"She's gone?" Frank raised his head, stared at Rich in disbelief.

Rich nodded as he caressed Frank's shoulder. "Do you want us to step out for a while?"

"Please." Frank rocked her like a baby. "I need a little more..."

Meredith felt Rich's hand on her back as they stepped out the door. "Let's sit here," he whispered and crumpled onto the porch step, still touching her.

We're crying together, Arlene! She leaned against him knowing her old friend would be cheering. When they heard Frank move about, they stood, and it was over.

The word spread instantly and people from all around— Including patrons of their favorite dancehall, Frank's paint customers, and a sprinkling of unsavory characters—descended on the center. Meredith watched Rich moving everywhere, meeting every need. He walked along the driveway holding Javier's hand and talking for a long time. He comforted women like Lupe who couldn't stop crying. He joked with several of Frank's friends who showed up with coolers of beer—instead of flowers—to offer support.

Arlene's only request was for her ashes to be spread over her garden. The weather celebrated with an unusual dry cool front and radiant sunshine. The crowd cheered the long rows of lush produce, a thriving image of the mural. "This bountiful fall crop is the sort of tribute Arlene would love," Rich said as he closed the memorial service.

Frank emptied everything except for a cot out of their side of the house. "I'll sleep here until I finish painting the school. After that, I'm gone."

Chapter Twelve

Meredith made it through the day on the one-year anniversary of 9/11 by working between her conversation classes to help eager parents enroll their children in the almost finished school. That evening, she returned to the kitchen to find Rich and Lupe watching Mayor Bloomberg rededicating the massive bronze Peace Sphere, a charred survivor of the collapse of the towers. Its scared exterior was placed temporarily in Battery Park. As the mayor lit the eternal flame at its base, he said it was in honor of all those who were lost, that their spirit and sacrifice would never be forgotten. Cameras scanned the dignitaries gathered for the solemn event. Her breath caught—a hit in the gut—when the background scene captured the charming old apartment building where their life had been happy. One of the last precious times was that evening just before New Year's. They had bundled up for a long walk along the river, stopped for an Irish coffee before bedtime and lovemaking.

The hand on her shoulder jolted her back to the kitchen. Lupe, at the end of the table, stared at the TV. Rich had moved to the bench next to her. "It's been a hard year." His words, only for her.

She leaned against him, swallowed the bile that churned from her stomach. "I'm trying...to accept what cannot be." She felt the absence of his hand. She had said too much.

"Yes," was all she heard. The distance could not have been more than an inch, but it felt like he had crossed a chasm.

The separation took on a permanence. For the next few weeks, he continued to go to chapel each morning before she got out to jog the caliche road to the highway. Despite going in the same direction, they did not cross paths. Was he deliberately avoiding her?

In early October, Meredith had jogged almost to the highway, when she realized the distant sound of sirens was growing louder. Flashes of red and white lights danced through the trees. A sudden invasion of police cars, a firetruck, and an ambulance whirled onto the road stirring dust into choking clouds. The entourage tore past the main buildings and halted in a cluster at the orange grove. Lights still flashing, men scurried onto the trail that was backlit with flood lamps.

When she reached the vehicles where motors idled a cacophony of noise and exhaust fumes, Frank emerged from the orange grove, scrubbing at his face with a handkerchief. "Don't go see it."

"What happened?" She touched his arm just below his sleeve. It felt wet.

"Rich and I stepped on the porch at the same time this morning and saw a bunch of lights flashing on the river. We got there in time to see three border patrol lift a man out of the water. Shot in the back of the head."

"Did you recognize him?"

"Naw. Some rich dude. Really fine suit and expensive shoes. And a ring the size of a marble." He kept shaking his head as they walked back to the kitchen. "Strangest thing. If the cartel threw the body in the river on the Mexican side, it shouldn't have washed up over here. The current cuts to the river bank on that side. Another thing...when Zetas shoot a man in the back of the head, it's because he's a traitor. This one had a hole up at his hairline where the bullet went right through. They had to have placed the gun right against his head to make a nice smooth exit. The other weird thing—that diamond was way too valuable to leave on a man they executed."

"Maybe they couldn't get it off..."

"Naw. They'd cut off his finger if they wanted it. We could hear the border patrol talking. They're saying somebody's sending a message."

They entered the kitchen where Maria had just made coffee. "I'll cook the breakfast. You and Mister Frank can talk."

Frank took a gulp of hot coffee. "Not like Arlene's." He shuddered as though jerking himself to the present. "The guy's hands and feet were bound, but the border patrol shined lights on that ring so the sheriff could photograph it. They couldn't believe what they were seeing." He grabbed a pen and a little book in his pocket and began drawing. "I'm including the fingers so you get a sense of proportion."

Meredith watched in amazement as the image—real as death—took shape in the sketchbook.

"I don't know anything about carats," Frank said. But that diamond covered most of that wide gold band."

The put-put of Don Gaspar's tractor announced the arrival of its usual morning riders. Javier rushed in, wide-eyed. "The sirens woke us. Mamá said we have to wait here to see what happened."

Don Gaspar stroked the boy's head, smoothing at his hair. "Patience is hard."

Javier bent toward Frank, then pointed. "That's *Papá's* ring!" His eyes became huge black orbs of excitement. "Where is he?"

Frank's mouth fell open. He stared first at Javier and then at Aleta, who walked toward him—a ghost floating with her hand outstretched. He pulled the pad against his chest and began shaking his head.

No one responded when Maria hurried out the door calling, "I'm getting Father Rich."

Aleta closed her fingers around the sketchbook and stood stone-still, her eyes absorbing the image. She lifted her chin. "You have a sharp eye. Captured every detail." She handed the book back to Frank and settled feather-like on the bench. The silence brought goosebumps to Meredith's arms.

"You saw it this morning? At the river?"

Frank appeared to regain himself. "There's nothing definite. We need to find out from Jeff...and Doc... Rich... Father Rich."

Javier leaned against Frank's knee. "Every night, I look for

Papá. Has he come back too?" His eyes caressed Aleta's face. "What's wrong?" He moved to her side.

"Nothing's wrong, *Hijo*. We have lots of questions." She looked up, and a flicker of a smile showed as Rich hurried in the door.

The churning diesel roar of firetrucks and other emergency vehicles announced their departure amid a cloud of dust. No sirens cut the air.

"Show *Papi* the ring. It belongs to my real *papá*." Javier reached for the sketchbook.

Rich's face did not change, only his eyes revealed the sorrow that he was beginning to comprehend. He held the book in one hand and pulled Javier against his leg with the other. "It's a good drawing, isn't it?"

"Yes, and we've got to find him. He's come back like my *mamá*."

"Jeff was on duty. But he probably can get back out here." Rich looked off toward the dust still stirring from all the traffic.

"I'll call Mister Jeff right now." Maria headed to the hall phone.

"He can help find *Papá*." Javier kept bouncing on his toes, excitement mounting.

Aleta reached toward Rich. "Don't you think Javier's *papá* is still up in heaven? Don't you think maybe he left his ring with a friend?"

Rich sat down, took Javier's hand. "I think she's right. We'll have to investigate. But we think your papá is still in heaven."

Javier's lip trembled, and he crushed himself again Rich's chest. "I want him back."

Rich lifted the child to his lap, rocked him, and stroked his wet cheeks until the tears finally stopped.

Javier ate some of Maria's eggs, pronounced them good. When Carmelita arrived to drive him to school, he appeared ready to go. "If you find *Papá*, come get me. Okay?"

Aleta nodded, held up her thumb, and kept back tears until Javier was out the door. She had reached for Meredith's hand after she looked at the sketch of her husband's ring. She was still clinging to it when Jeff kicked off muddy boots and hurried into the kitchen. Sweat soaked his green uniform and sheened down his face.

He listened, never taking his eyes off Aleta as she explained what she believed had happened. "The nearest medical examiner is in Harlingen. We send murder victims up there." He reached across the table but did not touch her trembling fingers. "Would you come to border patrol headquarters? Look at a photograph to make sure it's your husband? It appears someone wants him to be identified. We'd like to know—all you can remember—of his activities before you and Javier went to Veracruz."

"I need Shannon with me. Okay?"

Jeff looked at Meredith for the first time. A flash of recognition in his penetrating blue gaze. "Sure. We can arrange that." He looked around the room. "How about Father Rich? You okay with him coming along?"

"Oh, please."

Meredith realized she was still wearing jogging shorts. "Let me slip on some slacks. I'll only be a minute." She wished she could tuck her legs under the table as Jeff's ever-vigilant eyes scanned the raised purple scars clearly visible on her shins.

They climbed into the old red truck with Aleta squeezed in the middle. She continued, like a child, clinging to Meredith's hand.

Jeff's jeep pulled up to the border patrol station as they parked, and he met them before they reached the front door. "We'll go into a private room off the reception area."

Aleta lifted her chin, her black eyes wide—stared straight ahead—ignored a gust of wind that blew a veil of black hair across her face. She nodded a silent acknowledgment to the Patrol Agent, a dark-skinned man whose muscles strained the shoulders of his green shirt. Seated at the long table, she motioned Meredith to the adjacent chair.

After the ritual condolences, the agent who made Meredith think of Javier's brown bear bent toward Aleta. "May I show you a photograph of the ring we found on the victim?"

Aleta's hand flew to her mouth as though holding back vomit. She finally nodded and continued holding her mouth as she bent over the glossy print. Frank had captured a perfect image of the big, bold ring. "It was handed down from my *bisabuelo*. When I married Leonardo, my *abuelo* gave it to my husband. He said if we ever needed money, we should come to him. He would buy the ring from us." She looked at the faces straining toward her. "Now, my *abuelo*

126

has been disappeared..."

The agent was the one nodding now, apparently at a loss for more words of comfort. After an awkward silence, he fumbled in a manila folder. "I'd like you to identify the victim discovered this morning on the Gallegos' side of the Rio Grande."

Aleta squeezed Meredith's hand in a painful vise. She held the glossy up to her face as if she might kiss it. Then she dropped Meredith's hand and smoothed her fingers across the handsome face. A hole the size of a dime left a black rim on his forehead, below his hair line. "Do you think he suffered for long?"

"No, ma'am." The words sounded like a bark, a refusal to admit that the victim had felt anything. Nothing was said about the terror he must have experienced before the bullet blasted through his brain.

"Dona, will you sign a paper certifying the victim is your husband?"

"Yes, and I want to take his body with me. And the ring."

"Aw, well...the ring and his clothing are evidence in our homicide investigation. The victim is at the morgue in Harlingen." The agent began standing, a motion of dismissal. Then he suddenly sat back down. "Also, we're working with Mexican authorities. We have a few questions.

Aleta did not move. Her brows drew together. She placed both hands on the table. "Please stop calling my husband the victim. He is Leonardo Escondón."

"Of course, of course. Wasn't it the Gulf Cartel who took away your grandfather, kidnapped you, and your son? Took over your family's Veracruz land?"

"Zetas, too. They're working together."

"And now you're alone?"

"I have my son."

"Of course, we've heard he's bright as a dollar. Quite the young man."

"How did you know about Javier?"

The big man grinned, obviously proud. "It's our job to know about everyone along this twenty-five-mile-strip of border. Why they're here? What they're doing." His eyes took in Meredith.

He knows I'm a fake. She rubbed sweaty palms on her knees and did not blink.

The agent's eyes swept back to Aleta. "Your family had an airstrip and a boat dock. Correct?"

"They're abandoned. My father crashed his plane. Then a hurricane destroyed his boat dock. My *abuelo* let it go after that—"

"They're back in operation. Ideal location for shipments of Columbian cocaine."

"How do you know?" Aleta kept shaking her head.

"Like I said, it's our job to know."

Rich stood suddenly. "*Doña* Escondón has just lost her husband. Let's wrap this up."

"Sure. Sure. Just one more question...did you make your home in the wealthy suburb of Monterrey?"

Aleta stood, placed a hand on Rich's arm. "My husband was a leader who tried to keep our community safe." She sucked in a breath and looked at the agent who had also risen. "I want Leonardo's ring. You have a photograph for your investigation."

The agent looked at Jeff, shrugged, and nodded to someone at the door. "*Doña*, my advice is for you to remain here. We believe the Zeta's message is clear. You will be in serious danger if you try to return. Especially if you make any effort to reclaim your property."

"I have no plans to return." She smiled at Meredith. "Last night, I accepted the offer to be one of the preschool teachers."

Meredith felt like crying with relief. Javier would not be leaving.

They hurried out the door with Aleta clutching her husband's ring. She stopped on the front walk and looked around like a lost soul. "What am I doing? Leonardo's lying there naked in a morgue. I can't pay for a casket."

Rich guided her toward the truck. "I imagine *Don* Gaspar has already made arrangements. He knows as much about what's happening around here as the border patrol.

By that afternoon, Aleta appeared almost serene. Javier leaped from the car and raced into the kitchen. "Did you find *Papá*?"

She lifted the ring secured on a gold chain around her neck. "Your *papá* is in heaven. He left his ring for you."

Javier fell against her sobbing. "I wanted him to come back. Like you."

She held him, stroked his hair, whispering softly against his face. "In a few days, we'll have a Vigil, and you will see his body. His soul is already in heaven."

Meredith watched the mother and child, and she wished for someone to hold, to rock and comfort. She looked at Rich standing across the room. Could he be longing for the same thing?

Rich was right about *Don* Gaspar being in the know about everything. As soon as the autopsy was complete, the body was released, and *Don* Gaspar had arranged for the casket. He also sent word for the young priest from Immaculate Conception Cathedral to conduct the funeral Mass.

Meredith thought she was watching a metamorphosis as Aleta took charge. "We'll have a Vigil so that my son can see his father. He must understand that his *papá*, at long last, has gone to heaven." She did not wait for the priest to comment. "I want a simple funeral, no Mass. Father Rich can help officiate. And I want to bury him in the Gallegos' family plot. They've adopted us. We owe them the honor."

"I agree, *Doña*," seemed to be the only words in the young priest's vocabulary.

The night of the Vigil, Aleta stood on the chapel's narrow front porch—a different woman in a black silk dress, hat, and veil. The jogging shoes were gone, and she walked with ease in high heels and black hose. Even Javier looked comfortable in a suit and tie—a lifestyle far removed from the community center.

Javier dug his fingers behind his collar and pulled out the gold chain. "See *Papá's* ring! When I grow up, it'll be mine. I can wear it now. After we bury *Papá* out there with all those crosses, I have to put it away at the bank."

"I know you're proud to have such a treasure." She wanted to clutch him in her arms.

"Yes." He dropped the ring back inside his shirt and took Aleta's hand. When they stepped through the chapel's heavy wooden doors, he froze before the casket. "Is *Papá* in there?" He held up his arms. "Lift me up..."

Aleta clutched her son as he bent toward the body. His hand stretched out to touch the face—handsome—heavy makeup faded out the gruesome hole. "It's cold like playdough." He tucked his fingers back against Aleta's breasts. "That's not him. My real *papá's* in heaven—"

"Yes, he's watching over us."

Javier buried his face in Aleta's neck. "Let's don't look anymore."

Meredith's eyes swept the tiny chapel holding barely six rows of highly polished walnut pews. An over-sized Crucifix in polished gold dominated a simple altar draped in a black cloth. She stopped short at the sight of Rich dressed in a long white tunic tied at the waist with a cord. A black stole crossed his shoulders. *He is a priest.* She felt suffocated as the reality hit her. She closed her eyes and felt the hand on her shoulder.

"It's still me. I'm dressed for the event." Rich's eyes searched hers, and he smiled slightly before he and his hand moved away.

The Vigil and then the funeral and burial the following day went on forever. Strange rituals, all normal life put on hold. In the midst of all the people and all the hugging and caring words—Meredith had never felt so alone. The night after the funeral, people were still milling about the kitchen and into the almost finished school. Jeff sidled up wearing a navy blazer and blue tie that made him look delicious. "This has been an ordeal. But Aleta met the challenge."

"She's gone from a frightened little bird into a strong-willed woman. I'm sure it was there all along, but not showing." Meredith hesitated then said, "Do you really think she's in danger if she goes back?"

He leaned so close that she could smell his aftershave. "They'd kill her in a New York minute."

New York minute? A message? She hugged her arms around herself. "That's frightening. Happening right across the river."

"It's a war for control. And the cartels are winning. Corruption has eaten out the core of all the institutions. I have no idea how it's going to get fixed." He strolled away, and she kept holding herself.

The week leading up to the opening of the preschool in mid-October turned into a mad push—the cots for naps came late; rain delayed the construction of a fence around the playground, and they scrambled to register children of migrant workers who arrived at the last minute.

Meredith's coffee and conversation groups bulged with the new women. She helped with the school enrollment and in the kitchen. On the night after the grand opening, she started down the hall eager to fall into bed when Lupe opened her bedroom door. Her face was a puffy mask of tears. "I can't hold in no more."

Can I handle another problem? "Have you heard from Maximillian?"

"No. Father Rich wants me to get the Red Cross. Maximillian would get really mad if I did..." She wiped at her eyes. "I heard on the TV. Bush got the okay to go to war. Ever person here is so busy with the school. They never noticed."

"You're right. I've not seen the news in over a week. So, Congress has authorized him to use military force?" Meredith slumped down beside Lupe on her bed. "Remember. You don't know where Maximillian is right now. He may not be in any kind of danger."

Lupe wiped at her eyes. "I keep trying to believe. I pray ever day." She looked up with fresh tears starting. "My faith don't help."

Meredith finally crawled in bed after reassuring Lupe that her faith was strong even if she couldn't believe it would keep Max safe. What kind of faith did *she* have? She had demonstrated no faith in the truth. For over a year, she'd lived a lie. Now, the murder of Leonardo Escandón seemed to have brought the spotlight on everyone.

The concern about her secrets being exposed shattered in heartbreak the next morning when Carmelita arrived with Sarita. The stunningly beautiful girl whom Meredith believed to be a fast-track candidate for full college scholarships was pregnant.

"Maria's been working way too much in this kitchen. The board agreed that we've got to give her some relief. Sarita needs a job until we can get some support from the guy who knocked her up." Carmelita dropped both shoulders in submission. "I'm hoping this will be an answer for both of them." She looked at Sarita, who still had the bearing of an Aztec goddess.

"So, I gotta teach her to cook?" Maria rubbed both hands down her ample hips and eyed Sarita like she was a bushel of overripe grapefruit.

"Oh, I can cook. I've fed my brothers and sisters since I was eight." She rubbed both her hands down her narrow hips. "Only I don't eat everything I cook."

Oh crap! She wanted to scream at Serita not to start by stirring hostility.

Maria swelled like she was rising for a blow. Instead, she blew a burst of air and said, "Let's start lunch. The chicken's baking. How about you gathering some zucchini. Get it in the oven."

"Sure. Is the garden out back?" Sarita's glanced at Meredith for the first time. Then she kicked off sparkly blue sandals and padded barefoot out the door.

Meredith gave Maria a thumbs-up sign and rushed to her class, which had several new members who had arrived with the orange pickers. When she told them about the new preschool, they all hurried away—children in tow—except for one heavily made-up girl. Two dirty children clutched at her skin-tight jeans.

The girl looked around at the women waiting to start the class. "I checked it out. Who wants to drag out so early? Instead of doing the teaching, they want parents coming in all the time. Hanging around a school's the last thing I want to do."

Meredith decided not to argue. The gal would probably decide that hanging around learning English was also the last thing she wanted to do. She wondered if that was the future Sarita. Capable, but grabbing the moment for its pleasure.

Maria hustled in—all smiles—and kept the class lively with comments and her bubbly laughter. She stayed when the class ended. "I'm so glad to be back. Gotta admit Sarita can cook. Now, I've got time to be here." She pursed her lips and wiggled her shoulders a little. "You wanta hear my idea?"

"Sure!" Meredith realized how much she had missed Maria's enthusiasm.

"Sarita's gonna have a baby she don't want. Lots of us have babies we don't need..."

Meredith wrapped an arm around her shoulders. "So? What're you thinking?"

Maria pursed her lips, seemed to be mustering courage. "Ask Miss Maude to tell us about her pills.

Don't let her see shock on your face! "I bet she'd be glad to talk about how it works and how it helps."

"Will you ask her? I'll spread the word. Make sure plenty hear about it."

Probably bring the husbands and the priest down on us. And maybe Rich. "Okay. Let's try it."

Meredith watched Maria almost dance back to the kitchen. Thinking about getting permission created bubbles of tension in her belly. And Maude would have to be tamed, convinced that her role was education, not coercion.

Rich was in his office up-dating patient records. His smile made her glad to have an excuse to be alone with him. *What if this question separates us forever?* She stumbled through the request, watching his brows arch in surprise. He nodded. Was he agreeing or concentrating? He looked out toward the palm trees edging the sugarcane field. Then his eyes, so steady and penetrating settled on her. "It's probably the best way to help these women."

Meredith let out her breath. "I'm so relieved to hear that."

"You didn't think I'd agree?"

It felt intimate to sit three feet from him and talk about birth control—a man and a woman having sex. "I...wasn't sure. When I saw you at the funeral, it struck me that you're a priest. I'd not thought of you... in that way."

He leaned forward, forearms on his thighs. "It's been a struggle for me, too. Perhaps, one day, I can talk about it."

Talk about it now. "I know you've got to finish your patient charts. I'll see if Maude is still here."

"I want to talk to her beforehand." He leaned back in his chair. "She's qualified to provide exams and offer advice." He half smiled and shook his head. "It's just that she can be a bullhorn, or she can be a gentle soul. I'll try to prime the gentle part." His eyes softened when he grinned. "Come talk to me any time. You are not an interruption."

Meredith closed the door to his office and felt the fullness of his words warming her. She headed to the front of the clinic to find Maude.

Chapter Thirteen

"The Birth Control Class" as Maria and Serita called it was scheduled for a morning session and for the evening to make sure everyone had a chance to attend. When the day arrived, women lined up at the door thirty minutes before class. The library was packed with several women Meredith had never seen. Even as Maude began to speak, more—young ones and several too old for birth control—hurried in and settled where they could find space.

Maude spoke in Spanish and English, hanging large pictures on the board to explain how the human body—both male and female—functioned. When she displayed an erect penis, the group gasped, and a little twitter rippled through the room before they settled into hearing how that thing worked. A few of the women watched Maude's images with their hands over their eyes, peeping through their fingers. Others sat in rapt attention, absorbing every word. The hour flew into two. The questions started timidly and then came in rapid succession. Some were child-like: Can you get pregnant by kissing? How long before the pill is effective? And others were painful: How do you keep your man from running around?

Meredith wanted to hug Maude for showing her best self. She told them about birth control, showed how rubbers were used and how easily they could break. But she did not insist on using any type of birth control. Several said they wanted appointments to get "Maude's pills."

That night before she finished supper, Meredith realized people—men and women—were coming in cars and walking. She went around the table to Rich who was sitting with his back to the windows. "I better get over there. Looks like we need to spread into the gym."

He looked around and stood immediately. "I'll help. The priest's car just arrived."

Oh, Jesus! Had she opened a can of worms? She slipped on Arlene's navy broomstick skirt. It was the closest dressed-up thing in her closet, and she'd worn it to every funeral. Hopefully, tonight wouldn't fit the funeral category.

Her heart thumped—nerves jangled. Most of the women from the morning session returned, and several of them brought husbands. The young priest took his seat on the upper, back bleacher. What did it mean—above everybody or staying out of the way?

Rich pulled in the chalkboard and directed the hushed crowd— quiet as a church—to an area of the bleachers that had to be expanded twice. Maria and Serita had spent the afternoon baking cookies, and they set up the big coffee pot.

As she had at the morning event, Maude looked the part— starched white uniform, white hose, and shoes. And to Meredith's relief, she did not wait to be introduced. She took charge immediately and began to explain the purpose of the meeting. This time when she slapped the penis picture on the board, the only sound was the thumping of the big AC.

"Good God, this is R rated!" The man's voice made the crowd jump and sent a buzz through the gym. "So, you're selling birth control?" Another voice added to the rising mutterings.

"No, sir. I'm not selling. I'm educating." Maude could have been a drill sergeant if she'd had on the uniform. "This community center is here to help folks. The clinic offers immunizations and free exams. The store provides clothing. The kitchen feeds anybody who needs a meal. Volunteers keep the gym open after school. Father

Rich coaches four basketball teams. I might add that they are winning teams. Miss Shannon teaches English. We just opened a free preschool to give kids a boost. And now we're offering these classes so that women and men can learn how to manage their sex lives."

Sex lives! Oh, Maude, don't screw this up! In hopes of gauging the reactions, Meredith had taken a seat on the bottom row at the far end of the crowd. She turned her head in time to see two men move along the risers. Each one had a woman by the hand. The little priest had not moved, but the people sitting in that part of the bleachers had left a wide space around him.

"This is not what I want my wife hearing." The man had a belly that looked as large as his pregnant wife's. He looked up at the priest. "It's against the church. Against God's laws."

The rumble grew as more people began to move off the bleachers.

"I will continue with this class as soon as you quiet down." Maude's voice rose like a tsunami. She stood without flinching next to her chalkboard. Several women held back from their husbands' outstretched hands and nodded to her as they followed their men out of the gym.

When it was over, half the bleachers had emptied, including the priest's spot.

Maude continued to answer questions about pregnancy and birth control. She did not advocate for or against. The one-hour session extended for more than two. When it ended, Meredith was sweating, but Maude looked as crisp as ever. "I expect to be busy the next few days," she said as she erased the chalkboard.

Meredith looked at Rich, who had remained silent throughout the evening. "The Gallegos were conspicuously absent. Should I have asked their permission?"

"You asked me. That's enough." He looked tired. He waved an envelope. "I've got this invitation to meet the bishop at Immaculate Conception in the morning."

"Oh, Rich! I'm so sorry." She reached toward him as he turned away. Watching him leave the building made her chest hurt.

"There goes a conflicted man. He can't decide if he's a priest or a doctor." Maude turned back at the door. "This was a good idea, Shannon."

When she went into the kitchen to help with cleanup, Serita met her at the door. "I know I've disappointed you. I disappointed myself."

Meredith took the girl's arm. "Life's not over, sweet girl. You've added a big bump, but I'm confident you've got the smarts to get over it or get around it. And remember, you've got a lot of people in your corner."

Serita smacked a wet kiss on her cheek. "You're the best. And you know what? I'm not done yet."

Meredith laughed and went to bed smiling.

The next morning, she was finishing the last part of her run when she met Lupe coming out of the Gallegos' gate.

"You won't believe it. Father Rich's wearing his collar. I love him in that collar. Makes him look so special..."

It must be for the bishop's visit. "When does he wear it?"

"Hardly ever. But he's been praying so much. Maybe he's going to be more like a priest." She cupped her hand at the corner of her mouth, lowered her voice. "Don Gaspar was talking to him when I left. The old man never says a word at morning chapel. You think he's talking about those meetings? Some of them came in the store all excited about *birth control"* Lupe spit out the words.

Meredith felt like crying. "I don't have an answer for any of it, Lupe."

No answers were forthcoming at breakfast. Everything appeared the same except for Rich's white shirt with the stiff collar. Her heart sank when she saw him get in the truck wearing a black coat that completed his priestly appearance.

If the measure of success for Maude's presentations were the number of women seeking birth control, it was a slam-dunk. In regard to Rich's visit with the bishop, it stayed shrouded in mystery. Meredith yearned to ask, but Rich kept his distance—an island without a port-of-call.

She wished for Arlene, wanted to tell her that Maude's classes had been a mixed bag. Lots of rubbers and Maude's pills were dispensed, but many of the women who'd been faithful class members did not return. She could hear Arlene's raspy laugh. She'd probably say they were playing with fire. Gonna get some woman killed by an irate husband who thought the number of kids he sired proved his manhood.

Meredith remembered the imagined prophecy when Rich brought a young woman to class. She had stitches in her lip and a face distorted in a swollen purple mass. "I gotta learn English. Learn to use that computer. Get a job. Get my kids outta here..."

The room came alive with hands guiding her to one of the big stuffed chairs and offering coffee, water. The hum of acceptance melded the class and opened voices to dreams of better lives or better places.

Carmelita sat quietly all during the conversation, nodding as the women spoke. Just as the class ended, she hugged her arms together, rubbing like she needed to get warm. "I've been reading the *Times...*" She glanced at Meredith as a reminder of their secret. "Did you see it on TV? Priests in Boston have been shaming the Church. They paid $10 million for doing bad things to little boys. If you ask me, priests shouldn't be telling us what's right."

"Oh! No?" Two women began trembling.

"I hear stuff all the time...Never talked out loud. We got problems around here too. Something gets told. The priest is moved to McAllen or Mercedes or wherever...hear something else..." Her eyes moved to every woman in the room. "That's the way it's happening all over. Move 'em someplace else. Up in Boston, they've been talking." She slapped both palms on her knees. "I say we listen direct to God ourselves."

Everyone talked at once, but it sounded to Meredith like it was one thing to stand up to husbands, but not many were ready to buck the priest.

Meredith felt wrung dry by the time the last woman drifted away. Then she saw Maude headed to the library. Her eyes were red-rimmed. "You know that little gal with the split lip? She came for birth control. Swallowed a pill before she walked out. She's afraid to take them home. Says she'll stop by each morning when she drops her kids at school."

Without thinking of Maude as the drill sergeant, Meredith grabbed the woman in her arms. Maude buried her face in Meredith's shoulder and wept great, deep sobs. "I tell you, I was so scared the other night when all those folks started leaving. I feared the worst for those women." She lifted her head, dug out a tissue, and blew her nose. "That man beat the snot out of that little gal. All that violence woke up some of the tough women. They aren't taking it anymore."

The holidays from Thanksgiving until the New Year took on all the festive appearance that Meredith remembered from last year, but underneath it all, tension stirred. More than half of the early members of the conversation classes finally returned. Their rudimentary mastery of the language made conversations possible. Carmelita carried the torch for those who had not broken out of their submissive shell. "I own the store. But my ol' man made all the decisions. Being a man don't make you know stuff. I been speaking up."

"What's he saying about that?"

"Plenty. And it's loud."

"Being loud doesn't make you right."

A giggle passed through the room. But the talk shifted away and sobered when one of the older women shared that her son, due to graduate in May, had listened to an Army recruiter. "He'll leave in the morning. I've cried and begged, but he believes all this talk about Saddam Hussein getting ready to attack us again."

"You think that's true?"

"The inspectors said they can't find weapons of mass destruction." Carmelita spoke above the murmurs. "It's powerful people saying stuff. We gotta start deciding things for ourselves..."

"My husband says we're going to war. Doesn't matter what any inspectors find."

Meredith was relieved when the class ended. She didn't know any more about what was happening than any of them, yet they seemed to think the class was the place to figure out answers. And maybe it helped.

When she went to the kitchen to get started on lunch, she found Lupe near tears again. "Ever thing's a mess. All this talk of birth control. I think it's got Father Rich upset. He stays on his knees real long like a man who's suffering."

He was distant before the birth control talk. "I wish I knew the answer."

They had just finished eating when all eyes turned to look at a car with a military insignia on its side. Two soldiers came to the door, and the room fell silent. Maria and Sarita looked frozen in place. Rich rose from the table, his steps too slow as he headed to the door.

"Mrs. Lupe Castaneda?" The name was pronounced with the proper Spanish accent.

"Ayy?" Lupe didn't move, stared at the men—dress uniforms, chests heavy with ribbons and medals. A master sergeant and a chaplain—names fell away unheard.

"The Secretary of the Army regrets to notify you that your son, Maximillian Castaneda died in an attack on January 4, in northern Helmand Province, Afghanistan." He hesitated a few moments— time for his words to penetrate. "Private Castaneda's remains are being shipped home. The transport should arrive tomorrow in Corpus Christi." No one moved or spoke. Finally, he said, "If you wish to meet the transport in Corpus Christi, we can arrange that now."

Lupe did not look at anyone. "No. Bring him home."

Rich was the only one in the room who moved. He had stepped behind Lupe when the men came in the door. He kept both hands on her shoulders. Holding her together.

"Dona Castaneda, a casualty assistant will be here this afternoon. She will help you arrange the services—"

Lupe reached up for Rich's hands. "My priest will help me."

"Yes, ma'am. The casualty assistant will guide you through the benefit claim process."

"Claim?" Lupe's eyes swirled in tears.

"As Private Castaneda's sole survivors, you and your husband are entitled to a benefit settlement."

Lupe bowed her head and whispered, "My husband's in prison."

The chaplain directed his attention to Rich. "Our records show that half the settlement will be placed in Don Castaneda's prison trust account until he is released. If he dies while incarcerated, Dona Castaneda, as his sole survivor, will receive the balance." He took a deep breath—a man laboring to get through the ordeal. "We'll leave after she signs this agreement to transport her son's remains. Here's my card if she needs anything."

Lupe took the pen. Held it over the paper. "I can't remember... Maximillian showed me so many times. I always forget."

"Mark the paper however you are accustomed." The chaplain's soft voice cushioned his words.

Lupe clutched the pen, labored to mark a shaky X. "Maximillian would be so ashamed," she whispered. She looked at Meredith. "Will you help me learn?"

Don't cry. "Absolutely. Whenever you feel like it."

"Today." She bowed her head. "When they leave—"

"Yes, ma'am." The master sergeant reached for the form with the scrawled X, tucked it in a briefcase. "We'll be going along. You call if you need anything."

Lupe stood. "I got to learn to write my name. Before that other person wants me to sign."

Her back is bent like an old woman's. Meredith followed Lupe to her room.

She waved toward a little altar—candle, framed picture of Jesus, rosary beads, and a leftover Christmas poinsettia arranged on a cloth-covered box. "I pray here ever night." She stood before the shrine. "Sometimes in the day."

Before Meredith could think of what to say, Lupe smoothed a spot on her dresser. "If you make my name. I can copy it."

This is the most important thing since Carmelita started to read. Meredith wrote in clear cursive.

Lupe arranged her fingers around the pen. "Loop up and over. Then down and loop again." She bent over the page, slowly drawing each letter.

"You're writing an L then a U, P, and E. You have written Lupe, and it's clear as mine."

She looked up. "I'm done crying. No more being ashamed."

Meredith laughed. "I'm so proud of you, I could cry."

Word spread through the community so that when the body arrived in a flag-draped coffin, neighbors and strangers stood at attention along the drive and up the walk to the chapel. Some held little American flags, and the veterans saluted.

They filled the chapel and the yard again for the Saturday

afternoon Mass. Lupe arrived holding Rich's arm and wearing Aleta's black hat and veil. She stopped beside the coffin and bent to hug Javier, who had laid his hand on the flag. "Is your son in there?"

Lupe nodded, stroked his carefully combed hair.

"We can't look at him?"

"Let's be seated." Aleta tugged at Javier's hand.

"It's okay." Lupe cupped her hands around Javier's cheeks. "We don't need to see him. We know he's gone to heaven."

"Look for him shining at night...maybe he'll come back." The boy allowed Aleta to lead him to a nearby pew.

Faith comes in strange packages. Why not let the child have his? Meredith fought tears as she took Lupe's hand and walked down the narrow aisle to be seated.

The service lasted forever. Finally, Rich stood—a new thinness made his face look rugged. His words describing Max—a brilliant student, a physical powerhouse, and eager to serve his country—nurtured Lupe, her face softened by the veil, looked radiant.

He is not a man. He's a priest shepherding his flock. Comforting the grieved. Meredith clenched her teeth. When the service ended, she nodded at Jeff who was looking at her from across the room.

Even larger crowds than had come to the previous services converged on the kitchen and wrapped Lupe in kind words and long hugs. Meredith chatted with many of the women from her classes, but she mostly absorbed the image of Rich surrounded by admiring, respectful people. Did they see him as a priest? They were eager to talk to him but showed timid deference to the young priest—nodding and then skirting around him far enough to avoid a conversation. And then there was Jeff who moved among them all—comfortable and a little removed. He was their protector and the enforcer all at once. He encountered them the way they related to the parish priest—never stayed with him long enough to involve themselves in a conversation.

He was heading toward her. Had he realized she was watching? Did the cop in him trigger an alert?

"Glad to see you watching over Lupe. She's going to need support." His eyes pulled at her.

"She's been grieving since the day Max left."

He nodded, seemed to ponder his response. "She worshiped

him. Saw nothing but good in him."

And you didn't? Tension muzzled her. "I... I didn't know him very well."

"Yeah. You arrived not long before he left..." He started moving away. "I'll see you around."

Meredith watched him and realized she was sweating. His eagle-eye must have noticed.

By the time the well-wishers finally cleared out and they cleaned up and stored the left-over food, Meredith was exhausted. A quick shower and bed were all she could think about. When she started down the hall, Lupe called to her. "Please come to my room..."

Oh, not tonight! "Sure."

Lupe sat on her bed, patted a place for Meredith. "I have to finish this day. I buried my son, and this is the last thing..." She stood, reached behind the picture of Jesus on her altar, and withdrew a worn kitchen-size matchbox. "The day Maximillian left? When we emptied his room for Javier? I found my son's old sweatpants behind his bed." Tears ran unchecked off her cheeks and onto the front of her black funeral dress. "When I washed, I found this in his pocket." Her fingers trembled as she slid open the box.

Meredith clutched her chest, a reflex to the thud that hit her. She fought to compose herself as she stared at the little heart-covered cloth bag, the rescue packet from the women's center in the city.

Lupe withdrew the sack, held it out to Meredith. "I have prayed ever day that Maximillian would come home. Tell me about this. I kept it a secret, prayed it wasn't true."

Meredith used both hands to cup Lupe's face and wipe her tears. "I am so sorry you have carried this burden."

"I looked at them. They're beautiful. Very valuable." She choked and allowed Meredith to pull her tight against her shoulder. "I never found the money." She pulled back. "How much did he take?"

"I don't know. I meant to count it—"

"The sergeant lady helped me with papers. She said money will come soon. I'll pay you back—"

"Oh, please, no!" Meredith grabbed Lupe's shoulders. "That's your money. I have all I need."

Lupe pulled away. Stared at Meredith, eyes pleading for understanding. "I gotta get clean. Do the truth for my son. For Maximillian's soul..."

The truth? The pain crushed into her belly. *This simple, peasant woman knows about truth.*

"I will get $200,000. My husband, too. The prison keeps his till he gets out." She sighed, visibly stressed. "This summer."

"Oh, Lupe, are you okay with him getting out?"

"I want him to stay away. Father Rich says the law will keep him away... But I don't know. Father Rich says I need a bank account. Just for me. So, he can't get it. He says he'll help me fix it up..." She grinned, and fresh tears ran down her cheeks. "That's rich ain't it?" She slapped her hand over her mouth. "Not ain't! Maximillian would scold me."

"Yes, it's rich. And I'm not going to scold you."

Lupe touched Meredith's hand still holding the rescue packet. "You was rich, too. Them rings are the biggest I've ever touched."

I won't ask about the earrings from Mom. "They're an extravagance. I always wore them turned under." *Except when I was with Harvey.* She squeezed the little sack. The rubbers were gone. *The little turd used them, probably gave the earrings to the girl.* She pulled the string, watched the rings fall into her palm.

"Look at that diamond! He must a really loved you."

"So, he said." She remembered how he had bragged about using his last dollar to buy the rings. He said, "You've still got plenty. We'll be sharing everything." She'd shoved the worry aside, and they made love on her living room sofa.

"But he hurt you?" Lupe's fingers traced the sleeve of Meredith's jacket. "I saw the scars. And, your legs. Did you divorce him?" Her hand caressed, soothing the old pain.

A little truth. "No."

Lupe gasped. "You think he'll come here?"

Meredith shook her head and stood. "I'm safe."

Lupe cupped hands over her breasts. "My Diego will come. Father Rich say he's afraid to hurt me..." She leaned against her door as Meredith headed to the bathroom. "I'll pray to keep them men away."

Prayers are batting zero, so far... Meredith let the hot shower beat against her face and across her back. If she'd been as honest as Lupe, she wouldn't have run away. Her promotion included a terrific salary increase. She could have moved to the city. Roomed with friends who had rent-stabilized apartments. Even taken her own place. She could have hired someone to cook and clean for Harvey.

She stepped out of the shower and wiped the steam off the little mirror on the medicine cabinet door. But she didn't do any of that. Instead, she got pretty good at cutting her hair—her new disguise— curls like wiry springs. Her breasts were scrawny as her body, an image Harvey had called feisty. After the crash, he never looked at her again.

As she dried herself, she remembered the phone calls at work— dozens—even from the golf course. If she had moved into the city, the calls would have come all night. Tormenting, complaining, angry rants about whatever entered his twisted mind.

When she tiptoed across the hall to her room, the chill made her shudder. She'd forgotten to turn on the heat-pump. Pulling the heavy quilt up over her wet head, she tried to find comfort remembering the early days when she went to sleep with her head on Harvey's shoulder. No use, the curtain had come down, the drama had ended.

Chapter Fourteen

The red of Carmelita's flowing muumuu cast a flush on her beautiful face. She paced about the library as the women settled down for the evening class. Finally, she sat on the edge of a folding chair, her glitter-studded tennis shoes placed squarely, hands on her knees. "The time's up. Bush gave Saddam Hussein forty-eight hours to leave Iraq. Believe me, we're headed to war."

Shocked silence, then every voice erupted at once. "You think he'll really do it?"

"My man says we got to stop the terrorists."

"They probably coming in right now."

"But Jeff says he ain't caught any."

"Trouble is, our kids is joining up."

"Did you hear that Rodriguez girl left last week?"

Meredith had discovered that the women captured conversational English when they shared their feelings. Interrupting with grammar and sentence structure shut them down. Her role had developed into helping them express themselves—a close-knit group—sharing their lives and worries.

Carmelita, the de facto leader, kept glancing at her big, bold watch—a popular Levi brand she carried in her store. "I think we better get on home. I got a bad feeling we need to be watching TV."

Meredith realized she had been as disturbed as the other women by Carmelita's insistence on war. She hurried to the kitchen and found Lupe and Rich staring at the TV. Bush was speaking from the Oval Office. She sat down as he said something about needing to free the world from grave danger. "War?" she looked at Rich.

"Afraid so. It started at 8:34 our time. Bush said further diplomacy won't protect us. He still claims Iraq's behind the 9/11 attacks."

The television screen switched to Baghdad—still-dark early morning—flashes like fireflies sparked background darkness.

"That's the Tigris River," Rich whispered.

"The Tigris River in the Bible?" Lupe's voice sounded shaky.

"Yes. See the street lights reflecting in the water? Listen. The birds haven't given up. They're still calling."

Meredith wished they had a sofa, wished they could sit close, touch as the distant explosions sent up bursts of light.

Streaks flared across the sky as an announcer explained they were Tomahawk cruise missiles from ships in the Gulf and Red Sea. The ratta-tat sound of guns seemed to come from the city. As light crept onto the screen, explosions ripped debris into the air, sending billowing black clouds across the city.

Meredith realized she had been squeezed into a knot, her knees pulled up to her chin as she sat on the bench, staring at the upheaval on the screen. "I have to give up. Go to bed."

"Me, too." Rich rose, turned questioning eyes toward her. "I wonder how many people died while we watched..."

Two weeks later, the afternoon class had started in an uproar. The women scared each other about a shoot-out that morning in Matamoros. The discussion quickly fragmented into Spanish. "It was on Mexican TV... They captured that big drug boss, Osiel Cárdenas. I saw them shooting. Two soldiers got hit. Then, they arrested Cárdenas. He was handcuffed like a common criminal...You imagine? Big man like that. Bam! Then it's all over."

Another woman, eager to be included said, "They planned it for six months. All kinds of Mexican police and US cops were in on it, including the border patrol—"

"You suppose Jeff was there?"

"Ha! We'll never know." The woman's eyes grew big. "Unless he got killed—"

"No! Don't say that. Bad luck..."

Progress? Meredith smiled to herself. They never lacked for topics of conversation. Her challenge was keeping the focus on English.

When class finally ended, she headed to the kitchen wondering why the women didn't worry about the cartels crossing the river. Did they feel safe because they lived on the U.S. side?

She smiled at seeing Lupe rushing to meet her.

"I've got a check for you. Father Rich showed me how to write it." She stretched out her hand, proudly displaying the carefully drawn letters.

"Oh, no! I can't take $5,000. There's no way I had that much." She thrust the check toward Lupe.

Lupe pulled her hands up to her chest—refusing to touch the payment. "I don't care. That's what I want. Father Rich helped me." She looked up. "There he is. Father Rich, tell her it's okay..."

He shook his head. "She wants to do it, Shannon." He smiled at Lupe. "I don't think it's necessary, but if it helps her feel better, then you should accept it."

What are his eyes saying? "I guess I better open a bank account—"

"Father Rich can help you," Lupe said.

"I bet she knows how."

Please give me a ride. "You think Carmelita will drive me into town?"

"She'd be delighted." He filled a coffee cup. "Now, you'll have enough to go on down to San Miguel..."

The words jolted her. "Do you want me to go?" Her insides grew weak.

"No." His looked at her for an instant then looked into his cup. "I...we want you to stay, if you want to."

"I do."

"Then, it's settled," Lupe squealed. "We want to keep you. I been thinking I'd come to your night class. Learn to talk better English. Don't you think Maximillian would like that?"

"You bet he would." Rich started out the door and stopped to let Aleta in.

She looked distraught. "I asked someone to watch my class at playtime. I need to talk to Tita before Javier gets out of school."

As soon as they stepped into Meredith's room, Aleta flopped on the bed and bent double. "I don't know what to do. This is crazy. *Abuelo* Gaspar wants to send Javier off to school!" She began to rock. "He says the boy's too smart for our little schools. He must go where he can meet his potential." She looked up, her eyes wide with horror. "I can't let him go. He's barely five. A baby!"

Meredith pulled Aleta against her. "Yes, he's too young. Please don't let him go." She saw so little of him now, the thought of him going off to a boarding school made her chest ache.

Aleta pulled back. "I knew you'd understand. You know what else? He offered to marry me, to give Javier and me a legacy." She drew herself up. "I'll tell you a secret." She lowered her voice and leaned close. "The family accepts me now. I'm there to watch over the don. If they thought my boy and I might get part of the Gallego estate, all hell would break loose."

Meredith laughed and then Aleta began laughing. "You nailed it. But is the old man getting flirty with you?" It felt creepy to ask.

Aleta slumped. "No. It's just that he loves Javier. His sons aren't giving him a progeny." She giggled. "I bet they'd get busy and have a litter of kids if they knew what he's thinking."

"So, what're you going to do?"

She shrugged. "I'm making it clear. I'll keep tutoring Javier at night. I know you and Rich will help." She stood up. "If he can't accept that, I'll see if we can move back over here."

Meredith did not admit that she wished for that very thing. She missed Javier every day.

The next morning when the tractor sputtered to the kitchen door, Javier was sitting on the old man's lap, steering the tractor. "Guess what!" He announced as he stepped in the door. "I'm going to help *Abuelo* mow today."

Meredith glanced at Aleta whose face was a blank slate. *Rich needs to know what's going on.* She eased on the bench next to him. "May I sit here?" Her hands felt sweaty. She'd been careful not to push herself on him. Now, things were different.

"Sure." Rich moved his cup, made extra room for her plate. "What's up?" His voice stayed low.

"Can we talk for a few minutes after breakfast?"

"Come to the clinic." He kept his eyes on his plate and finished quickly.

She couldn't choke down a bite, barely sipped her coffee.

He was waiting in his office when she entered the clinic. He closed his door and motioned her to the big chair facing him. "What's made you so upset?"

He can tell? She quickly went through her conversation with Aleta. "Truth is, I'm afraid she's still so vulnerable. She might give in to Don Gaspar's proposals—"

"I'm glad she's talking to you. She needs your strength..."

My strength? "I don't know that I've helped at all."

He leaned forward, close enough that she could have touched his face. "I'm glad she's talking, because Gaspar's been talking to me."

"So, he's serious?"

"He was. I think I've convinced him it's not in anyone's best interest."

Meredith closed her eyes. "I have to admit that I've missed that child so much that the idea of him going off to school absolutely crushes me." She opened her eyes when she felt the touch of his hand.

"I confess the same." He sat perfectly still, smiling. Finally, he drew in a breath. "I think we both fell into the imaginary parent role. And I liked it."

"Oh, Rich, I did too." She stroked his hands that he had folded together between his knees. "I guess I better get to my class." As she stood, she watched him get up slowly, and for an instant she thought he was going to reach for her.

"See you at lunch."

Meredith sat on her bed staring at the carefully drawn words on Lupe's check. Banks required a photo ID to open an account. Even the Gallego's bank would expect it. She'd have to explain why she had nothing. Frank rarely came around since he finished painting and drawing murals for the school.

He picked up on the first ring, startled her into stumbling over her words. "I got your number from the school."

"Good hearing from you." He waited.

"I... I have two things... I mean two things to tell you."

"Fire away."

"Lupe's given me money. She believes Max robbed me..."

"Bless her soul. That had to hurt."

"It's pitiful. She's like a *Penitente*, beating herself for what that boy did."

"Arlene didn't like the kid. She thought he had a mean streak a mile wide."

"Lupe'll never believe that. But she feels compelled to pay me back." Meredith heaved a sign, "So, I need to open a bank account. And they'll want a photo ID."

"Not a problem in this world."

"Also, I need to put Lupe's check in the bank so I can pay you back."

"Ha! That's not gonna happen. Tell you what...I'll copy your picture from the foundation brochure. Be over there tomorrow afternoon."

"Plan to eat with us..."

"I don't know. Let me see how it goes. Things around there get to me..."

"Oh, Frank. I'm so sorry to ask this of you."

"No! No! Truth is, I also miss all you people. Be there about four. You'll have to sign it before I can finish up." He hung up before she could respond.

The next day, his old white van pulled up to the library before her class ended. She hurried outside and leaned in his window. "You're a miracle man."

"No, sweet girl. I'm a con-artist." He grinned, but his eyes looked dead. "I'll come back tomorrow with the finished product. Maybe I'll stay long enough to eat."

The next day, he returned while Meredith was helping with supper. She was surprised to see how slowly he climbed out of his van. Fingering the pocket of his shirt, he pulled out the little card.

She held the impressive ID stating that she was on the staff of the Gallego Community Center "It's amazing how you were able to cut my face out of that group photo." She hooked her arm through his. "Be honest. Tell me what I owe for this. When I open my account, I'm holding out enough to pay you in full."

"No charge. Here's what Arlene and I decided when you made your first weekly payment." He pulled a worn envelope from his hip pocket. "We saved all the ten-dollars. When you made the final payment, we planned to hand it back to you." His lower lip trembled before he pulled his mouth into a tight knot. "Arlene said you'd never save the ten bucks every week, but we could. That way, she figured, you'd end up with a little savings account."

"But Frank, you saved my neck. I could not have stayed here without that social security card. It cost you big time to hire that woman."

He patted her hand, still clutching his arm. "Listen to me. Lupe needed to get whole, and I do too. There was never a pricy woman. It was always me. I charged you a chunk. Made Arlene so mad she wouldn't sleep with me for two weeks." He started laughing and bent into a coughing fit. When he settled down, he said, "I didn't mean to tell that part."

Another honest person. Her voice broke. "I have schemed and connived and landed in a bed of honest souls."

"It is a good place, Shannon." He followed her into the kitchen and stopped abruptly. "There she is."

"It looks so real. I watch her working in that garden every day."

His shoulders slumped, and he turned his back on the mural. "I can't stay here with that. I'm not sure I could be in her kitchen even without her on that wall, tending her garden." He patted Meredith's shoulder, nodded at Maria and the kitchen helpers before he rushed out the door.

The farmworkers had moved on by the first of May to the cooler climes of Wisconsin for harvesting vegetables as they came into season. And Meredith moved through the days in a private torment—warmed by how close they had come to each other in his office and questioning what drove her. Was she attracted to the forbidden? Had she sunk to that depth? Arlene had been kidding when she suggested that seducing Rich would do them both good. But Meredith wondered if that was all she really wanted—to screw a priest?

She went to the kitchen every night after her class, dreading to hear another story about the looting in Baghdad, hearing claims of this being a world war that would go on for years, and the perpetual reminder that no weapons of mass destruction had been found. Yet, she had to go, she had to see him—quietly nursing half-cold coffee. His eyes always welcomed her. And she always sat across from him—the table safely separating them.

When she arrived that evening, Rich had just gotten off the phone.

"That was Sarita's mother. The midwife wants me. Keep the coffee hot and update me when I get back."

He's asking me to wait for him. Meredith could barely concentrate on the evening news running continuous coverage of Bush. He had ridden in the co-pilot's seat of a fighter jet that made a tailhook landing on the deck of the *U.S.S. Lincoln*. After strutting about in a flight suit—tight in all the right places—he changed clothes and stood beneath a banner reading *Mission Accomplished*. He claimed there was more to be done, but this was the end of major combat operations.

She kept glancing toward the windows and finally saw the lights of his pickup coming down the drive. He walked in grinning. "Sarita's got a fine boy. Both mother and son are doing well."

"Oh, bless Jesus. I been praying." Lupe jumped up the minute he stepped in the door. "Good news makes me ready for bed." She smacked a kiss on Meredith's cheek and waved to Rich.

"Catch me up." He sounded breathless, eager to be in the moment.

She related the news while the images on the television ran again. When she described the mission accomplished banner, he rolled his eyes. "Do you believe that?"

"No. Sounds like the place is falling apart."

He nodded. "I'm glad you waited for me. And I'm relieved that Lupe's gone on to bed. I wanted to tell you something that's going to be announced."

He's sharing with me. She watched his face—relaxed, almost serene.

"I've turned in my resignation. I'm no longer a priest. Tomorrow night, at the preschool graduation, Don Gaspar's going to tell the whole community."

"Oh, Rich." She reached for his hand and welcomed his grip on hers. "Are you okay?" *Why say that?* "I mean, is that what you want? Did you get in trouble because of our family planning meetings?"

He shook his head, held tight to her hand. "No. I've wrestled with the decision for months. I'm a doctor, Shannon. That's what I want to be. I was worried for a time that the Gallegos, being such strong Catholics, would want me to leave." He laughed softly. "Truth is, they want a doctor running this place. The priest part was extra."

"Thank you for telling me. I'm honored that you trust me." They were friends, for sure. Was it more than that for him?

"I... I thought I'd get back to jogging. Now...now that I've made the decision. I know you're running on the drive. If you want to get back to the river, I'll be there in the morning."

"I've missed our...the trail. The caliche makes an awful route. The gravel gets in my shoes." She thought she might burst with sheer joy. "I'd love to meet you in the morning."

"Well...if that's a deal. I'll see you then."

He squeezed her hand before he released it and stood.

They both waited awkwardly on opposite sides of the table. "Well...goodnight." He rinsed out his cup and hurried out the door like a man with his tail on fire. She wondered whatever made her think of that image.

Sleep would not come. He shared with her before the announcement. She rehashed every word, every gesture—the way he kept holding her hand, how he squeezed it before he let go. At three o'clock, she set her alarm fearing that if she finally went to sleep, she'd not wake. But her eyes popped open right on time, and she hurried into the near darkness to see him coming around the building.

"It's good to see you." His hand—light as a feather—touched her shoulder.

Does he want to touch as much as I do? "I've missed these mornings." She took a deep breath and fell into an easy jog beside him.

As light began shaping the trail, he exclaimed like a man seeing it for the first time. "Look at that great blue! He's standing in those tall weeds like he's one of them." Then he spotted the barn owl in the palm tree. This time, she also saw it.

"The trail's a lot more worn. Makes a smoother run for us." His breathing sounded labored. "Jeff said the violence has picked up, forced the border patrol to increase their surveillance."

"I catch myself watching the edge of the river, glancing to the other side for movement among the trees."

Rich grunted, "me too!" He stopped, bent over, breathing hard. "I've let myself get out of shape. I've got to slow down. Go on, if you want."

"No! We're jogging buddies. *More than buddies.* I'm not leaving you."

He grinned, gave her a thumbs up. And without speaking, set a slower pace.

She finished the run, more invigorated than she had been in months. But as the day wore on and she followed her usual routine of classes and help in the garden and the kitchen, she became more apprehensive. How would the people take it? He didn't officiate as a priest, rarely dressed as one. Yet, women like Lupe called him Father. Would they feel abandoned?

Chapter Fifteen

The graduation was for children like Javier, who would be going to public school in fall. They had made their own mortarboards—black cardboards with tassels that were glued onto ball caps turned backward. Excitement churned through the school all day. At every free moment, Meredith helped Maria and the school cook prepare cookies and mix punch for the festivities.

Before they finished supper, people from the community began arriving. Parents had decorated the gym in crêpe paper streamers. The bleachers filled by seven o'clock. The children entered to a taped recording of *Pomp and Circumstance*. Meredith's throat swelled at the site of the solemn procession. She blinked hard to keep back tears as Javier marched in and took his place. This was the beginning of a serious journey for the little boy she had imagined as her own.

There were ten "graduates" who walked across the stage riser and accepted a rolled-up diploma. After the lead teacher made introductions and assured the crowd that the school would continue with twelve new three-year-old students to replace the graduates, she handed the mic to Don Gaspar. He moved to the stage with the bearing of a Spanish Grandee. His elegantly embroidered white *guayabera* made his almond complexion glow. He stood very still, gazed with obvious satisfaction at the silent crowd spread before him—the *jefe* appreciating his domain.

He spoke in elegant Spanish, thanking and celebrating the accomplishments of the staff, the students, and all the parents. He also acknowledged all the members of the foundation's board. Then he breathed in like a swimmer readying for a long race. "Our beloved Ben Jacque Richelieu, priest and medical doctor, has faithfully served our community from its inception. Each of us can personally recount many times when he has been our benefactor—always with calm, care, and love.

Rich's head is down. He needs an arm around his shoulders. Get on with it, Gaspar. Meredith's eyes trailed along the bleachers watching the expressions—rapt attention, concern on every face.

"...in deep prayer for months, called on our bishop, our priests, and on me for guidance...has resigned from the Roman Catholic priesthood. His decision is final. He will continue to serve our community as our medical doctor and director of the center."

An audible sigh swept through the audience. Rich looked up for the first time, and a flicker of relief crossed his face. Meredith gripped the edge of the bleacher and held fast to keep from rising and going to him.

The volume of voices grew as shocked faces looked at each other for confirmation and then strained to see—many even stood—a glimpse of Rich. He looked directly into the faces and nodded—solemn, near tears, and alone.

Don Gaspar rambled on for a bit longer. Finally, realizing that the crowd was done listening to him, he reminded them of refreshments and dismissed everyone.

Meredith tried to move close to him, to hear what people were saying, to know how they were accepting him. She wasn't sure if she wanted to laugh or cry when she heard Javier's clear voice, "*Papi, can you get married now?*"

Those within earshot apparently had a similar reaction. She heard whispers of shock. Then voices near her shoulder, "You suppose it's his mother?"

"Her name's Aleta."

"She's a beautiful thing."

"A little young..."

Meredith looked around, saw Aleta hurrying Javier over to the refreshment table. She looked radiant, lush black hair pulled back, emphasizing a perfectly sculpted jawline. She was certainly an eligible woman. Could it be possible? Javier said daddy as plain as day.

Why had she thought Rich needed her comfort? Maybe he was attracted to Aleta. With her, he could be a real father. Meredith moved to a position at the refreshment table—replenished cookie trays and filled the punch bowl—where she could keep from thinking about anything except the task at hand.

The comments as people munched cookies sounded more curious than unhappy. Several said they never thought of him as a priest. He was their doctor. Women in her classes nodded at her, clear impressions that tomorrow's conversations would center on Ben Jacque Richelieu.

By the time the crowd began to clear, she felt a mild nausea. The kitchen offered a respite, an excuse to wash trays and get away from comments and speculations.

"Can you believe it?" Lupe sounded angry as she rushed in the door, grabbed an apron, and began drying the stack of trays. "He's my priest. I been praying in the chapel with him..." Her black eyes snapped as she stopped and stared at Meredith. "Did you know about this?"

Liar! Liar! "Not until last night."

Lupe blew out a silent whistle. "After I went to bed?" Her eyes narrowed. "What you think about it?"

Here goes. "You remember how worried you've been? You've seen him praying and even crying?"

Lupe drew in an indignant breath and nodded.

"I think that's what Don Gaspar was talking about tonight. When he said Rich had prayed about it a long time."

Lupe shrugged, looked around like she was conjuring up an argument.

"I think Rich needs our support. I think he's struggled..."

Maria, her helpers, and Rich walked in carrying the last of the cookie trays.

Lupe turned, held out both hands as she walked toward him. "Can I still call you Father Rich?"

He reached out, folded the crying woman into his arms. "You bet. And we'll talk whenever you want."

Are we friends, or more than that? Meredith turned back to the sink, squeezed her eyes shut.

Rich hung around, washed the big coffee pot, and helped get the school chairs back in place. Finally, he turned on the television and sat down with a cookie and a glass of milk.

Meredith kissed Maria on both cheeks. You need to get along home with your kids. I'll start the coffee in the morning and make oatmeal and toast when I get back from my run. Sleep late and come in when you feel rested."

Rich turned from the TV. "And I'll help her."

Lupe took off her apron and angled toward the door. "I better get to bed."

"Yes," Meredith called. "You've earned a sleep-in, too."

"Seems to me *you've* earned a rest." His eyes looked at her—tired.

"I'm too keyed up to quit just yet."

"Me, too."

She slid onto the bench across from him. "How was it?"

He massaged his temple. "Mostly good. A couple wanted to drag up my promise to God." He grinned. "Gaspar played *jefe* for me. Spoke up both times."

She reached out, patted his cupped hand. "You're loved."

He clasped her hand between his and held on. "I thought they might run me off."

No reason to tell him the gossip. "Aw, Rich, I didn't hear anything negative."

"You want to meet here in the morning? If we come early, have a cup before we run."

As she shut the door to her room, Lupe closed hers. Meredith slipped into sleep smiling. Lupe might not know about a lot of things, but she was alert as a guinea hen.

The next morning, when Meredith reached the kitchen, Rich was already measuring coffee into the big pot. He might feel out of shape, but his legs still looked terrific.

They sat across from each other sipping the hot brew.

"You know," Meredith said, "this is the best time of my day."

"Mine, too."

Summer closed in, hot and still. Routines did not change—morning jogs, English conversation classes that included school-age children, Aleta and Javier riding to meals on the tractor, and discouraging evening news from the Iraqi front.

Meredith could not detect anything of significance between Rich and Aleta, but there also was nothing of significance for her. Hand clasping, smiles, and gentle shoulder bumps—attention one might receive from a good friend.

The community celebration for the beginning of public schools took place in mid-August. Rich organized races and water balloon fights, music, and basketball free-throw contests. Jeff and his boys had arrived early that morning pulling his portable smoker behind his truck. Everyone brought food, laid out on tables spread across the lawn.

Meredith roamed through the crowd, felt warmed by the laughter. She had taken a chair to watch the races when Javier ran up to her—sweating and breathless—a boy having the time of his life. "*Tita*, you remember I'll ride the school bus to first grade on Monday?"

"I do. Is it okay if I come up to the gate? See you off on your first day?"

"Sure!" He hopped several steps away and then turned back and kissed her on the cheek.

"You better savor that. Once he gets in big-kid school, the public kissing stops." Jeff stood beside her chair, a beer in one hand, and a can of soda in the other. "May I serve you a cool one?"

Too bad he's a cop showing interest. "Thanks. Pull up a chair. They're about to have the 100-yard dash."

His boys were stars, and she enjoyed helping him cheer them to victory. Between races he leaned over. "Oyster season's underway. How about going to Port Isabel with me next Saturday? We can sit on the porch of a little oyster shack and watch the seagulls swoop around the Laguna Madre."

She could see Rich, his shirt soaked through with sweat, corralling kids for the next race. *A little social life might clear my mind.* "Sounds like fun. I don't have classes on Saturday night."

"It's thirty miles down there. How about picking you up at 6:00? We can watch the sunset glow on Padre Island. Should be a full moon over the Laguna Madre."

He's checked out the moon? "I've never been down there."

"Yeah. The boys and I meant to take you and Javier. Then his mama showed up. We took them down there fishing a couple of times."

"Did he love it?"

"Sure. That kid loves everything. Wish mine had half his gumption.

Sounds like my dad. "Aleta's a great little mother."

"Guess she told you the ol' man wanted to send him to a big-shot private school. I'm glad she's keeping him here."

Do I really want to go out with this man? "Me too."

Meredith slipped on a full-skirted blue sundress that had belonged to Arlene and looked at herself in the mirror over her dresser. It looked nice, better if she filled out the top like the original owner. She walked to the kitchen feeling pleased that the hand-me-down sandals showed off her carefully polished toenails.

"Look at you!" Rich's eyes crinkled at the corners when he grinned.

"Jeff's taking me to eat oysters." She poured a glass of iced tea and sat on the end of the bench.

Lupe turned, holding a large stew pot. "Get them fried. Raw oysters slip around in your mouth. It'll make you sick."

"I've never tried them on the half-shell. Oysters Rockefeller tasted good as I remember." *Isn't Rich going to say a word?* She looked at him, but he kept his eyes on the television—something about a letter criticizing the CIA director for poor intelligence before the Iraq invasion.

161

Jeff arrived looking terrific—blue t-shirt that turned his eyes to liquid, tan slacks that fit smooth over a flat belly. "I'll get her back at a decent hour." He spoke to the entire room, all of whom stared except for Rich.

Jeff touched her elbow as she lifted her skirt and swung herself up into the sky-high cab. Maria, her children, and Lupe watched the departure. Rich was not among them.

The radio played country music, and Jeff commented on landmarks along the way. The narrow, two-lane highway cut through scrubland stretching flat toward the horizon and the Gulf of Mexico. Lazy clouds hung in white puffs across a sky that looked like it had been painted a tranquil blue.

Jeff pointed. "Most of the ancient Sabal Palms that survive along the river are back in that preserve."

"I've seen some on the Gallegos' compound."

"Most landowners plowed the handsome things down to get a few more acres of cropland."

"What's that big granite marker off to the right?" She had relaxed against the contoured seat and enjoyed Jeff's chatty tour guiding.

"Ha! It tells how the Confederates won the last battle of the Civil War right along here. Trouble is, it happened two months after Lee surrendered."

"You're a real history buff."

He grunted. "I tried teaching history. Like to have starved to death."

"Border patrol is a long way from school-teaching."

He expelled a fake sigh. "Historians investigate what happened a long time ago. Border patrol investigates what's happening now."

"So, basically you're an investigator." *Investigator?* She felt a ripple of tension tighten her chest.

His eyes seemed to look at her extra-long before he said, "Yep. That's it."

They rode for several miles in silence, until he pointed. "Look ahead, you'll see the Queen Isabella Causeway rising over the Laguna Madre. It's the bridge to South Padre Island."

"Wow!" Meredith spoke in awe. "The sun setting behind us is giving it a radiant red hue. But isn't that the bridge that was knocked down by the barges? Right after 9/11?"

"Yep. Five killed, including the local fire marshal. A ferry was the only way to get people to the island. That put a bee in the governor's britches. We had a much safer causeway built before Thanksgiving. Wait till we get closer. You'll see how beautiful it is. And that same red glow will spread across the bay and onto the island."

The oyster place was indeed a shack. The staff knew Jeff and rushed them through an inside room packed with sun-scorched, beer-drinkers. Their prime spot was on the porch that leaned toward the water and the panorama of seagulls diving toward fishing boats and tugs shoving giant barges.

As soon as they were seated and placed their drink orders, Meredith leaned close enough to whisper, "Great view. Best seat in the house. You obviously have connections."

Jeff's lids drooped, and he whispered back, "Remember, it's my job to know everybody and everything that's going on."

Relax. Stop imagining threats. "Tell me about Laguna Madre. It looks like a beautiful bay."

"It's also the Intercoastal Canal. That's why those barges are being moved through here. Goes all the way up to Boston. On the other side of the causeway, those tall buildings are South Padre hotels."

The waitress appeared, beaming at Jeff, who seemed not to notice. "Their fried oysters and French fries are the best you'll find anywhere. How about it?"

Meredith grinned at the waitress whose shorts barely covered her butt. "Do *you* think they're the best?"

"Yes, ma'am. Jeff's right."

Ma'am! "Sold. And add a salad, please."

As darkness spread across the Laguna Madre, lights in South Padre created a sparkling backdrop. The moon, flaming in the sun's last reflection, cast a glow on the gently rippling water. The staff lit candles protected by little chimneys on each table as Jeff finished his over-sized order. When Meredith couldn't eat all of hers, he speared the leftovers one-at-a-time, until he'd cleaned her plate.

He leaned back, swigged the last of his beer. "So, what's your plan?"

Her heart rate picked up. "What do you mean?"

"Your future? Are you going to hang around the center? Teach English forever."

The cop is loose. "Why does it matter? Do *you* have some kind of plan?"

"I do. Raise my boys; do my job. Maybe find a good woman someday."

"Well, I don't have children. I like my job. And I have no plans to marry." She tried to see his expression in the candlelight. "Did I pass muster?"

He sucked in a long breath and blew it out with the words, "not really. See, I know that Shannon Staples does not exist except on a fake social security card."

A flash hit her—fear or fury? "Are you going to arrest me?" The bastard had tricked her.

"Naw. I don't want to arrest you. I figure you're running. You been here long enough for the ring mark on your finger to fade out. The scars on your arms are clearly cigarette burns, and they're looking better. I can't figure out why your shins and ankles are so beat-up—"

"You mean with all your police experience you don't know how wheelchair footrests can cut up legs? Goodness, Jeff, I thought you had a handle on everybody's business."

"So, he's a cripple? You ran off instead of divorcing him—"

"Is that a crime?" She wanted to get up, run out the door, and never stop.

"Listen," he leaned into her face. "I've got a friend who is suffering over you. I want you to either tell him what's going on with you or clear out..."

The pain in her chest made her tremble. "Are you talking about Rich—"

"Of course. For God's sake, the man quit the priesthood. Struggled over the decision for months..."

"Did he tell you that?"

"Hell, woman. He didn't have to. Haven't you seen how he looks at you? Didn't you notice tonight that it almost killed him to see you leave with me?"

"So, you brought me here to tell me this? You could have told me without all this fanfare, showing off your connections—"

He threw money on the table and stood. "Look, whatever your name is, I needed time to talk to you. I hoped to convince you to get your life in order. Get yourself straight with Rich. Give that man the love he needs. Or move on."

Arlene said to take Rich to bed, be good for both of us. "Okay, take me home."

They rode in silence. No radio. The tires whined on the pavement. Clouds moved in, covered the moon—somber as the atmosphere in the truck. The headlights gouged a glaring path out of the darkness. She gripped the arms of her seat growing more tense the closer they came to home. What if he was horrified that she'd crippled a man and then abandoned him? Jeff the cop, was horrified. Jeff the do-it-right-all-the-time-guy, was horrified.

When they pulled up to the door, she could not see Rich.

"I'll go in with you."

"No need." Light from the kitchen shown on his face, rigid, sure of himself. "Do I have to give you a report?"

"I'll know." He shifted into reverse. "See you around."

The kitchen felt like a tomb. One row of florescent lights shown down the hall. She sank on a bench waiting for her nerves to settle down. If he'd been here, waiting, she probably would have burst out with the truth. But she couldn't trust Jeff not to take matters into his own hands. Sucking in breaths like a jogger back from a long run, she rose and stepped into the humid night. A ray of light creased the grass toward the rear of Rich's duplex. He might be in bed, reading. Maybe asleep with the light on.

She stepped onto his porch and knocked, listened to stirring.

"Just a minute..." He stood in the open door—pants, bare chest. A beer bottle in one hand. "Shannon?"

He must sleep naked. Or in shorts. "Do...do you have a minute to talk?" *Stupid question.* "I mean...may I talk to you? More than a minute?"

"Sure." He pushed open the screen door. "Come in."

She stopped short, taking in the place. Professor came to mind—a gray sofa and two mis-matched chairs facing a scarred coffee table. The walls were lined to the ceiling with a jumble of books. Sarita had been right, it looked like a book morgue and smelled of old paper.

He extended the bottle. "All I can offer is beer..."

"I'd like one." Her tongue felt like a wad of cotton. Might as well expose herself all the way.

"I've got several..." He squinted and motioned with his head. "Ah...why don't you pick? I sort of collect different kinds."

She followed him—iron bedstead in front of the window AC. A night table held a tower of books and another of medical journals overseen by a crookneck reading lamp. She stopped at the kitchen door. A library storeroom—books in cabinets and stacked along the counter.

"It's my overflow collection." His eyes trailed the room, so small it could have been a closet. "This place is mostly for storage...night-reading...sleep." He opened an under-cabinet refrigerator. Close to a dozen bottles of brand names and craft brews lined two narrow shelves. Several pieces of string cheese lay in the door tray. He raised up, shrugged. "Besides the books, I'm sort of a beer geek. I like to try the new ones."

"Give me what you're drinking."

He grabbed a bottle, twisted the top, and never took his eyes from her face. "You didn't come here for beer."

"I've... I have to tell you. Jeff took me out for a reason."

Rich frowned, stood still holding both beers. The refrigerator door wide open.

"He's investigated me." She wrapped her arms around herself. *Look him in the eye!* "My real name's Meredith Haggerty. When we met, I was running away from my husband. He thinks I died in the North Tower..."

Rich placed both bottles back in the refrigerator and shut the door. He pulled her hands from around her body and held them. "You were so traumatized. I figured you'd been there."

He's still holding my hands. "That's not all. I'm responsible for my husband being crippled. I was driving the car... I planned to run for years."

He lifted her hands, kissed her fingers.

"Aren't you repulsed? I'm telling you that I'm a fake and a liar."

"I'm telling you that I love you, Meredith Haggerty." He reached for her, crushed her against his bare chest. Held her against the hardness of his body, kissed her neck, and stroked her back.

"I love you, Ben Jacques Richelieu." She reached for his face, held it in both hands, kissed him quickly, and pulled back.

His mouth moved over hers, hungry and gentle, then eager. He pressed her against the wall. His hands moved over her body as she clung to him responding to his touch, allowing the pent-up desires to consume her.

He mumbled, "May I take you to my bed?"

"Please, yes." They moved together, fumbling to undress each other.

When her clothes fell to the floor, he gazed at her. "I don't know the proper way to do this. All I know is that I want you. I've wanted you for so long."

She pulled him onto the bed, forgetting everything except his body and his lips and his hands. They came together with an eagerness and intensity that drove her to an aching pleasure. When he finally groaned and fell against her breathing hard, he laughed softly. "I never dreamed it would be like this."

"Me either." She gripped him against her.

They dozed off and awoke well before dawn to arousal that carried them both to exhaustion. He lay beside her, stroking the damp hair off her face.

She finally scooted out of bed. "I need to get out before Lupe wakes. Meet me on the jogging trail?"

"I can't wait." He looked at his clock. "See you in fifteen minutes."

Cool water didn't ease the soreness—the memory of his body entering her made her alive to every move. Her shorts touched her where he had been; her t-shirt lay soft against the places he had kissed.

When they met and began the very slow jog into the grove, she reached for his hand.

"Do you believe what we've been doing?" He sounded like a man in awe. "Meredith. Meredith, I tried my best not to love you." He wrapped an arm around her waist, and they slowed to a walk through the darkness. "From that first day on the bus, I was attracted. I've been around plenty of beautiful women. I saw them but never had a desire. You were like a magnet, always pulling me."

167

"You stayed away so often."

He bent, kissed the top of her head. "I was trying to keep control."

Chapter Sixteen

For the next two nights, they waited until Lupe went to bed before Meredith slipped over to his house, and each morning she hurried back to change clothes before they jogged along the river. On the third night, they had drifted into contented sleep when a buzzer ripped through the air, jerking them awake. Rich raised up immediately and slipped on his pants. "It's the bell at the clinic. I'll get back as soon as I can."

"May I help?"

"You better stay here." He kissed her cheek and was out the door before she could argue.

She watched him trot toward the clinic and into the hazy light spreading from the security pole. There were no cars parked out front, no one stirring around. She walked out into the yard far enough to see him through the clinic windows talking to a man sitting on the examining table.

Life of a doctor. She crawled back in bed and dozed fitfully until she felt him slip in beside her. "What was it? Was he hurt?"

He pulled her against him. "No. He's looking for work. I gave him some dry clothes, filled him with coffee, and packaged up peanut butter and crackers from Lupe's store. He's beating it up the road toward town by now."

"How often do you get waked up like this?"

"Night's the best time to cross. Once or twice a week someone shows up. If they're sober and not strung out on drugs, I give a boost. Otherwise, I call Jeff."

She felt cold all over, pulled him tighter. "That's dangerous. How do you know they won't attack if you call Jeff?"

"You heard how the buzzer rings when they push the clinic bell? There's a button on the wall in the exam room that calls Jeff. You'd be surprised how fast he gets here."

"All this time, I didn't know you were going to the clinic in the middle of the night."

"You weren't supposed to know, sweetheart. It's Jeff's and my little secret." He stroked her cheek. "Now that I've thoroughly scared you, can you sleep for a couple of hours?"

"I'm going to try." She lay still, felt him relax against her. The AC cut off, an owl screeched, and she wondered who else might be climbing out of the river and lurking in the shadows?

The evenings belonged to them for the next two nights—sweet talk, gentle exploring. Then the screech of tires and banging on the front door jerked Rich from the bed and outside so quickly that it was hard to believe he had been asleep.

"They shot my boy! Shot him in the back..."

Rich ran between three cars whose headlights played on a couple carrying a body toward the clinic and others milling about in panic.

She threw on a shirt and jeans and made her way between a gathering crowd of people, some of whom she recognized from community events. Jeff's jeep and three sheriff cars with lights flashing, sirens blaring, arrived in a burst of white dust.

"He's dead. Boy didn't have a chance. Happens when they get with them older kids." It was all said in hushed Spanish as she hurried into the clinic.

Three older boys, none of whom she recognized, were being held in a death grip between four Mexicans who were soaking wet—sweat or the river?

Rich stepped out from behind the curtain, his face drawn, angry. "He's gone. The bullet got him in the back of the neck." His eyes whipped to the boys. "He was only twelve!" His nostrils flared, his fists clenched. He looked for an instant like he might hit them. Then he saw Jeff and turned away as though repulsed by the sight of them.

Jeff and the sheriff began handcuffing, walked the boys toward the squad cars.

Lupe rushed up to Meredith, threw her arms around her. "Here you are. I thought you was sleeping through all this."

Meredith shook her head. "Too bad it's not a bad dream."

"That poor woman. Her ol' man left her to raise that boy." Lupe choked, suppressed a deep sob. "That coulda been my Maximillian. They say the boy was their mule. Carried drugs across, easy. No one suspected one so young."

Daylight crept over the trees as the crowd loaded into cars, followed the vehicles carrying the boys. Rich stayed behind the curtain with the dead child's mother who kept saying he was a good boy, never in trouble, only wanted to have friends.

Meredith moved through the day in an exhausted fog, watching and worrying about Rich who looked as fatigued as she felt. Relieved that everyone headed to bed early, she hurried to his house and welcomed his tight embrace.

As they undressed for bed, Rich said, "I didn't get the whole story. It seems those older kids decided after the arrest of Osiel Cárdenas Guillén...you remember the guy that was head of the Gulf Cartel? He got arrested after a shootout in Matamoros." He sat on the side of the bed, staring at her and shaking his head as he talked. "Those dumb kids decided that they'd cut into the big boys' game. Apparently, they convinced the twelve-year-old to tote the drugs across the border for them. When he realized he'd been caught, he ran, tried to swim the river. He wasn't fast enough." Rich sighed, "Unless it comes out in the trial, we'll never know all the story."

"Jeff won't tell us?"

"Not in a million years. Please sleep with me. I'm too tired for anything else."

"Me, too." She crawled onto the bed and fell instantly to sleep in his arms.

They had another week of restful nights before rapid knocking shook Rich's front door. He jumped up, slipped on some pants, and she heard him say, "What's wrong, Lupe?"

Meredith dressed in the dark, peeked into his living room at Lupe sitting on his sofa wiping at tears.

"He called. The phone kept ringing. Shannon didn't ever hear it. So, I answered." She burst into tears again.

"Did he say what he wants?"

"He say I'm his wife. He means to live with me." She wiped at her face. "I'm scared. I tried to wake Shannon before I bothered you."

Meredith slipped into the dark kitchen, fingered her way along the rows of books until she found the back door, and stepped into the chilly night air. She had put on her pajamas and crawled in her bed when Lupe knocked on her door.

She held the crying woman and listened again to her story. "He'll be here this afternoon. He's a devil. Always whipped me and Maximillian—"

"We'll call Jeff in the morning. Get him to send someone. If your husband's on parole and acts up, he'll find himself right back in prison."

"I hope so. He wants my money. He'll be mad when he knows I gave the church a tithe." She laughed. "If I wasn't so scared, I'd like to see his face when I say 'ten percent is gone.'"

The next morning, Jeff contacted the sheriff who explained that he couldn't post anyone on the place. But he'd have a deputy keep an eye out. Call if it looks like trouble. Maria and Lupe spent the day pacing the kitchen and watching the road. Near sunset, a taxi stopped out near the highway, deposited a man, and drove away.

"That's him, Lupe whispered. "He walks so mean." She turned terrified eyes on Meredith. "Please call the sheriff before he comes in here."

"I'll call," Maria was already headed to the phone.

He swung a little suitcase, casual as someone home from a day at the office. As he approached, Lupe's breathing grew louder. "He's looking old, ain't he? Still greases his hair, but it ain't black no more.

172

Got kind of a limp. Must a been beat up in the pen."

The sheriff's car eased down the road and a young deputy stepped out. He nodded at Lupe's husband.

Diego ignored him and stepped inside. He stood perfectly still and stared at Lupe. "You ain't changed a bit. Must a been a good life here." He spoke in rapid Spanish.

"I don't want to live with you, Diego. Go someplace else." She glanced at Rich, who had moved beside her.

Diego stepped forward, and the deputy moved up. "The *Doña* wants you to leave. How about I call a taxi?"

"Get your ass outa my way, boy. I'm talking to my wife." His words snarled from a mouthful of yellowed teeth. He took a step toward Lupe, and Rich slid, smooth as a shadow, in front of her.

"Who the hell are you?" Diego's eyes looked like his son's— droopy lids, thick black lashes that had seduced a younger Lupe.

"He's Father Rich." Her position behind the priest emboldened her voice.

"So, you're a priest? Where's your collar? You been messing with my woman? Keeping her satisfied while I'm getting my ass kicked in the pen?"

The softness she knew—tenderness that made her heart sing— disappeared. Rich's face contorted, his body swelled—a steam boiler about to explode. That's when she heard the click—sharp, metallic. It flashed silver, long, thin as Diego's hand extended.

The explosion shoved him forward, mouth open, eyes walled back. Blood sprayed from the front of Diego. It splashed on Rich, and he bent forward to catch Diego. Reaching, fingers splayed.

"I had to do it. I had to..." the startled deputy looked wild, gripping his gun, almost paralyzed.

Rich wasn't helping Diego. He was lying on top of him. Their blood ran together on the floor. "Call an ambulance," Meredith heard her voice. It was loud, and it made the boy move. She knelt beside Rich feeling a strong pulse. "Get some cup towels!"

Lupe was there helping her reach under Rich. As they lifted him off Diego, the switchblade clattered against the floor. She shoved her hand into the wetness on Rich's side, used the dike of towels to stem the flood. "Open your eyes, sweetheart. Open your eyes."

The grin barely moved his lips.

Sirens pierced the air. Crowds seemed to swarm, calling out Rich's name, crying loud words of damnation. Skilled hands, wearing gloves. Stripped away his shirt, jabbed wads of gauze into him and lifted him away from her.

They stepped over Diego, face down, spilling blood across the floor. The young deputy had holstered his gun. He paced, shaking. "I didn't mean to kill him. I meant to stop him."

"Please take me to the hospital." Meredith clutched the sleeve of an older deputy who looked down at the blood-smeared print she made on his shirt. "Ma'am. We're not equipped..."

"Carmelita will take us." Don Gaspar stood there—pale, shaken.

They watched the ambulance pull slowly along the drive. "Why don't they hurry?" Did anyone hear her?

Carmelita scooped an arm around her, guided her to the car. The horn blared as they sped past traffic. Meredith and Don Gaspar bounced against each other, squeezed between people in the back seat.

"He's going into surgery." The woman at the ER desk barely lifted her head. "Does he have relatives here?"

Carmelita pushed Meredith forward. "*Señorita* Staples is very close to him."

She knows? Meredith leaned toward the window. She could feel Carmelita's strong hand against her back, holding her up.

"The waiting room is through those doors. The doctors will come out when they get him patched up."

"Patched up?" Meredith formed the words.

The woman looked up from her computer screen and offered a brief smile. "We'll let you know when we can."

They sat on cold plastic sofas. A handful of silent, scared souls staring at the double doors to surgery like a herd of deer waiting and watching for any movement. Each time the doors opened, they flinched, ready to bolt. Finally, the doctor came toward them, his scrubs were green and clean. His mask hung around his neck like a stiff scarf.

"Miss Staples?"

Carmelita helped her stand, moved her toward the smiling, pleasant face.

"He's going to be terribly sore. Got an appendectomy without anesthetic." He chuckled at his joke. "Seriously, he's a lucky man. Got a strong body. No major damage. Lots of blood, but you people were quick to slow the flow."

"Can we see him?" Meredith didn't mean to say 'we'. She wanted to be alone with him.

"He'll be in recovery for a while." He grinned again. "I hear the other one wasn't so fortunate."

The other one? "I forgot! Where's Lupe?"

"Maria's taking care of her. I'll go out there when we get him in a room." Carmelita stroked Meredith's back. "Right now, I'm going to the gift shop. Maybe they have a robe for you."

Meredith's hands ran down her shirt and along her pant legs. "Rich's blood."

Carmelita returned with a heavy chenille robe. "Go put this on for tonight."

She knows I intend to stay. "They may call me."

"I'll stand outside the bathroom door. Watch for you."

The lavatory water paled his blood from her hands and nails. Her t-shirt and pants bled red stains down the drain. She'd put them back on when they dried.

They walked, arm in arm, back to the waiting area. "All that blood. We could have lost him."

Carmelita whispered. "I can't imagine God letting that happen to you two."

She knows. Meredith squeezed her dear friend's arm as they sat together on the hard-plastic sofa.

She froze at the door in rigid shock. The overhead lights exposed him—faded gown left open—crossed by a tangle of tubes moving fluids. Orange antiseptic smeared up into the thin patch of hair along his chest. His face looked sharp, drawn like chalk. He opened his eyes. "Come close."

She bent, slipped her lips beneath the oxygen ring and kissed him for a long time. "I'm here for the night. Right now, we must let *Don* Gaspar and Carmelita come in."

"If we have to." His eyes slipped shut.

Don Gaspar kissed Rich's forehead. Carmelita did the same. "The sheriff's waiting. He gave us one minute."

Meredith pulled the heavy robe around her and stepped aside as the lawmen swarmed in.

The officer held his big Stetson over his stomach. "We'll be talking to Doctor Richelieu, ma'am. Please step in the hall and speak to my deputy."

The partner looked the same: round in the middle, pink cheeks, and a hat covering his belly. His eyes trailed over the big bathrobe. "We'd like to get your account of what happened this afternoon, Miss."

Miss? Meredith went over the events. And she emphasized that Lupe was afraid of her husband.

As soon as the officers left, the head nurse bustled in. "Your friends have filled the waiting room. I'm placing a NO VISITORS sign on your door." Her eyes took in Meredith.

"I want her to stay." Rich raised his hand, then closed his eyes, surrendering to exhaustion.

The nurse wiggled her shoulders. "The recliner's all we have."

There would be no questions if we were married. Meredith cut the lights, kissed Rich's responsive lips, and curled into the plastic-covered recliner. She had screwed up her life. Made marriage impossible.

The next morning, Javier stood in the doorway holding a cluster of red Turk's Cup bound together in wet paper towels. "*Abuelo* let me pull these off his fence." He made a fake grin to show a missing tooth. Then he shoved the flowers to Carmelita and bound across the room. Meredith grabbed him, loved the feel of his hot little body as she lifted him up to the bed.

"We waited and waited last night. They wouldn't let us see you." He scrambled onto his knees and stretched his arms very carefully across Rich's chest. "I was scared when they took you off."

"I'm almost well. But look at you. What happened to your tooth?" Rich stroked the child's head.

"I pulled it myself. Last night." He sat back. "Can I see where he cut you?"

"It's sewed up now." Rich pulled back the sheet.

Javier's frown deepened. "What's that tube for? Are those black things where they sewed you up? Did it hurt?"

"Oh, no! They put me to sleep." Rich pulled the boy against his shoulder.

"Will they take out that tube?"

"Probably tomorrow. Aren't you supposed to be in school?"

"*Tía* Carmelita's taking me. I wish I could stay here."

"Tell you what," Carmelita said, "I'll bring you back this afternoon."

Javier climbed off the bed, looked at Meredith's robe. "Where're your clothes?"

"I had to wash out the blood. They aren't dry."

"That bad man got blood all over the kitchen. It made *Tía* Lupe cry a lot." Javier sighed liked an old man carrying a great burden. He reached for Carmelita's hand. "Tell my teacher not to put me on the school bus this afternoon."

"I'll remember," Carmelita said as they turned to leave.

Visitors came in a steady stream all day. Most were as curious about Meredith's presence as they were about the attack. "We're glad you could be here." "Did you spend the night?"

When they were finally alone, Meredith whispered, "It's good that Carmelita brought me some clean clothes. Saved explaining the bathrobe."

"Word spreads," Rich said. "By the time we get home everybody will know."

"You've been loved for so long. I hope I'm not causing trouble."

"The women love you. They'll keep the peace."

I hope you're right. She helped him stand, arrange his gown, and take another walk down the hall.

That afternoon, they were about to walk again when Javier arrived with a book under his arm. "My teacher gave me this story about being in the hospital. Want me to read it to you?"

"How about taking me for a walk? Then read to me?"

"Sure." The boy eyed Rich's hospital gown. "You don't have on clothes."

"It's okay here. Lots of patients wear these little dresses."

Meredith and Carmelita stood at the door watching the boy

holding one hand while Rich used the other to pull his pole of dangling tubes.

"I'm so glad you brought him. Rich loves that child..."

"It was a necessity. Javier brought you two together."

"You noticed?"

"Honey, everybody noticed. We watched you both suffer when Javier and Aleta moved to the big house. It was like your family was torn apart."

Meredith grinned, slipped her arm through Carmelita's. "It feels good to be accepted."

"Ha! Tell me about it. You didn't raise an eyebrow when I admitted I couldn't read." She bumped her soft hip against Meredith. "Only you didn't need to admit anything. We could see it."

The welcome home began with Lupe coming to Rich's apartment. Her lips quivered as she stopped just inside the door. "I been too embarrassed to look at you. That man shamed me and Maximillian..."

Rich reached for Lupe's hand. "You had no control over Diego. Promise me you'll stop blaming yourself."

Lupe nodded, lifted swollen eyes. "I been so upset, I forgot to tell you I'm glad you can be a real man." She ducked her head. "I mean...you know priests can't be like others—"

"That means a lot. I was hoping for your blessing." Rich held onto Lupe's hand until she finally stopped crying.

The next morning, the women munched cookies and giggled. The struggle to speak English got in the way of questions about a wedding date. She stumbled and hedged and felt relieved when the hour ended.

The evening class opened with a jolt. Three of the long-time members arrived with their husbands. The women fluttered, avoided looking directly at her.

While she helped arrange extra chairs, she noticed a man who towered over the others. Everything set him apart—handsomely chiseled features, impeccably dressed in starched khakis, topped off by an air of superiority. When the class started, he remained standing. "We have some questions." He looked around, indicating the entire room was part of the *we*. "What's all this business about English and birth control?"

Why did they wait all this time? Her body went hollow as she watched Carmelita step outside. She wanted to call out, beg not to be abandoned.

"What kind of place you running here? Since you came, thing's changed." His eyes kept circling the room—corralling support. "This English you're pushing. What's it for? You turning our women into feminazis?"

Talk radio junkie. She reached for her glass, swigged a long drink to relieve her cotton-mouth. *Do I look terrified or in charge?* Setting down the water, she looked at each face—sneering men, women who appeared in pain—and finally found her voice. "Most members hope for better jobs. Speaking English opens a lot more doors."

Emboldened, another man, leaning back on spindly chair legs said, "What's wrong with what they do? That's all they know."

All eyes turned to the door where Carmelita appeared with Rich. He looked pale, drawn. Was he hurting from the walk or angry?

"If you need help with your family income, don't you want your wives to make more money?" She watched the insult soak in.

"They don't have to work." The leader glanced down at his wife and drew himself even taller.

Meredith grinned. "Okay, ladies. If you don't need to work, we'll dissolve this night class. You can join one of the daytime groups."

Several women snickered, hands flying to cover their mouths.

The leader sniffed. "That ain't all. You push birth control. It's against decency." His eyes cut around to Rich who leaned forward, absorbed in the conversation. "You know what we mean...it's the church...even the priest." As though drawing new energy, he said, "And what's all this between you and Father Rich? It ain't right for a priest—"

"I'm not a priest anymore." Rich's first words. "You'll have to go to town to speak to a priest." Rich's eyes never left the man who slumped a little.

That's his soft spot. Meredith didn't move. The room became eerily still except for the steady hum of the AC.

"Let's go." He reached for his wife's hand. She pulled it away but followed him out.

When the door slammed shut, Meredith waited for the absence to be felt. "Shall we start our discussion?"

It became a rehash of the morning class—questions about Lupe's husband, Rich's knife wound, and their relationship—all in English. The four remaining husbands squirmed, unable to understand most of the English. All the women struggled to keep from slipping into Spanish. And no one left.

When it ended, Carmelita said, "I'm getting my car. You don't need to walk anymore tonight."

"No, no! I feel invigorated. Things are going to work out just fine."

As they walked back to Rich's apartment, she took his arm. "I keep shoving away the truth. I'm hurting you in this community."

"I love it here, Meredith. But I love you more. Let's not fret. See how this plays out."

Chapter Seventeen

Within days Rich was back in the clinic—a few hours at first. In two weeks, he had returned to fulltime.

That night he pulled her on his shoulder. "We were swamped again today. Not for medical problems. The questions keep being about us. Even Maude can't get over the charm."

"We're more titillating than their romance novels. I'm embarrassed that it's you and me they're salivating over."

He ran his hand across her breasts. "Let's get married. Put a stop to it."

She covered her face with both hands. "That adds bigamy to my other crimes." She sat up, faced him in the dark. "You and Lupe and Frank have all been honest. It makes me ashamed of myself. I've decided to call Harvey. He'll be wild with fury. But I'm going to ask him to divorce me. For abandonment."

Rich raised up, shoved pillows into a mound, and pulled her across his chest. "You think he'll do it?"

"No. He'll want me jailed for insurance fraud." She sighed, "But I've got to try."

The next morning, Rich sat close while she punched in Harvey's number. It rang twice, and the operator said it was no longer in service. Surprised, she called again. Same message.

"He hated people, but I can't imagine him cutting off the phone. I'll call the condo office." She stopped. "What if he died? All by himself, alienated from the world..." She felt Rich's hand stroking her back as she punched in the number.

"Harvey Haggerty? You say number fourteen? The Rogers have been in there since I came here. Let me look in the files. He sold in February 2002. Anything else?"

"You don't have a forwarding address?"

"No, lady."

The new girl who answered at the clubhouse didn't know of a golfer named Haggerty. She shouted his name, but no one remembered where he moved.

"He vanished. Like I did—"

"Last report I saw, over a thousand were still missing. Perhaps the city of New York will tell you how to contact the next-of-kin."

She began searching for the number, pulled the phone to her chest to quiet uneven breathing. "I'd like to forget this. Pretend I didn't exist until I became Shannon Staples."

He kissed her shoulder. "Me, too."

Finally, she got through and reached a cheerful voice asking how to be of help.

"I'm trying to locate the next-of-kin of Meredith Haggerty...she...was in the North Tower—"

"Sorry, hon, we can't give out that info. Oh, wait. Did you say Haggerty?"

"Yes...yes?"

The muffled sound of her hand cupped the receiver. "Hey, is that wheelchair guy at Ground Zero named Haggerty? Yeah...yeah, that's it. Hon, we don't give out contact info, but there's a guy named Haggerty at the recovery site every day. Rain or shine. I've only seen him once." She lowered her voice to a whisper "He's looking for his wife. Nutty, huh?"

"Yeah, thanks," Meredith whispered.

A pause. "Anything else?"

"Oh...you've been very helpful." She hung up, trembling.

"Please, hold me as tight as you can."

"I could hear." He rocked her until she settled down.

"If Frank can sell my rings, add that to the money Lupe gave me, I should have enough. I'll find him and start divorce proceedings." She squeezed her eyes shut. "Or, go to jail for insurance fraud."

"If he's looking for you, maybe he hasn't filed."

"First thing, I'm going to see Jerry Morganstein." She laughed. "He's the only one who knows about all those years. He was my friend, internist, and psychiatrist. Called me a damned fool at every visit." She grinned, shook her head. "Thought I was crazy not to divorce Harvey." She cupped her hands on Rich's cheeks, kissed him hard. "But you know what? I'd have never met you if I hadn't been a damned fool and run away." She began to laugh, pulled him back onto the bed. "I'm so glad I found you. Even if I end up in jail—"

"No, no! Your doctor may be the answer. He should have a record of your visits."

"He charged me enough. Surely he kept something..."

"Okay, you're getting a plan. And I'm getting a wife." Rich rolled on top of her and began smothering her with kisses that grew more urgent. "Let's make love. Give us a little moral boost."

Frank whistled while he looked through his loop at her rings. "You've got some rocks here. That man must have had plenty of cash."

"Yep. And he spent it all on those rings."

Frank laughed. "Then you had to pay the bills?"

"Nutty as it sounds, that's the way it turned out. But I had gorgeous rings!"

He stuffed his loop and the rings in a little felt sack. "You're going to get screwed. There's no way I can get what these things are worth. How much do you have to have?"

"Whatever you can get. I'm using it to divorce the man."

"Ha! Then, Doc and I need to hurry this along."

So, he knows too. "Thanks for saving my neck. Again."

"It's a great neck to save. Besides, Arlene would kill me if I didn't do this. See you in a few days."

It was only two days before he returned with five thousand dollars. "They're worth five times that. You think this will get you through it?"

"I hope so. If you're still talking to Arlene, ask her to kick in a word for me. I know she's somewhere with connections."

Frank's lips puckered. "I can't let her go."

Meredith squeezed his hand. "I bet you a hundred dollars that she'd tell you to get out. Go dancing. Look around for some gal who can boot scoot. Probably not as well as Arlene, but dancing just the same."

"I know. I know." He grinned. "Maybe when you and Rich get hitched, I'll be so inspired that I'll do a little scouting."

"Oh, Frank, I hope it's soon."

She watched his old van rumble up the road and then hurried inside to begin making arrangements for her flight to Newark.

As she folded each pair of hand-me-down slacks and tucked in two turtle-neck sweaters, she whispered thanks to Arlene. "You'd be cheering me, girl. I'm scared as shit, but you'd shove me all the way."

Rich wrapped his arms around her, cupping a breast in each hand. "I hear you talking to yourself. Are you practicing?"

She gripped both his hands. "Maybe you'd call it praying."

He kissed her neck. "I vote for that."

She turned to face him. "I know Arlene would tell me to put on my big girl panties and get going."

"Yep, that's exactly how she'd say it."

She slammed Rich's suitcase shut. "Thanks for the loaner. I aim to get it back to you as fast as I can."

"It's a piece of junk, but if that's what brings you back, I'll call it a prize."

She swung onto him. "I wish we had time to make love."

"We don't. But keep it in mind." He kissed her nose and grabbed the old suitcase.

Lupe and Maria had stayed out of her room, given them the last

184

few minutes alone. But neither of them had fully understood why she wanted to get a divorce. Lupe had said over and over, "forget that man. You got Father Rich now. New York's far away."

Maria had echoed the sentiments. "I got divorced so he'd have to pay. You don't need no child support. Besides, he may say no."

When they stepped in the kitchen, Carmelita had joined the farewell group. "Sure you don't want me to drive you to the airport? You're dressed for New York temps. Rich's truck will cook you."

Meredith didn't respond. Instead, she reached for all three women and folded them into a group hug. Her voice broke. "Watch after Rich for me. Okay?"

The nods were all silent as they fought back tears and followed along to Rich's truck.

When they turned on the highway, he reached to adjust the side windows. "I'm being selfish, making you ride in this hot rattletrap."

"I want it to be just us." She pulled open the throat of her sweater and scooted against him. "We can pretend we're teenagers."

"If teenagers are as horny as we are, they're in trouble."

You missed all that? She laid her head on his shoulder and tried not to think that this might be goodbye forever.

When they reached the airport, he cut the motor, lifted her face, and kissed with such urgency that she had to pull away. "This isn't the end. I'll be back. Believe with me that I'll be back."

"I do. I do. One more kiss."

She could feel his tears, and she could not stop hers. "I'm leaving you here. Security won't let you go past the door. If I look back, I'll chicken out." She jumped from the cab, grabbed the suitcase from the back and half ran into the terminal. Once inside, she had to stop, to see him one last time. He stood beside the red truck staring after her.

The check-in was as harrowing as she'd heard—nothing like it used to be. Her flight was finally called, and her heart dropped in disappointment when she found her seat in the cabin on the opposite side from the terminal, cutting off the possibility of seeing him one last time. The plane finally filled, and they backed out, taxied down the runway. She stared out at the flat scrubland spreading on forever. Then they made a sweeping turn, hesitated an instant, and began to move, picking up speed. The terminal rushed into view and as the plane lifted, nose up, she saw over the rooftop, the red truck. Rich stood, raising his arm in the air.

She clutched Arlene's over-sized bag to her side and did a speed-walk through Houston's labyrinth of terminals until she arrived breathless at her gate with ten minutes to spare.

Rich had insisted that she buy a phone so she could call him. He would be in clinic so she left a message. "About to board Houston flight. Love, love, love!"

Just as she took her seat, the phone pinged, and she heard his message, "I'm loving you every minute."

The plane rose above clouds—away from Rich, away from her life—suspended in a clear blue world. It was best not to see the plowed fields, the cluster of towns, the spiral of roads—not to know how rapidly she was moving away from all she loved.

When they touched down in Newark, she felt like a switch turned, plunged her into a surge of momentum. Hunger that felt more like nausea gripped her. The plan, keep to the plan. Get the shuttle into the city, check into a pricey hotel near the Battery, and call Rich. Yes, Rich's voice was what she needed.

Glad for a seat all to herself, she gripped the metal armrest as the van driver jerked through traffic. Her pulse took on the staccato rhythm of flashing lights, interrupted by the sharp jolt of a blaring horn or squalling brakes. She shut her eyes and remembered her mom whispering, "Ride 'em cowboy," when they reached another foreign country and were being hurtled through madcap traffic to the place they were supposed to call home.

Had she forgotten the energy of the city, or was it fear of what lay ahead that made her tremble—a steady low-volt urgency. The shuttle tore at breakneck speed next to the Hudson—black and still, pocked with sparkling tour boats and lumbering ferries. Then the Battery—their first home—loomed into view. Did she ever live in this tight cluster of buildings? Did she and Harvey really walk arm-in-arm along the river, feeling the fog wet their faces? Watching for the Statue of Liberty to appear in the distance?

She breathed in the wet night air, dug out a tip for the driver, and registered for two nights. Can I get a divorce started in two nights? She moved, numb as a robot into the elevator and up to the eighth floor, along thick carpeting to her room. Hot, small, and way over-priced.

His voice came on strong. "Meredith? Are you in for the night?"

"I'm missing you something awful."

He laughed. "I keep looking up, expecting to see you walking to your class. Javier came to see me at the clinic. Maude put him in my office. I found him standing on the ottoman gazing through the spotting scope."

Meredith held the phone, closed her eyes to imagine the boy and man together, looking for birds.

"He finally sat down, looked as serious as old Gaspar, and said, "I'm missing my *tita.*"

"Maybe we'll know by tomorrow." She shuddered, crawled in bed, and pulled the comforter up to her chin. "I'm freezing. I wish you could warm me up."

Morning came quickly. Still dressed in the clothes from yesterday, she went out in the chilled early light and ran along the newly landscaped Promenade. The potholes were gone, and the benches facing the river looked new, but the lights of Jersey City still made her think of a birthday cake. In the early days, Harvey had teased her, insisting she never had enough birthday parties to know the difference.

At nine, she stopped at the door where gold letters read:

JERROLD M. MORGANSTEIN, MD
INTERNAL MEDICINE, PSYCHIATRY

It felt like she had come home. The familiar cozy living room, soft music shutting out street noise from below. Two large Chagall prints dominated one wall. Thick carpeting, a sofa, and two chairs clustered next to reading lamps. Shirley pulled open the glass, a pleasant smile that the doctor's wife offered to every patient. Her mouth formed an O. She leaned forward into the opening.

Meredith nodded. "It's me, Shirley."

"Jerry!" It was a scream. "My God, it's Meredith." She ran through the door and the two women tumbled against each other. "Jerry, you were right. She's alive!"

The little short man with wire-rim glasses perched halfway down his nose ran up the hall. "I told you, didn't I! I told you she wasn't gone." The three of them clung to each other.

He pulled back. "Come on. Let's get in my office before someone comes in. Tell us how you did it."

"I'm locking the front door." Shirley, who was even shorter than Jerry, flipped the lock. Within minutes, she returned with cups of coffee on a tray.

Huddled like conspirators, they listened to Meredith tell her story. "I was sorry not to let you know I was alive. I needed a complete break."

"Yes, baby. You had to do it clean." Shirley's hands were twisted with arthritis and soft as feathers when she stroked Meredith's arm. "We pored over the lists of victims, always praying we wouldn't find you."

"So, you think he'll divorce you? I've seen him a couple of times down there. He's so wrapped up in whatever's going on in his head that he doesn't see me." Jerry grunted a disgusted sound. "I've never tried approaching him."

"Then you think I'll find him?"

"Of course! He's a fixture along Church Street."

"Have you kept records of my visits?"

"Oh, sure, sure."

"I'll need proof of his abuse if I have to do the filing—"

"I'll copy it all right now." Shirley was already standing.

"While she's doing that, let's go see Travlos. He kept the Stage Door Deli open after the attack. Only two businesses on Vesey Street survived. He's had a time of it. We try to eat there several times a week."

"Don't you have patients?"

"I'm cutting back. Mostly see people in the afternoon."

It felt good to walk beside an old friend. "I hope I'm not crazy to feel relieved. Now that I've decided to confront him—"

"You know my view. He didn't deserve all those years you gave him." Jerry took Meredith's arm, "I'm glad you've found someone who'll love you." Grinning, a little tear showed at the corner of his eye. "It's always been special for Shirley and me. We wish that for you."

They turned the corner onto Vesey, and she froze, struck by the emptiness, the filmy haze, the unpleasant tinge paling the air. She spoke in gasps. "I saw it falling..." She looked at Jerry. "I kept running from it...and from him. But to see it like this—nothing."

His old-man eyes looked red-rimmed and weary. "It always feels like death's lingering. The sky's as empty as our hearts, and the smell won't go away."

They stood arm-in-arm gazing at cranes, bent like long-legged yellow grasshoppers, stalking the space above the construction fence. Then—upward to nothing where the towers had been. She felt cold, pulled her jacket close, turned up the turtle neck.

The deli occupied an old building crammed between hollowed-out businesses that had faced WTC 5. They stopped at the entrance, and she looked back across the street at the high fence. "The largest Borders in the city took up three floors of that old glass building. I bought many a book in there."

"Yeah, when the towers fell, red-hot debris destroyed its top floors. Nothing's left."

She realized her mouth was open, her body growing weak with loss.

"Hey, Travlos, look who I found." Jerry's voice startled her. He had stepped in the doorway, shouted to the little Greek proprietor working behind the back counter. "You got any lox and bagels for this gal?"

Don't cave now. She followed Jerry into the deli.

"If it's not that Haggerty woman. I thought the towers got you, girl." Travlos threw off his apron and barrel-hugged her. "Where you been all this time?"

"Naw, naw!" It's a tale for another day. Just a *nosh* for now."

Jerry knows how to control the conversation. "I'm glad you're still in business, Travlos."

"Yep. Been a hard time. So few suits in here these days. Used to get forty for breakfast; hundred for lunch; calls all day and night for delivery." His eyes looked tired, watery. But we're holding on...thanks to the likes of Jerry and Shirley." He stopped, turned

189

around. "You come in here with a beautiful goy. Where'd you put Shirley?"

"Ha! I got her working. Package up her snack. We'll take it to her."

The familiar neighborhood tastes came back as she nibbled. She tried not to rush, but she wanted to get on with it. Harvey was probably right around the corner. But she needed Jerry's files before she made another move.

When they returned to the office, Shirley shouted, "Perfect timing. I got a pile of good notes." She stacked and stuffed papers in a folder. "You want to read them before you go?"

Meredith sighed. "I can't. I feel like I may explode. Thank you for everything. Especially for your love. Now, I've got to get this over with." She stuffed the folder into Arlene's bag.

"*Gei gezunterheit*, my dear." Shirley and Jerry took turns hugging her.

She walked back toward the empty hole, trembling. It was along here that she ran with Marty Savage, lifted the injured woman. Smoke poured from the giant, and it bulged before it rained down debris. She looked at the passive faces hustling past. If she stood around, might she spot Marty Savage? Would she even recognize him? All that ash turned them into anonymous strangers bonded in horror.

Suck it up! Get on with it. She turned the corner onto Church Street and was startled to see how many tourists were stopped all along the block. They huddled before the viewing wall—a galvanized steel fence—separating the movement far below in the pit where the towers had stood. Placed too high to touch, panels told the site's history beginning with business on West Street in the 1890s to the Singer Tower when it was the tallest building in the world. The attack on the Pentagon and the crash in Pennsylvania looked so real that she wanted to turn away.

Then she came to the list—those who perished on 9/11 and those who died in the '93 bombing. She had read the names every time they were posted in the *Times*, but this was different. This was the place where it ended. Her eyes started at the bottom of the first row, moved up, along the names, seeing familiar faces—comrades by day who would never again step into her office for a friendly talk.

Then, Pierre Abbe stood out like a bold shout. *Why did you turn back? You could have survived!*

Once more she scanned the rows for Haggerty. It had never been there all the times she'd read the list before, but it should have been. Why did she make it out? She had no children who were orphaned. She had no family left bereft.

Oh no, a panhandler! Headed my way. She always attracted them. As a child, she heard that hobos left a mark on houses where they found a good handout. Every panhandler in the city knew she was an easy mark. His beard hung to his chest, hair flying as his arms worked to propel the wheelchair along the sidewalk, scooting in and out between people who had stopped to gaze at the historic panels. She kept her eyes forward. No need to encourage him with eye contact. Besides, he was moving with such intensity, he must have some lucrative mark in sight.

"I knew you'd come back!" The bellowed words echoed.

The sun glinted on a metal crutch as it heaved toward her and struck with such force that she staggered backward. Clutching her face, she felt the ooze of blood between her fingers. Then she saw him inside all that hair. "Harvey?"

"Damn you! I told them you weren't dead."

The crutch came again, cleaving her raised arm, ripping the bone like the crack of a torn tree limb. *Get away! Get away!* She whirled, the blood-curdling screams threatened to impale her as his wheelchair thumped off the curb behind her.

The orange walk-light flashed one second. She raised her arm toward the bus as it slammed to a stop. Horns blared, brakes squalled, and he kept shrieking—guttural, furious. The crash, the volley of metal and thud of flesh. Then silence. An instant of nothing except her breath.

Arms grabbed her. "It's okay, lady. You're okay, lady. He's hit. He can't get you no more." The arms were black, tattooed, and muscular. "It's okay, lady. Settle down. Here, let me hold my handkerchief on your head. It's clean."

As the blood smeared away, she saw him crumpled—discarded trash blocking Church Street. "Harvey, is it really you?" The words, a whisper as she stared in rigid disbelief.

"You okay?" A man in a hardhat, dust making goggle marks

around his eyes, leaned close. "We thought he was harmless. He never bothered nobody." The words came breathless as he kept turning back to look again at the bloody pulp in the street.

"It shouldn't end like this..."

"Bus didn't see him tearing across...Crazy as a loon. Told anybody who'd listen that his wife didn't die in the attack..."

Sirens wailed—were the towers burning—from all directions. A cop with his whistle between his lips bent over Harvey, then ran toward Meredith. "You know that guy?"

"My husband..." A wave of nausea and her body felt light, cold. Hands gripped her, held her upright.

"Hey man, I saw the whole thing. Never saw him move so fast. Then he swung that crutch. Clobbered her. Came down on her again. I tell you; he was powerful."

"God, lady. Where you been all these years? He's loitered around here forever." The cop didn't wait for an answer. He stepped back and let the EMS descend on her, cradling her arm, lifting her onto a gurney.

"It's just some blood—"

"Your arm's broke, and you gotta have stitches. You're still bleeding."

"What about his body? I need to do something..."

"No, lady. They'll find you soon enough."

Harvey had disappeared beneath crowds, staring, gasping. She closed her eyes to shut out the faces straining to see her as she was lifted into the ambulance. A spectacle. Subject of conversation. The thing moved, whined to open a path as she slipped away.

"We're giving you a little blood." A man in green clothes bent into her face. "You're lucky the city's best plastic surgeon is here this morning. He works miracles on faces..."

She tried to thank him, but she couldn't form the words.

Her arm throbbed; her head pounded and floodlights glared through her eyelids. She heard him talking, sharp questions. Her name. What was her name?

He was a cop, thick Yankee accent. Boston? "We need a name, lady. You got two names in your bag."

"Meredith Haggerty." She could barely speak. "Water?"

"Try a little ice." The eyes—black mascara—smiled.

"Who's Shannon Staples. You got her social security and ID card."

"Fake. I ran away."

"Now you're back?" He had angry eyes and cigar breath.

"Excuse me, I'm Doctor Jerrold Morganstein, Mrs. Haggerty's physician."

"Jerry?" She tried to lift her hand and gritted her teeth to keep back tears of relief.

"It's okay, sweetheart. The cops called when they found my papers in your bag." Jerry's voice brought an infusion of calm.

"We got lots of stories playing out here. And we've got a dead man who seems to be part of it—"

"I ran away...from him. I came...for a divorce." Did she say it clearly? Did she sound as crazy as Harvey?

"The folks with the Victims Compensation Fund say Mister Haggerty claimed you weren't dead. Insisted your name not be listed with the missing. He said you'd come back if he took any of the victim money." The cigar breath got stronger. "Is that why you came? You thought he'd gotten rich?"

"I was afraid I'd go to jail..."

"Apparently, the poor guy didn't have a dime. Lived on disability—"

"Just a minute. You got my name from Mrs. Haggerty's files. Didn't you see all the times her husband burned her with cigarettes? Rammed his wheelchair into her legs? Have you even looked at the scars she still carries?" Jerry's voice had risen to a shout. "And how about his attack this morning? Doesn't any of that count for you?"

"Sure. Sure. We just need to get all the facts clear—"

Quit letting Jerry do all the talking. "Now that you have the story, may I leave?"

The kind, painted eyes appeared. "No, sugar. You lost too much blood. The doctor wants you to stay over. Make sure you don't get an infection." She smiled, pulled her mask down to reveal glossy-red lips. "The anesthetic will wear off, and you'll be needing a little help."

"It doesn't take much. I'm very susceptible to pain meds..."

"Let them take care of you, sweetheart. We checked you out of the hotel. Your things are at our apartment." Jerry moved close and whispered, "The plastic surgeon is an old friend. We'll get arrangements made on the bill."

"You're wonderful...please call Rich...in my phone."

"It's done. Assured him you'd call when you wake up. Sleepytime now."

194

Chapter Eighteen

She floated on the river, nestled against Rich, feeling his fingers soothing away the haze of pain searing her head.

"Good morning, my beautiful woman." He whispered against her ear.

"Are you really here?" She tried to see him, but something obstructed her vision.

"I got here about daylight. They said you slept all night." He touched her face. "He must have hit you terribly hard."

"Is he really dead?" She pressed her lips to stop tears, and pain blasted her skull. "I didn't want it to end like this...him smashed to death..."

He stroked her throat. "It was instant, sweetheart. He was gone so fast he didn't know it was happening."

She pulled his hand to her lips. "I'm glad you're here."

They've only given me enough time to wake you. The police want to talk."

"Stay. I don't want to lose you."

"I'm permanent."

Two men in suits walked in, said they were from NYPD.

Focus. Calm. She reached to shake hands, realized her arm was in a brace. She fumbled for the button to raise the bed. Her head throbbed, wanted to topple forward.

Only one man talked; the other stood back and stared, raising eyebrows and nodding like he was part of the interview. "We found Mister Haggerty's residence. Appears he's been in the city a couple of years. Living off disability. Witnesses said he was looking for you. Said you'd come back if he accepted any of the survivors' payout."

She sighed and felt her energy melting. "I came back to get a divorce." She tried to see their eyes, to see if they believed her, but they looked hazy.

"He lived like a pauper. But we found a stash of cash." The officer leaned close like he had caught her in a lie.

"I paid off our condo before..." She shrugged. "He must have sold it."

"Don't know how much is there. It's stuffed in drawers. Even under his mattress."

"As soon as I'm released, I'll close the apartment, pay off his debts."

"It's not an apartment, lady." His nostrils flared. "It's a room off a back alley—"

She nodded, clearly heard the distaste in his words. "I'll take care of things..."

"We need to let the coroner know what to do with the body."

"He'd want to be cremated."

The man opened a folder. "You'll need to sign for the cremation. You can get a city service for about a thousand. The number's listed here. They'll provide death certificates." He held the document out to her.

She strained to focus, gripping the pen increased the ache in her arm. She couldn't keep her name from scrawling up from the line. She struggled to add her address at the clinic. "I don't know what happened to my bag...my money..." She looked around the room, slow panic setting in. What if it got lost?

"You'll get a bill. We've noted Mister Haggerty's address on your copy."

Please leave. "I should get out today. Take care of everything."

"You returning to South Texas?"

"Yes. *Didn't you notice what I wrote on the paper?* "That's my home." She looked at Rich leaning against the window and saw his smile.

"Well... there's a month of back rent. Landlady's pretty uptight." The cop's mouth twisted. "Generally, I lean toward the one that got abandoned." He stuck out his chin, stretched his neck like his tie was choking him. "From the looks of you, I'd say you were wise to get out."

Did he tip his hat? He isn't wearing a hat. She watched him, and his silent partner bump into each other getting out the door.

She slumped against her pillow. "Do I look that bad?"

"Your forehead droops down over your eyes, and your face is a deep blue. The plastic surgeon is a miracle man. You have twenty stitches, and not one shows. You're still my beautiful woman." His lips touched her cheek, made her flinch. "The radius in your right arm is cracked all the way through. You'll wear that brace for six weeks."

They both looked up in response to a brisk rap on the door before it flew open to a male who looked like a rock star—tanned all the way down the open front of the silk shirt to a patch of hair. His jacket—thrown open—revealed a flat belly. He stopped, ran his hand over a thick mop of hair edging gray at the temples and shouted, "Rich, is that you?" The two men fell against each other, beat one another on the back. "Haven't seen you in twenty years. Where you been?"

"Running a medical clinic in the Rio Grande Valley." Rich's eyes ran down the quality–cut jacket. "Looks like all that sewing you learned has paid off."

The doctor arranged his coat. "Yep, it's been good. But what're you doing here?" He pivoted toward Meredith and morphed into her doctor, pulled a stethoscope out of his pocket. "You probably don't remember that we met yesterday. I'm Doctor Seth Rosenburg. I'm the one who sewed you up."

"I don't remember. I hear you did a fine job."

"You were in a lot of pain. So, it's good you don't remember." He swung around to Rich. "How're you two connected?"

"She's my girl." Rich reached for her hand.

197

"Well, I'll be damned." The doctor kept shaking his head, looking from Rich to Meredith. "This guy saved my ass in med school." He hung an arm over Rich's shoulder and grinned, obviously waiting for Rich to tell the story.

"You'll have to make you own confession. I'm out of the business."

"You quit? Well, thank God." He offered Meredith a sly grin. Rich was already a priest in med school. We tried ever-which way to break him in."

"Don't paint me as a pansy. I went out drinking with you guys."

"Ha. That's all you'd do." He slapped Rich on the back. "I've got to admit, I was damn glad to see you show up wearing your priest collar. I'd probably still be in jail, if not for you."

"That was a long time ago. It's obvious a lot of doctoring and good stuff has happened."

Seth leaned close to Meredith's face. "That's a beautiful sewing job. Ordinarily, you lost so much blood that I'd have you stay one more night, but Jerry said you're going to his place. And if this guy'll be there, you'll be in better hands than hanging around here."

"I can't thank you enough."

He waved his hand. "It's my pleasure to see you healing and to know I've returned a long overdue favor." His smile disappeared. "Seriously, Rich's a jewel, a real keeper."

"I know, and I intend to hang on."

Seth turned, slung his arm over Rich's shoulder as they walked to the door. "I've got to finish my rounds. I'll get over to Jerry's tonight. I want to hear about that medical clinic.

Cushioned in the soft comfort of the Morganstein's guest bed at the rear of the apartment, Meredith drifted into medicated sleep. She roused occasionally to the touch of Rich's hand. The window framed lights in buildings across the way, the steady hum of traffic drifted up ten floors, and then he scooted into bed against her. The next she knew, a dull light filled the window.

"Do I see you opening your good eye?"

"Mmm. My other one also sees you."

He pulled her onto his shoulder. "That's a good sign. How about some breakfast?"

"I want to go to Harvey's room. Get it over with."

"Your body had a big-time trauma. How about paying the rent and returning on Monday to clear it out?"

"Let's go home. I miss Javier...and our life." She didn't want him to see her cry like a big baby.

"Let's call Javier this afternoon. Tell him we'll be home the end of the week."

The Brownstone had been handsome at the turn of the last century, but it's Victorian trim had either fallen off or rotted in place. Peeling tape secured the sagging brass door knocker. Meredith rapped hard on the beveled glass inset. Waited and knocked again.

"Yeah?" The woman oozed garlic. Her eyes, sharp as a weasel's, took in Meredith and Rich. "I ain't got nothing right now."

"Wait! I'm Meredith Haggerty...Harvey's wife?" *Not anymore. It's over.* She worked her lips, tried to moisten her tongue, to ease the mounting tension. Then she felt the soothing touch of Rich's hand on her back.

"Ha! So, you're the wife. I saw it on the news." Her brows worked her forehead into deep wrinkles. "I told the cops you'd have to pay the rent before I'd let you in." She fingered a wad of keys dangling from a belt holding up over-sized men's trousers.

"I understand he was a month behind."

"Three." She held out a white hand and raised her chin enough to show a patch of whiskers. "Three grand."

For a room in this flophouse? Meredith's heart raced as she pulled open her bag and watched the bills fold into the woman's palm. "I'd like to go to his room."

Rich's hand stayed firm against her back as they followed the woman. The only sound was the thud of their feet and the keys jangling as they walked along a dark hall—wallpaper, yellowed with years of misery and four doors shut tight—to stairs that led to a trash entrance overlooking the alley.

"It's down here. He could get in without bothering me." She ran a key in the lock and shoved open double doors. "It stinks all right. He scooted up and down the stairs on his butt to get to the bathtub. Never used it except when he brought in a whore." She cackled, adding her garlic breath to the stench. "They probably insisted he clean himself up first!" She flipped the switch for the overhead bulb to light an alcove tucked behind a row of dumpsters.

Meredith clasped the doorframe, stared at tangled sheets and curled-up pillows twisted across Harvey's motorized bed. His overhead lift bars dangled, lifeless. Along the floor, beer bottles and food-crusted plates crawled with roaches—the picture of his existence. She felt Rich stroking her back, soothing her as the woman's laser eyes took in the room.

"Ha! I thought he was an old bum. That bed cost a piece of change. And that TV's twice as big as mine."

My last Christmas gift for him. "We'll get things out and return the key on Monday."

Hands on hips, the woman gauged the cramped circle of clutter. "That TV could fall off that fancy little table."

"That was my mom's table..." *Where she settled each morning for her first highball.* Rich's hand pressed tight against her.

"You want this other crap? I can use the sheets. An old man who flops upstairs needs the nasty clothes."

"We'll gather it up for you." Rich pointed the woman out the door and shut it behind her.

Meredith pressed fingertips to her lips. "I don't know the person who lived here." Her eyes fixed on a corner toilet, stained brown, anchored by his old handgrips. It sat next to a sink crammed with fast-food scraps. "That's where he washed himself...reduced to this..." She kept shaking her head and leaned into Rich's arms.

"You need to sit." He pulled a little chair out from under the table.

She smoothed her hand over the seat. "Mom's exquisite needlepoint is beneath this filth. She worked for years to teach me how to do it."

"You don't need this. Let me take you back to Jerry's." He circled her in his arms. "I can clean this out."

She pulled away, forced a grin. "Remember, I'm supposed to be wearing my big-girl panties. "Let's find the money before we leave.

That landlady's itching to nose around."

"Okay." Rich reached for a box of garbage bags. "I'll stuff the sheets in a sack, and we'll see what's under that mattress." When he pulled off the old cover and lifted the mattress, he stopped—mouth open—gazing at stacks of twenties arranged in a long row. "Lord help him, Meredith. The man had a fortune..."

She slipped her arm around his waist, fought nausea. "I can't believe he kept this bed. He hated what it represented. I had it delivered the day he came home from rehab. He accused me of welcoming him with an insult—making it clear that he was a cripple."

"I wonder how he maneuvered in this cramped space," Rich mumbled.

"He was strong as a bull in his upper body. If something got in his way, he went over it or through it." She swung around. "The cops said there were drawers of money...and that's my dad's English tall chest backed up to the toilet!" She scooped a yellowed t-shirt from a pile of laundry on the floor and wiped the chest's oily surface. "I used to stand on a chair to lock and unlock every drawer. I wonder if Harvey kept the key..." She opened the top drawer. "Look, a stack of twenties behind this jumble of socks."

Rich shook crumbs out of a plastic supermarket bag and lay the bills inside. "We need to count this."

Facing the chest, shirts draped like curtains over a clothing rack topped with shelves holding boxes and porn magazines. "He's stuffed more twenties in my old shoeboxes." She stared at Rich. "Why all twenties? Was he always crazy, or did I make him crazy by running away?"

"He was sick. He hurt you before you left. He would've hurt you a lot more if you'd stayed." He turned her back to the chair and squatted, holding her hands. "You shouldn't be touching all this. I'll get it cleaned up." He pointed at the bed. "That thing's not damaged. Let's rent a truck, take it, and all your family treasures back home."

She cupped his face between her palms and grinned. "The two of us bouncing home in a truck? Let's do it."

"Sit here. Watch how fast I get this mess cleaned out." He began sorting items in the chest and on the clothing rack. "Two more boxes of bills. And look here! Was Harvey in the army?"

"That's my dad's old trunk!" Leaping from the chair, she ran her hands along the brass binding as Rich set it on the bed. "Dad bought it in London when I was about two. It's a British officer's campaign trunk, commissioned in India." Her fingers trembled as she lifted the latch and was struck by the leathery scent of the teakwood. "I stored all our papers here. I can't imagine Harvey keeping it."

She curled her fingers around a little bottle with a cream-colored top that sat in one corner of the tray. "I had a business trip to Dallas about a year before...I brought him this cologne from Neiman Marcus."

Rich laid his hand over hers. "He didn't hate you as much as you imagined."

"He must have been horribly tormented." She lifted the tray and gasped. "My death certificate..." She ran her hand down the page, "Cause of death, Victim, September 11, 2001." She clutched the paper, stared at the words. "Why did he deny it? Turn down the compensation?"

"Here's the answer, sweetheart." Rich lifted the sales contract. "He needed the death certificate to sell the condo. Look at that, five hundred thousand."

"What?" She stared at the page. "I only paid three..." She sat down hard in the chair. "No wonder he has money poked everywhere."

"The condo sale gave him enough to survive. Wait for the day you returned."

She shuddered. "And try to beat me to death."

"Here're two life insurance policies. A million each." Rich held the instruments, shaking his head. "The man never made a claim..."

"But he kept the trunk." She lifted more files. "These are old tax returns. The last I filed for 2000. Looks like he cashed the check for the condo and disappeared, even from the IRS." She laughed, "And here's my birth certificate buried underneath it all."

"My girl, born on December 18, 1962, Brooke Army Medical Center, San Antonio. She weighed seven pounds, eight ounces." His finger traced the black smudge of her footprint.

"Dad was in Vietnam. It was a year before he came home."

"That was hard on your mother."

Dear, dear Mom. "Yeah. It's amazing how much people can

suffer and continue to look like the model American family."

"Now, all you'll need for a driver's license is your social security card and this birth certificate. Think you can shift the gears in my truck?"

"Yep. Dad taught me to drive in his old jeep on the back roads of Puerto Rico."

Rich moved her to the chair and knelt, taking both her hands. "If you'll have me...all Texas requires for a marriage license is your photo ID and a birth certificate."

"Oh, Rich! What a proposal—on your knees in the midst of Harvey's crap." She pulled him between her legs, crushed his face into her breasts. "You are so damn romantic. I can't wait to be your wife."

He looked up, grinning. "I don't want to make love to you in the midst of Harvey's crap, so you better let go of me, or I'll throw you on that lousy bed."

She giggled and pushed him away. "Let's get out of this joint."

She squeezed her eyes shut, imagined seeing Javier as he ran squealing to the phone. "*Tita*, are you in the hospital?"

"No. *Papá* and I are at a friend's apartment. We should be home by next weekend." She smiled at Rich who was snuggled against her.

"*Tía* Lupe said your husband hurt you really bad—"

"Oh, precious, I'm okay now." Her throat convulsed. *He's not my husband anymore.* "Tell me about you. What have you been doing in school?"

"Nothing. I only think about you. I want you and *Papá* to come back."

Don't cry! "We're trying to hurry home. We miss you so much." Her voice choked and she whispered. "You want to say hello to *Papá*?"

Javier was crying. "Please, thank you."

Rich wiped his eyes and took the phone. "Your *tita* is almost well. I'm taking good care of her." He stroked her back as though she were the child he was calming. By the time he hung up, they had all stopped crying.

"Why don't we join Shirley and Jerry? They've ordered some terrific-smelling Italian food."

Jerry met them in the kitchen. "We've got a bottle of old champagne we've saved for something special. We can't imagine a time more special than this." Jerry held the bottle up like a prize. Then he looked over the top of his glasses. "Don't tell me you're still teetotaling. That's as dumb as being celibate. Excuse me, Rich, that's not meant to be a slur on Catholicism."

Rich burst into laughter.

"I'm saying that Meredith is no more an alcoholic than I am...well, I'm more of a candidate for AA than she is." He bent close to Meredith. "As your former physician, I prescribe one toast. If you throw yourself into a fit and grab the bottle, we'll prise it from your clutches. Guaranteed!"

Shirley applauded. "Stop preaching and pour the drinks, darling."

They stood in a circle around the stove-top island. Jerry very formally lifted his glass. "Here's to people who should have been together long before this."

"*L'chaim*," Rich lifted his glass.

"*Salud*," Shirley and Jerry said together.

"Cheers," Meredith shouted. "Thank you, dear people." She sipped her champagne and looked at Rich who was watching her. "It's very tasty. Other than being so excited, I'm stable as a rock."

"That's what we needed to hear," Jerry said. "Let's move into the living room. There's nothing we'd like more than to see you folks married. Would you consider doing it here?"

Rich slipped his arm around Meredith's waist. "I've checked that possibility—"

"When?" Meredith squealed.

"I made a lot of calls while you slept. "We're lucky your birth certificate was in that campaign trunk. But New York also requires a social security card."

"Will it be hard to get a new card?" Shirley finished her drink and held the glass for a refill.

"I talked to our foundation lawyers. They suggest trying to replace her original card. The clinic will start using the replacement.

See how that sits with the feds—"

"I've made a mess of things." Meredith finished her drink and waited for a refill. "But I never would've met Rich if I hadn't run off."

"Cheers!" Jerry lifted his glass and kissed Shirley on the cheek. "Couldn't have happened any other way. Let's go eat. I have a great Sangiovese to go with the grilled vegetables and pasta and Bolognese sauce."

When they were seated and Jerry began to fill wine glasses, Meredith declined. "I'm excited to be back in the social world, but I feel those two glasses of champagne—"

"That's what we want. Relax and enjoy—"

"I need to talk business. The only thing I remember before Seth sewed me up, was you saying not to worry about the bill..." She reached across the table for Jerry's hand. "I want to know how much I owe you, sweet man."

"Not a thing! It's taken care of. We've got a mutual agreement—professional courtesy—we take care of each other."

"But, Jerry, I'm not in your circle—"

"Yes, you are! And so is Rich."

"What about Seth?"

Rich leaned close. "Seth's part of Jerry's circle, and he's an old friend of mine."

Meredith pulled her napkin to her face. "I can't believe I'm benefiting from all the comradery."

"A lot of docs don't do it anymore." Jerry circled his arm around Shirley's shoulder. "We remember the price tag for medical school. And we remember how many years it took to pay it off."

Stop spoiling the celebration. "Okay, I'll try a sip of your Sangiovese...just to be social."

All during dinner, Jerry continued excusing himself to answer the phone. As they finished, he pushed back his chair. "I hate to be a kill-joy, but I've got to see some patients early tomorrow." He kissed all around and headed to bed.

Meredith and Rich helped clear the dishes before they went to their room.

He closed the door and pulled her into his arms. "I've missed touching you."

She kissed his cheek. "I'm not done worrying. Let's talk before we go to bed. Harvey didn't pay taxes. I've got to fix that. But I have no idea about penalties..."

Rich sprawled on the chaise lounge and pulled her onto his lap. "The Gallegos are looking into the social security problem. They're our best bet on the taxes." He slowly rocked her. "Let's get home as soon as we can. I want to marry you before you notice that I'm not rich like Jerry and Seth."

"I haven't seen suits as fine as Seth's since I left the city..."

Rich rubbed his cheek against her hair. "I figure Seth makes in one day of surgery as much as I make in a year. From the looks of this apartment, I bet Jerry makes my salary in three months..."

Is he measuring himself? "I love Jerry and Shirley, but our life brings more satisfaction than all this fine living."

"I want to take you home and ravage you for hours."

"Since I can't drive, you'll have to stop that rental truck along the way at cheap motels. Perhaps we can practice."

He laughed. "I really wanted to take the bus. Enjoy remembering those glorious three days I spent with you.

She giggled, decided not to tell him that back then, she wanted to get away from him. "It's a long way home, sweetheart, and I can't wait to get there."

CPSIA information can be obtained
at www.ICGtesting.com
Printed in the USA
BVHW042302090223
658261BV00002B/33

9 781644 565612